THE SWAMP

A Levi Yoder Thriller

M.A. ROTHMAN

Primordial Press

Paperback ISBN-13: 978-1-960244-26-0
Hardcover ISBN: 979-8-8381913-8-0

ALSO BY M.A. ROTHMAN

Technothrillers: (Thrillers with science / Hard-Science Fiction)

• Primordial Threat

• Freedom's Last Gasp

• Darwin's Cipher

• Multiverse

Levi Yoder Thrillers:

• Perimeter

• The Inside Man

• Never Again

• The Swamp

LitRPG:

• The Plainswalker

• Sage's Tower

YA Fantasy:

• Agent of Prophecy

• Heirs of Prophecy

• Tools of Prophecy

• Lords of Prophecy

"The Social Responsibility of Business is to Increase its Profits"
—Milton Friedman 1970

"Greed, for lack of a better word, is good. Greed is right. Greed works."
—Gordon Gecko 1987

"If the [Ukrainian] prosecutor isn't fired, you're not getting the money."
—Joe Biden 2018

CONTENTS

This page left purposefully blank.

CHAPTER ONE

With his heart beating through his chest, John pulled the minivan into the parking spot nearest to the third-base line of Simpson Field. It was early morning and the dew still glistened on the grass. He had a clear view of the congressional baseball practice, and they'd already fielded the players.

In his rearview mirror, he saw someone approaching on the driver's side. The man rapped his knuckles on the window and motioned for him to lower the window.

John glanced at the badge clipped to the man's belt and complied. "Yes?"

The man leaned down, his eyes quickly roaming across the interior of the late-model Toyota minivan before settling on the driver. "Sir, I'm Agent Sanchez from the Capitol Police. We have some congressmen practicing on the field today, so if you want to watch them that is certainly within your rights, but you and your vehicle will need to be searched ahead of time."

John was twenty, and he looked like an innocent white kid from the upper-middle class—but he didn't trust the cops. He tried to keep his voice steady as he turned off the car and unbuckled his seatbelt.

"Is there a problem? I used to come here with my brother and we didn't have to be searched." He unlocked the doors and stepped out of the minivan as another agent appeared at the passenger-side window. John looked over his shoulder at the other agent. "The door's unlocked. I have nothing to hide."

Sanchez motioned for John to lift his arms. "We had an update to our security policy after the congressman was shot in 2017. Arms out to the side."

After a quick but thorough pat-down, Sanchez looked over to his partner, who tossed him a thumbs-up as he slid the minivan's door closed.

"Okay, sir, you're good to go. Enjoy the practice."

John smiled as he walked past the bleachers and pulled out a newspaper clipping from the *New York Times*. He looked back and forth from the article to the players on the field. At least one of the men—no, two from the article were on the field. One red-headed and fifty-something, the other with a drooping left eyelid. There were probably more, but he'd have to get closer to get a better look.

No way was he going to risk it.

Besides, he didn't need a closer look. These men were all traitors to the country his father had fought and died for in Afghanistan. These congressmen were living large on the taxpayers' dime. They were liars and cheats, all of them.

He gave his surroundings a quick scan and saw that the cops were clustered around the press box and the dugout, just as he'd expected. They were out of his way for now.

Stuffing the article back in his pocket, John walked over to some shade trees just out of sight of the field. At the base of an oak tree he found the little patch of dirt he was looking for. He took another quick look around, then used his hands to move the loose dirt until he uncovered the item he'd buried here two days ago.

He pulled the ammo box out of the ground, flipped open the latches, lifted the lid, and smiled.

Inside were an old Smith & Wesson revolver and a Heckler & Koch MP5 submachine gun. Both had once belonged to John's father.

He slipped the revolver into his waistband, then slammed the filled magazine into the MP5, pulled back on the gun's charging handle like he'd seen his dad do countless times, and chambered the first round.

As he flipped the fire select to "auto," he recalled the details of the *New York Times* article, and his face burned with anger. The headline had read: "The Citizens of the World Are One Day Going to Feel the Effects of Today's

Vote in DC." The article had gone on to identify the traitors who'd crossed party lines to join the opposition.

John muttered under his breath, "Some citizens will feel those effects today."

Slinging the MP5's carrying strap over his shoulder, John tucked it under his windbreaker and strolled toward the field.

The game was in session. A pitch was thrown, and the batter at the plate made contact with a resounding *whap.* As the ball sailed into the outfield, heads turned to follow it.

With the loud thudding of his heartbeat drowning out all the other noises on the field, John pulled out the submachine gun, lined up his first shot, and pulled the trigger.

Sitting on a park bench on the north side of Lincoln Park, Levi Yoder waited for his contact to arrive. It was the middle of a bright and sunny day in DC, and though the risks of COVID infections were almost nonexistent in the open air, most people wandered through the park wearing their face masks. It was a strange time he was living in, one where politics and science were often confused.

Levi hadn't had so much as a cough since beating cancer a few years back, but he too wore a mask. Not because he thought it would do him any good, but because if he didn't, he'd stand out—and that was the last thing he wanted.

As one of the only made members of the Italian mafia who wasn't actually Italian, Levi had long ago embraced a life of obscurity and shadow. But today he wasn't doing anything for the Bianchi family. In fact, if Don Marino knew what he *was* doing… well, there'd be a lot of uncomfortable questions.

His phone vibrated and he tapped the Bluetooth receiver on his ear. "What's up?"

"Levi, it's Brice. I'm calling to give you a heads-up that the FBI's gunshot monitors just triggered an alert in your area."

Levi pressed his lips into a thin line. "I haven't seen anything out of the ordinary."

"Shots were fired just across the river from you, around two miles from your current location. The computers say it was automatic weapons fire. I don't have any police scanner traffic yet, but the Capitol police are going to lose their minds over this. Don't be surprised if all public venues around DC get slammed shut in the next fifteen minutes."

"Does this change my plans?"

"No, that's still on. Just wanted you to know that there's some stuff going down nearby and you might see a surge of activity in the area."

"Roger that."

Levi hung up and sat back against the park bench with his senses on high alert.

Brice was the chief tech guy for a place called the Outfit,

a part of the government nobody ever talked about. The Outfit was also his second "employer"—in a weird sense of the word. He didn't exactly pull a regular paycheck from them, but occasionally they had things they needed done that required Levi's more unconventional skills and resources.

Today was exactly such a day.

He glanced at his watch and frowned. It was two minutes past the scheduled meeting time, and that told him a lot about the person the Outfit had sent him to meet up with.

In the society of which Levi was a member, you were never late to a meeting without having a really good reason. And if you were late to a meeting with someone of a higher rank, that was equivalent to a slap in the face. People had gotten whacked for less.

But this wasn't some mafia capo he was meeting with, or even a business acquaintance. This was a DC stooge of some kind, and like most federal government workers, they always thought they were the most important people in the universe.

His phone vibrated again. "Yup?" he answered.

"Walking toward the statue of Mary Bethune and the two kids." The man's nasal voice reminded Levi of Paul Lynde, the voice of Templeton the rat from the *Charlotte's Web* cartoon—and perhaps a bigger star from game shows in the seventies.

"You're late."

"I know, sorry. I just got—"

"I'm sitting on the northernmost bench."

Levi hung up and scanned the park for his contact. In the distance he heard multiple sirens.

A minute later he saw a thin man dressed in a dark suit fast-walking in his direction. The man was in his forties, and the suit lay well on him—it was tailored and likely above the price point of the typical government worker.

The two men's eyes met, and the contact gave Levi a nod as he approached.

He sat on the other side of the park bench, then turned to Levi and said with a grin, "What's your favorite way to hide a corpse?"

"Medium rare, slathered with garlic butter and paired with a nice Chianti." Levi glared at the man. "What the hell kind of question is that?"

The man shrugged, thrust his chin forward, and looked down his nose at the mafioso. "I was just trying to break the ice. I know who you are, Mr. Yoder. I also know about your connections to New York and the other families on the East Coast. You've acted as a CI in the past, and I'm glad to hear that you're willing to help *us* out again."

It took everything Levi had not to throttle the man sitting just outside arm's reach. The only law enforcement he'd ever worked with in DC had been the FBI, and at no point had he ever been an informer. "I don't know what kind of stuff you think you know about me, but if you're implying that I've been a confidential informer for you or anyone in the past, you're sadly mistaken, Mister…"

"Smith. Just call me Agent Smith."

"Okay, Smitty. What is it you want?"

The agent frowned. "I'd assume your person would have told you what I'm here for. Do you have it?"

Levi sighed and shook his head. "I don't know what kind of training they're giving you people in the FBI Academy, but this isn't how it works. *You're* the one looking for a favor." He leaned forward and growled, "What the *hell* is it you want from me?"

Smith's eyes widened slightly, but otherwise he kept a calm demeanor. "I was told you have some photos for me."

"Very good, Smitty." Levi gave the man an icy stare. "Now tell me what kind of photos you think I have. You want the naked ones of you with your neighbor's daughter?"

"What?" The agent shook his head and snorted derisively. "I don't even know who my neighbors are much less whether or not they have kids. I was told that there's compromising photos of a certain congressman's wife."

"And why would you want such a thing?"

The agent lowered his voice to nearly a whisper. "I can bring the full force of the FBI to bear if need be. I don't need to explain why."

"Baloney. I don't care who you think you are, you don't have the authority to do jack."

Levi wasn't the least bit intimidated by the man's hollow threat. He couldn't imagine why the Outfit had okayed giving this pompous ass *anything*. But in the end, he had to trust their intel on the matter.

He pulled an envelope from a pocket on the inside of his suit jacket and handed it over. "There you go, Agent Smitty. Is that what you wanted?"

The agent peered into the envelope and pulled out a set of polaroids. As he flipped through them, a smile grew on his face. Levi couldn't fathom what might be so entertaining to an FBI agent about pictures of some woman snorting white powder.

Smitty put the pictures away and got up from the bench. "Thank you, Mr. Yoder. You've done a great service for your country." Then he turned and walked back the way he came.

Levi's phone vibrated, and he tapped his earpiece. It was Brice.

"I've been watching through one of the park's security feeds. You're all done?"

"That guy is lucky I didn't kneecap him, but yeah, he's got the photos. Was there something else before I head back to New York?"

"Yup, Mason wants to see you. Now. If you can head over to Georgetown, I'll meet you at a bar called the Rooster and Bull. I just texted you the address."

Levi shook his head as he got up and walked back to his rental. "I wouldn't have thought you to be the bar type, Brice. I'll be there in twenty minutes. What's this about?"

"Honestly? I have no idea. All I was told was that

Mason wanted to meet with you today. Management, like God, works in mysterious ways. They don't always share their agendas."

"Well, whatever Mason has planned, I'm going back to New York tonight. I've got an appointment that I'm not going to miss. You tell him that."

"Roger that, Levi. I'll let him know."

There were cops everywhere along the route from Lincoln Park through the National Mall and past Foggy Bottom on the way to old Georgetown, where Levi was to meet Brice and Mason. Whatever the shooting was that Brice had told him about, it hadn't hit the airwaves yet, but Levi sensed the tension in the air as he drove through the heart of the country's capital. There were at least twice as many cop cars on the road as normal, and in Georgetown he spotted a pair of flatfoots walking the beat every other block. Something had definitely stirred up the hornets' nest.

Levi pulled into an open spot on the side of the road, hopped out, and put coins in the meter. As he did so, he caught the eye of an old man in dirty threadbare clothing staring at him from across the street.

"Do you have any food I can have?" the old man yelled.

Levi shook his head and walked south on 31st Street until

he spotted what he was looking for: a faded sign featuring a profile of a rooster on the left, the head of a longhorn bull on the right. He opened the door beneath the sign, and the smells of stale beer and wood polish wafted from within.

The place was like any other dive bar. Dimly lit, a few tables and booths, a gray-haired man behind the counter toweling a glass dry. It was obviously a slow time of the day, as there was nobody else in this place but one pudgy man at the bar. The man Levi had come to see.

Brice stood and held out his hand, gripping the edge of a coin between his thumb and index finger. It was a challenge coin. Such coins were popular in the military, usually to signify that the person holding the coin was a member of a particular group or campaign. This one was a bit different. It served the same purpose, but mere possession of such a coin wasn't all that was required to be identified as a member of the Outfit.

Levi gripped the other side of the coin. For a moment, nothing happened. But after a second or two, the coin grew warmer. The coin featured a pyramid, much like the one on the back of the one-dollar bill, and when the eye in the pyramid began glowing—signifying that both holders of the coin had passed a biometric identification—Brice pocketed the coin and motioned toward the unoccupied stool next to him.

"Mason should be here any moment." He waved to the

barkeep. "Get my friend a…" He glanced at Levi. "If memory serves me right, you're a teetotaler, aren't you?"

Levi looked up at the grizzled barkeep. "A seltzer would be great."

The barkeep placed a glass of sparkling water on the bar, and as Levi pulled out his wallet, the old man waved it off. "The drinks are covered. Your money's no good here."

Mason arrived a minute later, coming through a door at the back. "Levi!" he said as he approached with his hand extended. They shook hands vigorously, and the shorter man grinned mischievously. "I've been waiting for this day for quite a while."

"You have?" Levi frowned. "Brice did tell you I don't have much time, right? I've got a plane to catch."

Brice nodded. "I told him you have important plans."

The director gave Levi a lopsided grin. "Surely you have time to let me give you a tour of our headquarters."

Levi sighed. "I'm sorry, I only have time for a short meeting. You know the traffic is miserable out there."

"Then I guess it's a good thing we don't have to drive," Mason said with a grin. "You're standing in our lobby." He stepped away from the bar and motioned for Levi to follow. "Well, hurry up. You said you don't have much time, right?"

The director led the two men through the door at the back of the establishment and down a plain hallway that ended at two restroom doors. Mason pushed open the door to the men's room and motioned for Levi to enter first.

Levi stopped short. "I don't understand."

Brice walked past Levi, looking amused. "You'll see."

With Mason still holding the door open, Levi stepped into the bathroom.

Three closed stalls and two urinals were lined up on one wall, with an "Out of Order" sign taped to the door of the farthest stall. Just past the sinks, a white-haired man sat on a stool, dressed in tan slacks and a plaid button-down shirt. He nodded at Brice, then looked over his John Lennon-styled spectacles at Levi, as if sizing him up for a fight.

"This the new guy?" the old man asked.

Brice shrugged as Mason came in, the door closing behind him.

"What is this?" Levi asked. "Why are we gathered in a bathroom with an old man giving me the stinkeye?"

"Who you calling old?" said the white-haired man, crossing his arms.

"I wouldn't recommend pissing Harold off," said Brice. "He might give you the wrong one."

"The wrong what?" Levi asked.

"The wrong towel. It's only happened once or twice," Brice said. He accepted the towel that Harold was holding out to him, then went into the stall marked "Out of Order." "At least, that's what I've heard," he added as the door closed behind him.

From inside the stall came a loud metallic click followed by a long whooshing sound.

"Those rumors were never substantiated," Harold said loudly over the din of the flushing toilet. He held out another towel.

Mason motioned for Levi to take it, so he did. It was heavier than he expected, but otherwise it was soft and fluffy and… well, a towel.

Mason pushed open the door to the out-of-order stall. Brice wasn't inside. The stall was empty.

"What the hell?" Levi said. He glanced at his towel. Was this some kind of bizarre entrance?

"Put the towel on the lever and flush," Mason said. "But make sure the towel is in contact with the lever when you press down."

Levi stepped into the stall and shut the door behind him. He inspected the toilet, looking behind the tank and around the underside of the bowl. It looked like an ordinary toilet. He felt the towel in both hands, running it through his fingers, feeling for anything out of the ordinary.

"Put the towel on the flushing lever," Mason said from outside the stall.

Levi did as he was told. "And just flush like normal?"

"That's the idea."

"He's kind of slow, isn't he?" said Harold.

Levi shook his head and pushed down on the lever.

CHAPTER TWO

The instant the toilet flushed, the floor dropped—taking Levi and the toilet with it. He put his hands on the tank to steady himself as he dropped down some kind of elevator shaft.

His stomach lurched and his eyes widened as the brown walls of the toilet stall had been replaced by a blur of slate-gray concrete marked with alternating yellow and black stripes.

Then the walls fell away and the toilet-elevator slowed nearly to a stop, forcing Levi to focus on his balance as he descended into a featureless room about as large as the restroom above. The entire rig settled into a recess in the floor, and stopped.

"Surprised?"

Levi turned to see Brice smiling at him. "You could say that."

"Step over here."

As soon as Levi's feet cleared the platform, it launched itself upward, toilet and all, disappearing into the ceiling. A series of clicks echoed down the shaft as it locked into place above.

Levi shook his head and looked around. He stood in an empty, featureless room. There was a wastebasket filled with hand towels, but that was it. The only exit—other than back up the shaft, if that was an option—was a plain steel door. A panel beside it featured a stenciled outline of a hand.

This entire place reminded Levi of a fallout shelter. The air carried a musty scent and the aroma reminded him of an abandoned warehouse.

Hydraulic pistons hissed, and the toilet platform descended once again, bringing Mason with it.

Levi frowned. "What is this place, and why are we here?"

The director tossed Levi a mischievous grin and motioned for him to follow as he walked toward the steel door. "I've gotten dispensation to show you the Outfit's inner sanctum. This isn't something that typically happens with my people."

"*Your* people?" Levi cocked an eyebrow, not sure how to take that comment. He'd met a handful of others that were associated with the Outfit—people like Brice—but he had no idea how it was organized apart from the fact that Mason was some kind of recruiter or manager. He also knew they had access to some folks who were a sort of paramilitary group. An A-team of sorts, but without the normal military ribbons and markings.

"Yes, *my* people." Standing in front of the door, Mason turned and gave Levi a serious look. "I'm charged with recruiting people into the Outfit that are somewhat... out of the mainstream. And I take that responsibility seriously. But we tend not to share too much with the members of OCID—"

"OCID?" Levi interrupted. "That is..."

"The Organized Crime and Intelligence Division. That's the group you got recruited into. As I was saying, we tend not to share too much with... how shall I say this delicately, people in your line of work. Obviously, anyone I recruit has demonstrated a variety of talents that the Outfit finds useful. And you've all been vetted, of course, ensuring you have characteristics that are compatible with our needs.

"And though I've always believed that the people I recruit are trustworthy, those *above* me... they aren't as easily convinced. At no point do we forget where my recruits come from and what they do. So what we're doing here, and what you're doing here... is an exception. The higher-ups have allowed me to bring one of my recruits into the fold on a trial basis."

"And I'm that guinea pig?"

"You are."

"Why?"

"Do you remember when I called you an angel in wolf's clothing?"

Levi nodded.

"That wasn't just marketing hype on my part. I trust you to do the right thing, but our organization is an old one, it's very conservative, and it hasn't been around for as long as it has by taking risks. We're also not a very big group of people. Don't get me wrong, everyone within the Outfit is highly skilled and effective, but there just isn't that many of us.

"You'll find out more very soon. We're extending the trust envelope further for you so that we can expose what we really are to you. If things work out, this could become a permanent arrangement."

Levi furrowed his brow as he scanned his surroundings. "Those are all nice words, but I don't know what it means just yet. What exactly is down here?"

Mason grinned. "I'm glad you asked." He stepped up to the door and placed his palm on the smooth panel. A blue line passed back and forth underneath his hand, a green LED flashed, and a click echoed from inside the wall. The director stepped back, and three massive locking bolts slid out of their retaining blocks on the right side of the door.

"Stand clear," a digitized voice warned, and the door slowly opened outward.

Brice rapped his knuckles on the side of the door as it swung open. "Four feet thick, reinforced steel. This thing will stand up to a nuclear blast. Just don't get your fingers caught in it while it's closing. You'll be using your toes to paint with for the rest of your life."

Levi looked past the door and saw a plain concrete corridor that seemed to run straight for at least one hundred feet.

"How in the world did you get that monstrosity of a door down here?" Levi asked.

Mason answered as he led them down a plain, unmarked hallway lit by bright LED lights. "There's another shaft dug solely for the purpose of heavy transport. Still, it was no simple task. And I know, because they had to replace the original door about ten years ago. The thing weighs eighteen tons."

"How long has this place been down here?"

"It was all dug out of the bedrock in the late nineteen fifties."

They turned the corner, and the hall ended at another door. Mason put his eye up to a box on the wall, and after a green light flashed, the door clicked.

Mason pushed it open. "Welcome to the Outfit's US headquarters, Mr. Yoder."

Levi stepped through.

He found himself standing on a metal walkway twenty feet above the floor of a room larger than most warehouses. Cubicles were arranged in a grid below him, stretching as far as he could see, with men and women working busily at computer screens or talking among themselves. Up here, at Levi's level, metal walkways led to offices positioned all around the edges of the room, looking down on the central work area. Through the office windows, Levi saw more people working at computers.

In the very center of the room, four huge display screens, each easily fifty feet across, hung from the ceiling, displaying information, maps, photographs, satellite feeds, and more.

"This is like the bad guy's lair out of a Bond film," Levi said.

Brice stepped around Levi, and smiled. "I had the same reaction the first time I saw the place. It's a little weird at first, but you get used to it."

Levi's eyes widened as he spotted a painted image of a giant eye on the ceiling. "What's the deal with the big eyeball surrounded by words in Latin? It looks like the logo we have on our paper money."

Mason nodded. "That's the Eye of Providence. When our little organization was created, the founders created that logo since they felt it embodied who and what we are. *Novus Ordo Seclorum* means 'New Order of the Ages,' and *Annuit Coeptis* means 'providence favors our undertaking.'"

"Hold on," Levi stared at the image and was certain he'd seen it all over DC in one form or another. "Are you saying the Outfit preceded the founding of this country?"

"Is that such a shock?" The director said with a note of amusement. "The original members of the Outfit were the Agents of the Revolution. It was actually the original name of our organization."

"And what do the Agents of the Revolution do?" Levi said it with as even a tone as he could muster despite his rising skepticism.

"Originally, the Outfit was formed around the time of the Revolutionary War," Mason explained. "Hence the name. It started with a group of British officers that weren't particularly loyal to the Crown, along with the members of the original Continental Congress. They saw the need for an organization that could do things that needed to be done... but which couldn't be done in the view of the public."

"Like what?" Levi asked.

"Like assassinate the king of England."

Levi raised an eyebrow. "I'm pretty sure the king of England was never assassinated."

Mason nodded. "The war ended before they got into position to pull it off. But it was in the works. At the time, it was believed that King George the Third was mentally ill. His son, George the Fourth, was old enough to take the throne, and he was a much gentler soul—a regular patron of the arts. Washington himself signed off on the operation.

"But that was just the beginning. After we'd won the war, the founding fathers knew they'd continue to need the Outfit. They'd seen how much arguing went on in Congress over even the simplest issues, and they realized that if they ever needed to act quickly, they'd have to be able to get around that bureaucratic nonsense."

"So even back then, there was too much red tape."

"Exactly," Mason said. "You've seen what it's like—in your world as well as ours. Often the good is bogged down by the weight of bureaucracy. The Outfit is a way to cut through all the nonsense for the betterment of all.

"But this is DC. Everyone wants their hands in everything; they all want their say in decisions. So we have one mandate: if it's actionable, we act. It's as simple as that. We don't need to build an airtight case for court, and we don't need to convince politicians somewhere on some golf course that a particular target needs taking out. We just do it."

A sense of curiosity welled up within Levi. "That sounds dangerous. Like an anarchist's wet dream. What about if you're wrong, or one of your people goes rogue and abuses his power?"

"Rogue agent?" Mason shook his head. "It's never happened. As to whether we make the right call, of course we need to be positive that we're on the side of the angels before any action takes place. The difference is we don't need to convince layers and layers of bureaucrats. We just get clearance from within the group."

Levi frowned. "It's hard to believe you never had a bad egg in the group."

"Well, it's true. But remember, we have two types of human resources at our disposal. The type *I* most often deal with are our contacts within organized crime—men such as you. *I* trust them, because I've personally vetted them, but the organization doesn't. Therefore, they never get a full picture of what's going on, they're used for specific tasks and that's all. You've obviously experienced what that's like."

With a wry expression, Levi nodded.

"And then there are the agents who we bring into the fold. There's a different level of trust for those on the inside. You're now within that trust boundary. As I mentioned, this is something of an experiment. To use your words, you're a guinea pig of sorts. We know you maintain loyalty to your mob family up in New York, but we expect that you also do the right thing by your country and its citizens."

Levi's brow furrowed. "Why me? And why now?"

"We need some help," Brice said.

Mason shot him a hard look, but then nodded. "Brice is right. We didn't ask for your help getting those incriminating photos of a congressman's wife because we're suddenly branching out into politics. There's something serious going on in DC—something that could destabilize our government. And we suspect those pulling the strings might be associated with foreign criminal organizations sponsored by their own governments."

Levi's curiosity was piqued. "The Chinese? The Russians?" He had a history with several of the syndicates in Russia as well as the triads. Heck, he was occasionally sleeping with the former mistress of a now-deceased triad gang leader.

Brice shrugged. "We don't know yet, at least not for certain. Those photos you passed onto the congressman's chief of staff—"

"Wait a minute," Levi's jaw tightened. "That bastard at the park wasn't FBI?"

Mason looked at Brice, who shook his head.

"Did he say he was?" Brice asked.

Levi frowned. "He certainly implied it." He now had a strong desire to scare the crap out of that pompous ass.

Mason grinned. "Well, that's a convenient little felony. Impersonating a federal officer is punishable by up to three years in jail."

"That was stupid of him." Brice held a surprised expression. "The guy's name is Tony Banks. He's been around DC longer than most of the politicians. Just another member of what we like to call the swamp."

"The swamp, eh?" Levi had heard the term used in the media before. "So there is such a thing."

"Oh, without a doubt." Mason sniffed with disdain. "Everyone knows about the people who get elected. They're the ones who get in front of microphones or TV cameras all the time and spout nonsense. But they're not the real power in DC, it's the so-called workers who facilitate things that are the real power. They're the ones who connect the dots and make things happen in the capitol. And these are the people you'll never hear about in the papers or on any news broadcast. Unfortunately, these people exist in almost all governments."

The director glanced at his watch and motioned to Brice. "I have to get going, but he'll take you through the rest of the tour and fill you in on where we might need your help."

Levi shook hands with Mason and the short, enigmatic man fast-walked down the flight of metal stairs to the ground floor and was quickly out of sight.

Levi turned Brice. "Okay. Now what?"

Brice motioned for him to follow. "Let's head down to my lab. I'll fill you in there."

The entrance to Brice's lab was an unmarked door on the bottom floor. Brice swiped a finger on a pad, and the door cracked open with a click. "Sorry about the mess," Brice said. "I'm not exactly set up for guests."

The place looked like a tinker's workshop as much as a science lab. A huge table at the center of the room was covered with scraps of metal, wire, soldering tools, and random bits of electronics. But Brice ignored all that and led Levi to a desk in the corner, where he flipped open a laptop.

Levi pulled up a chair beside him. "This place doesn't look much different than Denny's back room," he said.

"That doesn't surprise me. He's just as much of a gadget nerd as I am." He chuckled as he tapped at his keyboard. "Back at school, Denny was always tinkering with the dorm's phone system. We were still mostly analog back then and..." He cast a sidelong glance at Levi. "Let's just say we never paid long-distance charges when calling home. A sign of things to come for him, don't you think?"

Levi grinned as he thought of his longtime friend back in New York. Denny was an electronics genius and Levi's gadget person.

"Sounds like Denny," Levi said. "But I'm surprised you took advantage of that. You seem the type who'd never cross the line into a gray area."

Brice shrugged. "You're not wrong. But Denny and I go way back, and... I guess I never thought of what we did back then as crossing a line. We were just two nerds messing around and realizing that some things weren't designed for folks like us."

A flat-screen monitor on the wall showed what Brice was doing on his laptop. As Brice typed, a terrain map was displayed, with a river cutting through the center and a red dot blinking near the shore.

"See that?" said Brice. "That's Tony Banks with the Polaroids you handed him. Looks like he's heading to a remote spot on the Potomac." He tapped a few more keys and brought up the same map, but with a wider angle and a red line drawn across it. "This is the path he's taken. Looks like after he left you back at Lincoln Park, he took I-395 S and eventually turned onto Wisconsin Avenue."

"Wisconsin?" Levi said. "Isn't that right around embassy row?"

Brice's fingers became a blur on the keyboard, and he pulled up some sort of street-level video footage. A traffic cam, or perhaps outdoor security for some business. There was Cyrillic writing along its bottom edge.

Brice fast-forwarded, then stopped when he found what he was looking for: a black Mercedes captured in the center of the frame. "There's his car, driving past the Boris Nemtsov Plaza video camera."

"Russian embassy?"

Brice nodded. "He drove right past the entrance."

Levi's eyebrows went up as it dawned on him how easily Brice had gotten access to the Russian embassy's security tape. "Okay, our guy buzzed by the embassy on the way to his fishing spot. That could be a coincidence. Maybe his nav system just took him that way."

"No chance," Brice said dismissively. "Passing by there added fifteen minutes to his trip. I'll bet you our guy has some kind of passive proximity sensor; when he drives by the Russian embassy, it sends an alert to an asset with some preset instructions. Either that or there's a burst communication happening as he drives by, though I'd thought the Russians had stopped using that method. I'll have to check on it."

Levi frowned. "So what's our Polaroid guy up to now?"

Brice pulled up another video feed. This one showed someone walking down a slope toward the shores of the Potomac. But the view was from too far away to make out much.

Levi squinted. "Is he carrying a fishing pole?"

Brice zoomed in, but doing so resulted in an image that was heavily pixelated. "I think so? Unfortunately, we don't have any cameras closer than this. This one's a traffic-monitoring feed, almost a quarter mile away on the Chain Bridge."

"Well, I don't see him carrying a bucket or anything," Levi said. "Just a pole. What kind of fishing is he doing?"

"No clue. But this is the second time our guy has visited this general area."

Levi glanced at Brice. "You have his car bugged, I take it?"

"Not bugged, but we have an active transmitter on his car. There's also something on the photos themselves. And I've got things set up to run all of his calls—he has a government-issued cell phone—through the Utah Data Center to monitor for anything suspicious. Our guy is cagey, though. He's clean on the phone. Still, my Spidey senses are tingling like crazy."

Levi cocked an eyebrow. "I'm thinking you probably didn't ask permission from a judge to do any of this."

Brice snorted. "Remember our motto: if it's actionable, we act. And besides, if this guy has nothing to hide, us knowing where he's going and who he's talking to isn't going to harm him."

Levi liked the implications behind the Outfit's motto. It was sort of how he'd always lived his life. He wasn't big on asking permission, and though he did his best to abide by the law, no law had ever prevented him from doing what he felt was the right thing to do.

"What set you off on this guy? And what does it have to do with me? You still haven't told me why I'm here."

Brice leaned back in his chair. "This hasn't been on the news for obvious reasons, but two confidential informants for the FBI went missing six weeks ago. And then, just last week, an FDA meat inspector detected something odd with an imported batch of meat destined for a pet food manufacturer. Further investigation detected human DNA in the ground meat sample."

"One of the informants," Levi said.

Brice nodded. "Anyway, I traced the source of the meat to a French horse farm."

"*Horse* meat? I didn't think it was legal to import that."

"Oh, it's legal, just nobody in the US likes to think of eating one. And it was for pet food in this case anyway. So after a little more digging, I found that the owner of the farm has business ties to some rather unsavory characters out of the Eastern bloc. These associates... they're folks with a similar background profile as yours in some ways. Anyway, we don't have all the threads unsnarled yet, but we think we're going to need your special kind of help. So we want to give you the bigger picture in order that you can be most effective."

Levi had both worked with and fought with Russian mobsters before, and he knew they were a calculating and volatile group. They wouldn't hesitate to grind someone up. Hell, his own mafia family had a history of doing some rather unsavory things in their day as well.

Brice watched the monitor, where their target still stood by the shore. "You know there've always been leaks in DC. It's part of the culture. We have a saying: if more than one person knows something, it's gonna leak. A small exaggeration, but lately, it's been closer to being accurate.

"I'll give you an example. Just last week a *New York*

Times article included a bit of highly classified information that was known to only five people. All five of them were subjected to lie detector screenings, and all passed."

"Passing a lie detector isn't a big thing," Levi noted. "I've done it before."

"Agreed. But now all five of them are on my watch list. So we'll see. And that shooting earlier today? Long story, but that was triggered by another leak that got published. It's getting worse and more frequent."

Levi sighed. "I'm not political, so I'm not big on who's saying what in the papers. Is there a theme to these leaks?"

"We've looked into that. Unfortunately, the leaks are all over the map. Still, the ones we're most interested in are the international ones, if only because the domestic issues are less prone to getting people blown up or taken hostage. Usually, anyway. And there's been a lot going on in the international space now that the president's playing hardball with some leaders in the former eastern bloc nations. The Ukrainians and the Russians have been causing trouble, and there's lots of talk regarding sanctions, either adding more, lifting them, you name it. Plus there's all sorts of turmoil even between friendly nations. Normally stuff like this, cabinet-level discussions in the White House, doesn't hit the press. But it is."

"I assume you've looked at the reporters," Levi said. "How are they getting the data?"

"It's never on the phone. If it was, I'd know, because

I've got just about every reporter on staff with a major paper on watch with the UDC. Our understanding is that these leaks arrive in an unmarked envelope, always anonymous. Practically untraceable. And of course the reporters don't even want to help. The papers nowadays are nothing more than glorified trade rags more interested in clicks and getting paid than they are focused on real journalism, much less national security."

"But somehow you've been led to this guy Banks," Levi said. "How'd he get on your radar?"

Brice reached into a desk drawer and handed Levi a file folder. "This is a copy of his FBI case file."

"So he's on the FBI's radar as well?"

Levi flipped the folder open and began scanning the contents.

"Not that unusual in DC," said Brice. "Lots of staffers have some kind of file on them. The FBI has had him under surveillance ever since he was suspected of foiling the surveillance of a suspected Russian plant in the White House. It turns out they noticed Banks in some video footage, did a facial recognition, and that's when things got exciting."

Levi cocked an eyebrow. "What kind of video footage?"

"I didn't see it, but I heard from a source that our guy was filmed near a Russian dead drop." Brice motioned to the case file in Levi's lap. "Evidently our weasel tossed a half-eaten snow cone into the trash and *accidentally* dropped his cell phone in with it. This just so happened to have occurred right after someone who the FBI suspected was spying for the Russians had used the trash. They think Banks retrieved whatever had been left in the dead drop."

Levi frowned. "Did they think Banks was the Russian agent who the other guy was communicating with?"

"At first they didn't think anything of it, because they had someone else in mind and Banks evidently made a good show of just being clumsy. But eventually they ran a full investigation on him. Despite his status, they ransacked his apartment, the works. They found nothing. It was a dead end.

"But… that brings me back to the *Times* leak I mentioned earlier. Our guy works for a senior congressman who happened to be one of those five people who were privy to that bit of classified information that got leaked to the *New York Times*. Like I said, all of them passed a lie detector test. None of them leaked it—not intentionally anyway. But one of them did admit to sharing the info with someone else."

"Banks's boss told him."

"Bingo."

"Isn't that illegal?" Levi asked. "I thought you needed to be cleared to receive classified information."

Brice snorted. "Of course it's illegal. But it still happens. These congresscritters are all the same: rules for thee and not for me.

"So Banks again fell under scrutiny. He was given a lie detector test of his own. He passed. Another dead end. Except this time, he'd done enough to get on *my* radar." Brice smiled. "And let me tell you, you don't want to get on my radar."

"What did you find?"

"First, he's not as stupid as he seems. In fact, much to my chagrin, he's another MIT grad. Got his MBA there, and he's been working in DC ever since. He's developed quite the network in his time here—lobbyists on K Street, members of Congress, he even has the ear of a Supreme Court Justice or two."

Levi closed the FBI file and handed it back. "And those photos of the congressman's wife? Was that for some kind of DC blackmail?"

Brice shrugged. "I honestly don't know, but you would have to assume so. Her husband is the chair of a powerful subcommittee, so yeah, that's leverage to be exploited."

"My type of folks could certainly get some use out of it," Levi said with a smile.

"I don't doubt it."

Levi pointed up at the screen, which still showed the same pixelated image. "He's not really fishing, is he? Is that even a fishing spot, or is he the only one?"

Brice zoomed back out, revealing one other fisherman, on the opposite side of the river, about fifty yards away.

Levi squinted again. "It doesn't look like Banks even

cast out into the river, he just plopped the tip of his rod down into the water. Zoom back in."

Brice did so, and Levi nodded.

"That rod and reel..." he said. "It's hard to see, but I think that's too big for fresh water. That's a deep-sea rig."

They both watched as Banks did something with his left hand while holding the rod in his right.

"What was that?" Brice said. "It looked like he was clapping his hands together."

Just then Banks pulled his rod out of the water and began disassembling it. He walked away from the shore, paused, and knelt on the ground. There was a flicker of something bright at the man's feet, and then he stood and continued up the slope, leaving behind what looked like a small fire.

An indicator in the top corner of the monitor flashed red. "Oh crap," Brice said. "We just lost the signal from the photos."

"*That's* what's on fire?" Levi stared at the monitor. "Zoom out. What's our guy across the river doing?"

Brice zoomed out. The fisherman on the other side of the river was gone.

"You have any other cameras on that side of the river?"

Brice shook his head. "Coincidence or on purpose... a mystery wrapped in an enigma."

Levi glanced at his watch. "Well, this has been interesting, but I really do have to get going. I can't miss my flight."

"I understand. I'll escort you back up to the bar."

"You don't need to monitor this?" Levi asked, gesturing to the screen.

"The computers will automatically log Mr. Banks on whatever cameras pick him up. It's actually easier if I just wait till it puts it all together for me."

As Brice led Levi out of his lab, he said, "So—do you think you can help?"

"It depends on where this leads and what you need done. But if you get something solid pointing to my kind of people... I'll see what I can do."

"Thanks, Levi. This guy's annoying me; he's slippery. And I think Mason's right about you: once you get your teeth sunk into something, you're not going to let it go. Speaking of—what's so urgent up in NYC?"

Levi shook his head. "You know better than to ask. Let's just say it's much more important than a guy burning up some Polaroids."

CHAPTER THREE

Levi breathed in the thick smell of new leather as he leaned back against the plush seats of Vinnie's new car, a Mercedes Maybach S580. He looked out the passenger's side window and immediately recognized where they were. They were just southeast of Lancaster, having turned off of Leaman Road onto a hard-packed dirt road. He'd walked this rural road countless times when he was a kid. Levi glanced to his left at his longtime friend and the head of the Bianchi family. "I'm thinking this might be the first time a Mercedes like this has wandered the rural backroads of Amish country."

Vinnie ran his finger along the center console and grinned. "Your people speak German, this is a German car, it's all good. And I can't exactly show up in a jalopy, I've got a reputation to uphold."

"Just don't spoil the kids too much." Levi smiled as he

remembered the last time Vinnie had come with him to the farm. Unbeknownst to him, the man had brought a ten-pound bag of hard candies and by the time Levi's mom figured out what was going on, the mob boss had handed it all out to not only Levi's kids but any other kids that happened to have wandered by. Vinnie had instantly become very popular with the youngsters in the area. "Control yourself with the candy this time or I'll never hear the end of it from my mom."

The mob boss motioned dismissively at Levi's comment as the car swerved to avoid a black horse-drawn carriage, common transportation in the Amish-populated sections of Pennsylvania. "A little treat here and there won't hurt them. Those kids of yours are growing up right, just like you did, with dirt under their fingernails."

"Boys, we're just about at the turn off." Paulie spoke just loud enough so that his ear piece could pick up his voice over the blowing air condition.

Vinnie glanced through the rear window and then leaned forward. "Hey Paulie, what's the story with the Beemer? I don't see it."

Beemer? Levi turned to look out the back window. From what he could see were two large Cadillacs following them, which carried the normal muscle that accompanied the mob boss wherever he went.

The driver looked in the rearview mirror at Vinnie and

smiled. "Don Bianchi, Richie asked if he could stop to fill up the tank before delivering the car. I told him to go ahead."

Vinnie nodded. "Just make sure he doesn't get lost."

"Wait a minute," Levi turned to face his longtime friend and boss. "What does he mean deliver? You aren't thinking of giving Alicia a car, are you?"

"Pfft." Vinnie made a dismissive noise and shook his head. "Of course not. All I've got is candy to give out."

Levi's gaze narrowed as he stared at Vinnie and knew he was up to something. But he knew better than to pry into whatever the head of the Bianchi family had going on. He was as stubborn as a mule once his mind was set on something.

The car turned onto a long dirt path that led between two fields, one growing tobacco and the other lay fallow for the season.

Levi noticed a brand-new Bentley Continental parked in front of his mom's barn and winced.

Vinnie noticed the car and had a huge grin on his face as he pointed in its direction. "I'm pretty sure that ain't your mom's. Is that your dragon lady's?"

Levi spotted Lucy in the distance near the small schoolhouse. She turned in their direction and even though she was too far away, he felt her unblinking eyes staring directly at them.

"I wasn't expecting Lucy to be here."

Paulie set the parking brake and hopped out of the car, opening the door on Vinnie's side.

Vinnie playfully punched Levi in the shoulder. "She still trying to put her brand on you?"

Levi shrugged. "It's complicated."

"I'll bet." The mob boss laughed as they both got out of the car.

The sound of kids screaming "Daddy" echoed across the grassy field as a dozen girls ranging from age twelve to seventeen raced in Levi's direction.

He was almost knocked off his feet as the girls slammed into him and they had a big group hug. He hadn't seen them in a couple months, so there was a fair share of some tears and clinginess that usually accompanied some of his longer absences.

The dozen Asian faces all beamed with smiles as they talked all at once and jostled for his attention.

These girls were Levi's life. He'd long ago rescued them from a living hell on the streets, and thankfully, some had no memories of their time before coming to the farm. The others had been scarred but not broken by their past experiences.

As far as the kids were concerned, they were normal Amish girls living on a farm. That they were of Asian descent and had an adoptive father who was a "fixer" for one of the New York City mob families was immaterial.

Vinnie walked up to the gaggle of girls with a bag of

cellophane-wrapped candies. One of the youngest yelled out "Uncle Vinnie!" and gave the mob boss a huge hug as the man began handing out candies.

"Girls!" Levi's mom yelled in Pennsylvania Dutch from the front porch of the house he'd grown up in. "Help me set the tables for our guests. Alicia, you relax and take it easy. It's your special day today." She wagged her finger in Levi's direction and yelled, "Lazarus, you tell your friend, 'No sweets before supper.'"

As most of the girls hurried over to help their adoptive grandmother, Levi chuckled and watched as his mother, who was approaching seventy, hustled the girls into the house. "Vinnie, we've been here three minutes and you already have me in trouble."

The man patted him on the back. "Just like back in the old neighborhood." He turned away and walked toward Paulie, who was just a few inches shy of seven feet tall, and they talked in hushed whispers.

Alicia, his eldest, approached Levi with a brilliant smile. "You got your braces off! Baby, you look fantastic."

She did. Even though she was turning seventeen today, Levi couldn't believe how mature and put together she looked. In his mind she was still the brave ten-year-old he'd rescued from a sex-trafficking ring.

Even though she wore the modest clothes of a typical Amish girl, with her long black hair tucked into her white prayer cap, he could see that she'd grown into a beauty. She was tall, nearly five foot nine, and had the prominent cheekbones and facial structure of a model.

The boys were going to be go crazy around her.

Alicia gave Levi a bearhug and whispered, "*Ahbah*, I've missed you more than you can know. I think I made a choice on school."

Ahbah was Cantonese for father. Alicia was one of the ones who hadn't forgotten a thing about her past. In many ways, the girl was amazing. From the first moment, she'd taken it upon herself to help the other younger girls and had been there for them when he couldn't be. Levi held her out at arm's length and asked with a hopeful tone, "Did you hear back from Princeton?"

The young girl frowned. "No. It kind of sucks, because I even called them. I figured since I didn't get any letter at all from them, not even a 'sorry, you suck' letter, that maybe some wires got crossed. I couldn't get anyone in admissions to give me a straight answer. But the good news is that I got accepted by Stanford, which is still a really good school." Alicia tilted her gaze down a bit and said with a concerned tone, "It's really good, but it's almost eighty-thousand dollars a year and I didn't get any scholarships. If that's too—"

"Hold up, little lady." Vinnie came over to her, held out a cellophane-wrapped toffee, which she took, and asked, "Didn't you say you wanted to go to Princeton?"

Alicia held her head up and with a matter-of-fact tone said, "I did, but I didn't get in, so I have—"

"Are you sure about that?" Vinnie pulled an envelope from a pocket inside his suit jacket and handed it to her. "I had a sit down with a friend of mine who happens to be associated with that school. A dean of something or other… anyway, I told him all about you and what a smart kid you are. And since I'd be seeing you on your birthday, I wanted to know if…" the mob boss smiled "he could see about your application. It turns out that it might have gotten misfiled somehow." He motioned to the envelope that was now in Alicia's hands. "Go ahead, let's see what it says."

Levi felt a swelling sense of brotherly affection for his longtime friend. Even though he'd only mentioned Alicia's desire to go to Princeton in passing to Vinnie, the man had almost certainly pulled some strings.

Lucy approached the group and Levi had a hard time not looking at the statuesque Asian woman that he'd been dating on and off for a handful of years. As always, she wore a form-fitting dress and he knew from previous experience that there was nothing under that dress. She gave him a wink and then focused on Alicia.

The young girl's hands were shaking. "It's from the Admissions Office."

Alicia carefully opened the envelope, pulled out a sheaf of papers, and unfolded the cover letter. Her eyes darted across the paper and she let out what could only be described as an "eep" sounding almost like a surprised chick.

"Well?" Levi leaned closer. "What does it say?"

With her eyes shining with unshed tears, she held up the letter and said with a quavering voice, "Congratulations! The committee has reviewed your application and we are happy to offer you admission to the Class of 2023. Princeton received a record applicant pool this year and your academic accomplishments, extra-curricular achievements and personal qualities stood out among this strong pool. The committee was impressed with all you have done. Thank you for applying. We are delighted to be accepting you."

Levi smiled and glanced at Vinnie, who was also grinning from ear-to-ear. "That's awesome, honey—"

"But *Ahbah*," Alicia's eyes glistened with unshed tears as she scanned through the rest of the papers from the admissions department. "I probably didn't get a scholarship, so it's going to be really expensive." She looked up at him, her chin quivering with emotion and then looked down at her feet. "It's too—"

"Honey, it's okay." Levi stepped forward and wrapped his eldest in a hug. The girls didn't know what he really did for a living. As far as his mother or the girls knew, he was a businessman who took care of things for Vinnie's import and export business. "Baby girl, I've budgeted college for all of you kids, so don't even give it a second thought. It's covered."

"And this should help." Lucy smiled as she offered Alicia a red envelope. It was traditional in Chinese culture that people put cash gifts in a red envelope. "That should take care of some of your book expenses."

Alicia kissed Levi on the cheek and accepted the thick red envelope with a shaking hand. "I can't believe this. You guys are too much."

Lucy motioned impatiently. "Go ahead and open it."

Alicia opened the envelope and her eyes widened as Levi spied two banded packs of hundred-dollar bills. She glanced at Levi.

"Hey!" Lucy spoke abruptly in Cantonese, "You will *not* look to your father for approval on this. This is my gift to you; he has no say in this thing."

Levi grinned, nodded at Alicia, and then gave Lucy a look. "You really should talk to me before giving such gifts." He shifted his gaze back to Alicia and patted the girl's cheek. "Let's go inside and check on your grandmother—"

"Hold up, we're not done yet." Vinnie interrupted with a Cheshire-like grin and gave Levi a soft elbow in the ribs. "Your father has one more gift he forgot to mention."

Levi turned to the mob boss and stared blankly at the man, not sure what he was talking about.

Vinnie motioned for Alicia. "Follow me, darling, I had one of my boys bring it with us."

"Bring what?" Alicia voiced the question as they all

walked toward the front of the farm where the rest of Vinnie's crew had parked.

Levi's gaze focused on one of the mobsters busily buffing a side-view mirror and instantly he knew what Vinnie was up to. He didn't like spoiling the kids with material things, but the head of the Bianchi family had other plans today, ones that, given the circumstances, would be hard to undo.

Vinnie looped his arm over Alicia's shoulders and spoke in a conspiratorial manner. "Your father is a modest man, but he's been working on some big projects for me and got some big bonuses doing them. He wanted to make sure you had something reliable for when you go to school." The mob boss raised his arm and pointed at the shiny new convertible parked behind two Cadillacs. "What do you think?"

Alicia gasped as she approached the fiery orange BMW convertible. It looked very out of place in rural Lancaster.

Vinnie surreptitiously passed a set of car keys to Levi and winked.

He growled at the mob boss and the man laughed. "That's one cool color you picked, Levi." Vinnie said it loud enough for everyone to hear. "Is that the new Sunset Orange?"

Lucy whistled appreciatively and patted Levi on his arm. "That's the kind of car I'd expect a young lady to drive when attending an Ivy League school. I'm impressed that miserly father of hers actually opened up his dusty wallet for such a snazzy ride."

Alicia turned away from the car and looked at Levi with tears running down her face. "I don't deserve this." she sobbed.

At that moment, he knew that she'd be okay if he let her keep it. Adapting quickly to the situation, Levi tossed her the keys and said, "Come on baby girl, prove to me that you know how to drive that thing."

As Alicia raced to the driver's side of the car, Levi gave Vinnie a kiss on both cheeks and clapped him on his shoulder.

No words were needed between them.

"They're only this age once." Vinnie smiled and motioned to the car. "Go have a bit of fun."

"Lazarus!" His mom yelled from the front door of the house in Pennsylvania Dutch. "Ten minutes before food is on the table. Tell your friends to get washed up."

Lucy smacked Levi's backside and said, "I'll explain to your mother that you'll back be in time for dinner."

The BMW's engine roared to life and he jogged to the passenger's side and hopped in.

Levi focused on his eldest as she put the car into gear and slowly merged onto the dirt road.

One look at the unbridled expression of happiness on Alicia's face stirred something in him and he motioned toward town. "Let's go into Lancaster and loop back. Your grandmother will murder us both if we're too late."

As Alicia drove slowly on the bumpy road, she glanced at him and asked, "*Ahba*, I'm seventeen now, don't you think it's time you told me the truth?"

Levi turned in his seat and stared at Alicia's profile as she focused on the road. "Truth about what?"

"Isn't Uncle Vinnie's last name Bianchi?"

"Yes," Levi said with some hesitation. He didn't remember ever telling the kids Vinnie's last name. "Why do you ask?"

"Come on, I'm not dumb. You and Uncle Vinnie just drove here in a Maybach. Aren't those $200,000 cars? And I've known for years that Lucy is some kind of former mobster, or at least was married to one."

"Hold on," Levi frowned and felt a surge of anxiety building up within him. He hadn't expected to have *this* conversation. "Who told you that?"

"She did!" Alicia waved dismissively at him. "Girls talk, you know."

"I see." Levi muttered, not thrilled with where this was going.

"And you guys aren't exactly married, but I know she and you are kind of together."

Levi prayed silently that Lucy had enough sense to keep *some* things private between the two of them.

"Well, I did a reverse-image lookup at the library and

found out that Vinnie is the head of what some people say is the Bianchi crime family out of New York."

"You did a what?" Levi had no idea what a reverse-image lookup was. "Look, it doesn't matter. Vinnie is a very successful businessman, and there are always rumors of strange things with people like him. Baby, there's nothing you have to worry about."

Alicia laughed. "Oh, I'm not worried, I'm just wondering how it's possible for an Amish person like you to be part of the Mafia."

"Alicia!" Levi barked at her. "That's not something you should ever say aloud."

"So you *are* part of the Bianchi family?" Alicia's eyes widened and her mouth hung open in a shocked expression.

Levi shook his head and leaned it against the headrest. "I've always told you girls the truth, and I won't stop now. I'm really good at fixing problems, and that's what I do. Just realize something, this talk we're having, it doesn't happen again. Understood?"

Alicia nodded.

"I've known Vinnie for almost thirty years. The rumors in the newspapers about him are all junk, don't give it a second thought. As to what I do... I have some colorful friends—"

"I met some, they're all Italian, right?"

"Not all." Levi chuckled. "But a good number of them are. You've been to my place on the Upper East Side, not many Italians there, but realize that Vinnie and I and lots of his folks, we all came out of a part of New York City called Little Italy. But you've met Denny, he's about as Italian as you are Jewish. Anyway, I don't tell you exactly what I do, because sometimes what I do is classified."

Alicia's eyes widened once again. "Classified? You mean like government classified?"

"Yes. And that's about all I can say."

"Oh, great. Now you're telling me that my dad is 007?"

"I'm not telling you anything, but I've been called stranger things." Levi laughed and made a circular motion with his hands. "Let's start heading back, I guess those lessons I paid for did some good, you haven't wrecked the car and we're not stuck in a ditch. Anyway, as to college, are you still interested in science?"

"Actually, that's the cool part, Princeton has the Neuroscience Institute and that's what I'd hoped to focus on..."

She continued talking excitedly about school, and Levi breathed a small sigh of relief. Aside from his oath of silence regarding the New York family business, her not knowing anything for certain was more to protect her than anything else. And he didn't lie... mostly.

Levi's phone vibrated and he tapped his earpiece. "What's up?"

"Levi, are you good to talk?"

It was Vinnie. Alicia glanced at him and he motioned for her to keep her eyes on the road.

"Yup, I've got my ear bud in."

"Frankie just called, there was a disturbance at the Helmsley."

The Helmsley Arms was the Bianchi family's high rise luxury apartment complex on Park Avenue.

"And before you go all half-cocked, I'm taking care of this. You stay and celebrate your daughter's birthday and her good news; I'm going back with the boys."

"What happened?"

"Jimmie Costanza was dumped out of a car in front of the Helmsley. Evidently, he's a mess and some of the boys took him to Mount Sinai to get looked at. But whoever did it left a message pinned to his shirt. It was in Russian. They're looking for 'the fixer' and said they'll be back."

"Are you sure—"

"I'm sure of one thing, you're keeping your ass in Pennsylvania for the moment. Paulie is warming up the car now. Give your mom my best, and the dragon lady said she'd take you home. Again, don't worry about it right now, tomorrow is a different day."

"Okay, but if they were looking for—"

"Levi, I promise you that I'll try and save you a piece to handle yourself. I'm getting in the car, come up to my apartment when you get in, and I'll fill you in on the rest."

The line went dead and it wasn't thirty seconds later that the large Mercedes flew past them, going the opposite direction, followed by the other two Cadillacs.

"Where are they going?" Alicia asked as she turned onto the Yoder farm.

Levi imagined Jimmy's broken body lying on a gurney and balled up his fists so tightly that his knuckles popped. "Something came up back in the city, Vinnie sends his love."

One of Alicia's eyebrows arched upward as she parked the car and gave him a look.

Levi opened and closed his fingers and smiled. "Let's go inside before mom has an aneurysm."

CHAPTER FOUR

Levi stepped out of the elevator at the top floor of the Helmsley. The wood panels in the room gleamed with a warm freshly-polished glow and two thickset mobsters were seated on either side of the double doors to Vinnie's parlor on the penthouse level. "Luca, Giuseppe, what are you two palookas still doing up here?"

They both popped up from their chairs as Levi approached and Luca shrugged. "Since this morning's trouble with Jimmie, Frankie's taking no chances on us being ready for anything. He's doubled security and it's running 24-7 until he says otherwise. I think we get relieved at midnight."

Giuseppe, the shorter of the two, spoke with a heavy Italian accent. "The Don's expecting you." He rubbed a swollen cheek where Levi had left a bruise during one of their sparring matches. He made the sign of the cross. "Mamma mia, that *pezza di merda* is going to wish he wasn't born once you find him."

Levi approached Giuseppe with a sly expression, patted the man lightly on his swollen cheek, and said in Italian, "If I find him, he and I will discuss the future of his soul. Don't you worry."

A grin bloomed on the beefy man's face, and the two guards opened the double doors. The warm sound of opera enveloped Levi as he walked into the huge, lavishly appointed room.

The sound clicked off almost immediately as Vinnie got up from a plush leather armchair next to the lit fireplace and motioned to the men, who closed the doors behind Levi as he walked across the well-appointed parlor.

The room served as an office for Vinnie, and a sort of lobby that separated his family's living quarters from the penthouse lobby. The chamber was filled with ornately carved wooden furniture, beautiful paintings, and a museum-quality marble statue of the Venus de Milo.

On the statue, Vinnie had placed a fedora on Venus's head, a hat that the mob boss had begun wearing more often as his hairline receded.

Vinnie put a finger to his lips, motioning for silence, and pointed at his desk.

Levi spotted the black, pyramid-shaped stone object with a glowing red LED on its top. It looked like a decorative piece, but he knew differently. He nodded as he pulled out his cell phone and held the power button down for a few seconds to completely power the device off.

Vinnie stepped over to a minibar built into the wall behind the desk and refilled his crystal tumbler with a thick amber liquid. He then squeezed on the handle of a large metal canister—an old-style soda maker, the kind that ran off CO_2 cartridges. It gave out a loud whooshing sound, and Vinnie squirted freshly made seltzer into a tall glass for Levi.

The red light on the pyramid switched over to green, indicating there were no detected signals being transmitted in the area, and Levi tucked his phone back into his pocket.

Vinnie handed Levi his seltzer, glanced at the pyramid and gave a quick nod. "Your man, Denny, he does good stuff. He's still in business, right?"

Denny had redone the security systems in the building and the pyramid was one of the electronics whiz's contributions as well.

"Sure, you need something?" They both walked over to the fireplace, sat on the plush leather chairs that were facing each other, and Levi balanced his seltzer on the arm of the chair.

Vinnie dug something out of his pants pocket, leaned forward and handed Levi what looked like a USB dongle. "Frankie gave me that for you. It's a copy of this morning's incident from the security cameras out front. Frankie and I both scanned the video and saw the Lincoln SUV that dumped Jimmie in the gutter across from our front door. We couldn't make out the license plate or anything, so I was wondering if your guy was that kind of guy who could coax something out of the video we couldn't see."

Levi frowned, took a long sip of the seltzer and leaned forward. "I'll talk to him and see what he can do."

"When?"

"Well, I was planning on seeing Denny tomorrow after visiting Mount Sinai and paying my respects—"

Vinnie waved dismissively and curled his lip into a snarl. "I saw him today, don't bother going to the hospital just yet. Jimmie's in a coma, he wouldn't know if you were there or not. Hell, if the Rockettes were in his room swinging their tatas in his face, he wouldn't know it. The doctors give him a fifty-fifty chance of coming out of this okay. Bleeding on the brain, swelling isn't too bad, but he's in the ICU." The mob boss jabbed his pointer finger at the USB dongle in Levi's hand. "See if your guy can unwind what's on there and get us someone to pay a visit to."

"Do you by chance have the note that they put on Jimmie? Denny might be able to get some prints off of it."

"Actually, I do." Vinnie hopped up from his chair and walked to his desk. "Unfortunately, a bunch of the guys had their mitts on the note, so I don't know if your guy can do anything with it." He picked up an envelope and handed it to Levi. "The slip of paper is inside. I was going to have one of our boys see about prints, but if your guy can do it, then let him."

Levi put the envelope inside his suit jacket, leaned back against the armchair and felt a growing sense of anger bubbling up inside of him. Whoever had done this had to have known they were kicking a hornet's nest. Normally, just talking back to a made man was enough to have someone get his ass kicked. The idea of hitting a member of *La Cosa Nostra* was unthinkable. At the very least, you'd be visited by a goon squad who'd take pleasure in breaking a few of your bones. Whoever did this, they were dead meat.

"Vinnie, I'll call Denny right now and see what we can do. If he can't help, do you want me to see about pulling some additional strings?"

The mob boss tilted his head. "What do you mean?"

"Well, the Outfit might—"

"No." Vinnie shook his head and grinned. "You're new to these things with the Outfit, but this isn't something for them. Remember, those guys are pretty squeamish about what our folks do." He held up a finger and took a big sip of his amarctto.

Unbeknownst to Levi, the Outfit had recruited Vinnie many years ago. They'd done it back when Vinnie's father was still running the family. Even though Vinnie didn't really do much for that clandestine organization anymore, he was still part of that unusual group of outsiders. Levi had only in recent years learned that Vinnie had been involved in his recruitment to their cause.

Vinnie continued, "Unless this is a legit thing to investigate that isn't of our own doing, they might as well not know about it. Is there a reason the Russians would be looking for you?"

Levi shook his head and then paused. "Well, just before I came back to the business… there were those Russians that attacked me in prison."

"Wasn't that a setup?"

"It was, and I'm pretty sure the person who sent the Ruskies after me is now dead—"

"Sure, I remember that. You ended up messing up a bunch of those Russians in prison." Vinnie chuckled as he pointed his drink in Levi's direction. "They weren't expecting a freaking Tasmanian kung fu devil when they tried to give you a visit. You might have made some enemies back then that you don't even know about. This is our own dirty laundry, leave the Outfit out of it."

"Well, the note said they were looking for the 'fixer' so it sounds more like my dirty laundry than yours."

Vinnie held up his almost-finished glass of amber liquid and they clinked glasses. "You're a part of the family, so whatever issues some Russians have with you, they have it with us all." He motioned to the double-door entrance and said, "Go see what you can find out with your friend. We'll go from there."

Levi glanced at his wristwatch. It was just past midnight. Denny would be awake. After all, he ran a bar that didn't close until three.

He got up, the two men kissed cheeks and as Levi walked out of Vinnie's parlor, he knew one thing for certain.

Neither he nor Denny were going to get any sleep tonight.

———

It was almost closing time when Levi walked into Gerard's, a neighborhood bar located just off of Delancey Street, in New York City's Little Italy.

The place was nearly empty as Rosie, a thirty-something Puerto Rican girl shooed out an older man whose gait was a bit unsteady. She glanced at Levi, gave him an exasperated eye roll, and focused on the drunk she was helping out the door. "Pappi, are you sure you don't want me to call you an Uber or something."

"Nah, I'm good." The man dismissed the suggestion with an exaggerated wave of the hand and stumbled through the door that Levi had been holding open for him. "I'm Rosie... um, no, I'm just drunk. My building's only two blocks away."

Rosie looked up at Levi and motioned to the back. "Denny's waiting for you in the back, but can you lock up behind me? I'm going to make sure our buddy here gets home in one piece."

"Sure."

Levi watched as the bartender steadied the elderly man by holding onto his arm as they walked to Delancey Street. Rosie was a streetwise and mouthy lady who usually gave him a bunch of crap for taking Denny away from the business of running the bar, so it was interesting to see another side to her.

He locked the door and headed toward the back, past the bathrooms and hung a left into a poorly lit hall. The right-hand side of the hallway was tiled with a gaudy mural of a beach scene.

Levi had watched Denny press a combination of tiles to enter the back room, and as he reached toward the wall, there was a click, and with a whoosh of air the outline of a door appeared.

The door swung inward and Denny stuck his head into the hall. His normally close-cropped afro had grown out a bit, and he looked a bit haggard as he motioned for Levi to enter. "It's about damned time, I thought you were going to be here sooner than this."

Levi walked into the cavernous, well-lit room and tilted his neck from side-to-side, trying to loosen his stiff muscles. "I know, I could have walked here in less time than it took for the Uber to finally respond and bring me here." He panned his gaze across the room, taking in the countless shelves chock-full of electronic surveillance equipment, oscilloscopes, bits of dissected state-of-the-art security systems, and just about every gadget imaginable. He handed Denny the USB dongle and envelope he'd received from Vinnie. "I don't suppose you're ever planning on tidying this place up, it looks like a Radio Shack threw up in here."

"As if." Denny snorted, walked over to his desk and sat at the workstation. "No Radio Shack ever had some of this stuff, and besides, I don't think the Shack is still in business."

Levi pulled up a chair as the computer whiz plugged in the dongle and his fingers became a blur on the keyboard.

"Okay, this is a big file, let me transfer it to my RAID storage so I can process it more quickly." His fingers tapped a few remaining commands on the keyboard and shifted his attention to the envelope. He pulled open a desk drawer, retrieved some latex gloves and glanced at Levi. "So, you didn't tell me. What's the story with the dongle and letter? Do I want to know?"

Levi tilted his hardback chair backwards and shrugged. "Honestly, we don't really know much. Like I told you on the phone, the video is from our front stoop as someone dumped one of our guys on the street. Our guy isn't talking, since he's in a coma." He pointed at the envelope as Denny carefully extracted a bloodstained piece of paper with a pair of tweezers. "That note was pinned to his shirt."

"Got it." Denny opened a small plastic case and carefully

began sprinkling a fine black powder onto the bloodied note that contained the hand-scrawled Cyrillic message. With what looked like a delicate paintbrush, he lightly brushed away some of the powder and frowned. "Lots of people have had their paws on this."

Levi leaned closer and saw the variety of smudges all over the paper that the powder had highlighted.

Denny turned the note over and repeated the process, only to shake his head and point at the corner of the note. "Looks like we've got one partial here that I can try running against the FBI fingerprint database." Using a clear adhesive tape, Denny transferred a copy of the partial to a small square of white paper. He put the paper on a scanner and pulled up a website that had an FBI logo on it. After a few keystrokes there was a spinning logo indicating a search was underway. "I'm running it through NGI first, if we're lucky we'll get a hit on there."

"That works." He pointed at the dongle plugged into the large computer. "What about the video?"

Denny put the note back into the envelope, handed it back to Levi and removed his gloves. He then focused on the monitor and sighed. "What the hell kind of USB drives are your guys using?"

"Why, what's wrong?"

With a few strokes of the keyboard Denny snorted. "Remind me to hand you a box of USB 3.0 dongles before you leave, I haven't seen a USB 1.1 dongle since Y2K."

"Is that a problem?"

"No, it's just going to take thirty times longer to transfer the file." Denny stood and motioned for Levi to follow him. "That's fine, I've got something for you to try while the file is transferring."

Levi followed Denny past the rows of the metal shelves and stopped as the man retrieved a Fedex package from a long plain table.

He opened the box and pulled from the package what looked like a plastic contact lens container. He handed it to Levi.

"More contact lenses?" Levi asked. Over the years Denny had been a source of all sorts of gadgets and innovations that had helped him out of various tight spots in the past. Hell, he was wearing one of them. He now had five copies of this suit, which was matched to a thin power pack wrapped around his chest, like a belt. He hadn't made the suit itself, that was the brilliant work of several people to make it nearly bullet and stab-proof, Denny had hidden infrared light emitters along the dark-gray pinstripes. Those hidden emitters, paired with the power pack, helped Levi detect when someone was staring at him.

"Yes, more contact lenses, but this one is different." Denny pulled a laptop off a nearby shelf, flipped it open and began typing. "I'm pushing an app to your phone that will link to that lens. The last lens I gave you…" He looked up at Levi and furrowed his brow. "You still have that, right?"

Levi nodded.

"Good, anyway, the last contact lens I gave you streamed whatever you saw through the lens directly to your phone and I'd be able to access the data. Technology has evolved since I first created that." Denny pointed at the case in Levi's hand. "Go ahead and put that on while I explain."

Levi unscrewed the cap and examined the lens submerged in the contact solution. "This thing has more of the silver stripes running through it than the last."

"The design isn't too much different. They're fiber-optic channels interlaced with bundled arrays of carbon nanotubes. Trust me, you won't see them when you put it on. Put it in your right eye, since that's the one I had measurements for."

He scooped the contact onto the top of his index finger, and glanced at Denny. "And eye measurements don't change?"

Denny shrugged. "I guess we'll find out."

This was the part Levi hated. As he moved his finger closer to his eyeball, he wondered why anyone would willingly opt to wear contacts. The idea of putting something directly on your eye seemed nuts, yet here he was doing exactly that.

"You know the drill, just press it on gently and it'll just suction cup right onto your eye. It should automatically orient itself once you blink a few times."

Levi did as he was told, and the world turned blurry as

he blinked the excess contact solution away. He dabbed away the wetness, then looked around, not seeing anything out of the ordinary. "Okay, now what?"

"Grab your phone and the new app should be on your home page. Tap on it to activate it, and you shouldn't have to do anything else afterwards. As long as you have a signal or a Wi-Fi connection, you'll be good to go."

Levi pulled out his phone and the moment he tapped on the app he saw a *"linking"* message flicker into view in front of his right eye, just like a heads-up display. It was a strange sensation, because the text looked like it was just within arm's reach, but as he panned his gaze around the room, he could tell that the image must be somehow projecting into his eye. "Okay, it says it's linking."

He glanced at Denny and the engineer's face suddenly had a red square surrounding it with *"unknown"* flashing underneath it.

"Woah, when I look at you, it's highlighting your face and saying *'unknown.'*"

"Excellent!" Denny grinned. With a few keystrokes he pulled up an image on his laptop and showed it to Levi. "And now?"

Levi looked at the image, and just as he recognized the image, the face of the actor was highlighted in a green square and the text underneath it spelled out *"Nick Searcy, actor"* in glowing text. As he stared at the image, more biographical data began scrolling upward.

"That's pretty cool." He turned away and the focused back in on the image. It started over with the name and occupation. "So it identifies who I'm looking at and gives me some bio data if I keep looking."

"Yes, and I color-coded things for you based on a three-point assessment of where the identification came from, criminal associations, and active warrants or other similar types of alert flags. " With an enthused expression, Denny began speaking in a rapid-fire manner as he explained the invention. "I can do this now because of the latest silicon advances that allow me to quickly calculate hashes that I use almost like a fingerprint for the image you're looking at, transmit the hash to the phone, and then I can do quick lookups…"

Levi grinned and let Denny drone on as he explained stuff that was beyond his interest or comprehension. He pulled out his phone and browsed through random images. The prior contact lens he'd received, laid a transmitted image from a pen-based camera almost entirely over his right eye, and was useful but not practical in some ways. This gadget interfered much less with his vision and didn't leave him disoriented. As soon as Denny exhausted his stream of explanations, Levi asked, "So, most of the pictures I'm seeing here on my phone your lens is picking up and able to identify them, but it didn't identify you. Is there—"

"For the lookup, I'm using the backend APIs for accessing NGI, the FBI's next generation identification system, NCIC, INTERPOL, the passport image database through our State Department and about one hundred other country's passport services. Hell, I'll even fall back to Google's reverse image lookup if I have to." Denny tossed him a lop-sided grin. "However, I've pretty much scrubbed myself from just about any of those repositories, so the app doesn't work well on me."

Levi panned his gaze across the room as Denny put away the laptop. It was as if the lens wasn't even there, which was great.

Denny motioned for Levi to follow him as he walked back toward the front of the hidden storeroom. "Let's see if the video has spooled over to my system."

Pocketing the contact lens case, Levi let out a yawn as he followed Denny to his desk. He glanced at his watch and it was nearly four in the morning. Definitely past his normal bedtime.

The computer whiz pointed up at the monitor where an icon was flashing. "Hey, the database search popped up with something."

Levi felt a tingle of excitement course through him, chasing away the exhaustion he was feeling.

Denny pulled up the web site with an FBI logo emblazoned on it. "Yup, we've got a hit on someone." After a few keystrokes a page of text flashed up on the screen with a man's picture in the upper right-hand corner. "Do you know an Anthony Montelaro? Because that's who the partial belongs to."

He groaned. "I do. Tony was one of our guys manning security that morning. He had to have handled the note with his fingers."

"Not too much of a surprise if you think about it. I don't think I would have had the presence of mind to go find gloves given the circumstances." Denny minimized the browser's window and pulled up another screen. "Speaking of circumstances, the file finished copying, let me pulled it up and see what we're dealing with."

Levi watched Denny open some kind of application and within seconds he had the security footage displaying on the screen.

The two of them watched the footage in real-time, an SUV raced into view, screeched to a stop as the rear passenger door flew open, and Jimmie Costanza was launched head-over-heels into the street. The vehicle imme-diately lurched forward, vanishing from the screen, and seconds later a group of men wearing suits, the Bianchi security team, entered the picture and the video ended.

It was a miracle that the rear wheels didn't crush Jimmie's head as the SUV peeled away on the rain-slicked asphalt.

"Well, that was ugly." Denny remarked as he rewound the video to a point where the rear of the vehicle was visible. "Okay, let's see what we can see."

Frame-by-frame, he advanced the video as the car sped from the scene, and from what Levi could tell, there was no frame of the video that captured a full image of the license plate. And as Denny zoomed in on the clearest image he could get, the letters themselves were fuzzy at best.

Levi frowned. "I guess we need to look into improving the resolution on our cameras."

"Nah." Denny waved dismissively. "This isn't too bad, given the conditions. Looks like it was a rainy day, so the lighting isn't ideal, and it's not like security cameras are made to get perfect stop-action photography. We've got an excelsior license plate, so it's New York, and I can tell it's issued sometime after June of 2020."

Levi frowned as he stared at the blurred image. He could barely make out the gold blob at the bottom of the plate. "And the first part of the license plate seems to read 'KKL' but we've got nothing more."

"Heh, that's likely good enough." Denny scoffed as he switched windows and pulled up another site that looked like an employee's login page for the NYPD. After a blur of keystrokes and advancing through a few new web pages, the computer whiz typed in the partial license plate. "By the body shape I can tell that's a brand-new model Lincoln Navigator. So, let's see if we can pull up the DMV records for any car with our KKL partial, and with that model." After a few final keystrokes, he hit enter.

Levi watched as an hourglass popped up in the middle of the screen, and within seconds refreshed with three listings.

Denny pointed up at the screen. "That first one says the car is blue, let's skip it. The second is black, the right year, and registered to some woman named Marsha Springfield over in Canarsie." It showed her address and a phone number.

Levi pulled up a mental map of the local area, and he focused on Canarsie, which was in the southeast section of Brooklyn. A very middle-class area he'd visited a few hand-fuls of times over the years.

"And number three is the right model and color, regis-tered to an Alexander Rybakov—"

"Hold up, what can you tell me about him?"

After a few clacks on the keyboard, Denny pulled up what looked like a passport picture and some text began scrolling underneath it.

"Looks like he's holding a Russian passport. Born in the Ukraine, moved to a region just outside of Moscow when he was five, and is here on an expired visa." Denny tapped rapidly on the keyboard, the screen brought up a new set of logos and text, and he glanced at Levi. "Our guy is listed on INTERPOL. He has a petty criminal history dating back ten years ago. He served a year in..." Denny frowned at the screen. "I can't pronounce it."

Levi sounded out the words in Russian and he immedi-ately recalled the name of the prison from a documentary he'd seen a year ago covering the harshest prison in Russia. "It's known as the Black Dolphin prison. It's supposed to be the worst of the worst, and not exactly the kind of place you'd think a petty criminal would end up."

Denny shrugged as he continued scanning the pages of text. "The INTERPOL records don't say what he was in for, just the grade of the offense. Who knows, maybe he pissed off the wrong commissar in Moscow."

"Maybe. I've got Marsha's address; do you have one for our Ruski?"

The screen refreshed with the data Levi was looking for.

"It figures… Brighton Beach." Levi leaned closer to study the man's face. The contact lens on his right eye locked onto the image and identified the man's face as Alexander Rybakov.

"You want a printout?"

Levi tapped the side of his head. "No need. I've got it up here."

Denny shook his head and sighed. "That eidetic memory of yours has got to be one of the coolest things I can think of."

Levi stood and patted the computer genius's shoulder. "It's not as awesome as you make it out to be. Sure, I can recall images of things I've seen, but that's not the same as knowing what's there. For instance, I've been studying some of the law books recently—"

"You looking at becoming a lawyer?" Denny smiled.

"No, but it doesn't hurt to have a good working grasp of what the law says. If you ask me what's on page 205 of the bar exam prep material, I can tell you right away, but if you ask me a question that has an answer on page 205, I wouldn't necessarily have a clue that it's there. I still have to read what's there and study."

"Oh." Denny looked a bit disappointed as he stood, fist-bumped Levi, and let out a yawn. "You need anything else?"

"Nah, I'm good." Levi followed Denny out from the supply room just as Rosie walked into the bar.

Rosario Fuentes. His contact lens immediately popped up the identification.

The woman gave him her customary glare and focused on Denny. "Listen here, you're going to get yourself sick if you work day and night."

Levi chuckled, patted Denny on the shoulder and said, "I'm out of here, guys." He turned to Rosie and hitched his thumb in the computer whiz's direction. "Take care of him."

"I always do." She said with a dismissive wave of her hand as she stared at Denny, tapping her foot impatiently.

Levi walked out of the bar and breathed deeply of the musky scent of the pre-dawn streets.

The streets… they smelled of home to him.

Pulling out his phone, he dialed a number and in his ear bud he heard Frankie Minnelli's sleepy voice get on the line. *"Levi, this better be good."*

He grinned as he walked the darkened streets of Little

Italy. "It looks like I have a lead on those guys who messed Jimmie up. I need a pickup and a crew."

There was a rustling noise on the line and Levi imagined Frankie getting up from the bed.

The man's voice suddenly had a flint-like edge to it. *"Where you at, and where's our target?"*

"I'm in Little Italy, just outside of Gerard's. Our guy is at Brighton Beach. I've got the address."

"Hold on, I've got a crew working Pier 36 right now." Frankie paused for a moment. *"I texted them, they're in the car heading straight for you, should be five minutes or so. You need anything special?"*

"I'll need a quiet place nearby. You know… so our guy and me can talk."

"Gotcha. I'll pull another crew to act as backup. That area's full of them Russians. I'll have a cleanup crew on standby for when you're done. Also, just so you know… Jimmie didn't make it. I got word just about an hour ago from the hospital."

Levi stopped in the middle of the empty street, anger building within him.

Jimmie.

God damn it.

A car's headlights flashed as it came barreling down Grand Street and the Cadillac screeched to a halt fifty feet away. Carmine Ricci's head leaned out of the driver's side window.

"Frankie, they're here. I'll talk to you when it's over."

Levi disconnected the call as he walked over to the car. He hopped into the back seat of the large sedan and said, "Brighton 7th Street. Let's get there before things wake up in the area."

Carmine put the car in gear and slammed on the accelerator.

They all had an appointment in Brighton Beach.

There was a breeze coming from the east and Levi breathed in deeply, enjoying the scent of the salty air coming from Sheepshead Bay. It was just before five in the morning. Carmine was at the wheel of the Cadillac as Levi waited outside a brick duplex in Brighton Beach.

The rest of the crew, which included Gino, one of their top-notch second-story guys, and the Scarpetti brothers to act as muscle. Carmine was behind the wheel of the Cadillac while the rest had gone around to the back of the place. Levi stood in the front, a shadowy figure on the lonely pre-dawn street.

Levi panned his gaze from left to right, studying the layout of the buildings, taking in every detail. It was an eclectic area, like much of the city, and these Russians were living next door to a place with Cyrillic writing stenciled under the generic sign that said "Hair Salon" while next to it was another storefront advertising translation services.

Suddenly, Levi caught movement and the front door opened.

A chill raced up Levi's spine as he saw a tall thin man step out of the duplex's front door. He looked directly at him, smiled and called out to him in Russian, "I was expecting a visit, and you have not disappointed."

Behind the man was a muscularly-built behemoth with both of his hands in the pockets of his windbreaker. The pockets were plenty large enough to conceal a short-barreled gun.

Levi hadn't spotted any cameras outside, but how else would the Russian have known he was out here? And where were Gino and the boys?

The street was eerily silent as the man's voice travelled the fifty feet between them. "Lazarus Yoder, my boss would like to gain use of your services—"

The big man standing guard beside the speaker grunted as Gino dropped from a second-story window, directly onto the man's shoulders and plastered a cloth across the brute's nose and mouth.

The Russian speaker's arms slowly raised as one of the Scarpetti brothers aimed a revolver at his head.

Gino hopped off the large man as he collapsed, landing face-forward on the steps leading up to the duplex.

The Russian man's gaze focused on the gun being

trained on him as he yelled over his shoulder, "This isn't necessary, Mister Yoder. My boss is Yuri Popov. He wants to come to an understanding with you."

Gino walked up to the Russian and without warning sprayed something in the man's face, which caused him to stagger backwards and wheeze. Instantly, the mobster launched himself at the man, and with his arm around the man's neck, dragged him down to the ground, all the while slapping a cloth over the Russian's face.

The man groaned as he struggled, but went limp within seconds.

It was done.

Levi walked up the steps as Gino talked into his wrist-mic, "We've got three for transport, make it quick, the neighborhood's going to be awake soon."

Levi patted down the Russian, retrieved his wallet and flipped it open. There was a laminated card filled with Cyrillic and the French phrase *PERMIS DE CONDUIRE*.

It was the driver's license for an Alexander Rybakov.

An unmarked panel van pulled up in front of the duplex and the Scarpetti brothers began dragging the unconscious bodies toward the vehicle.

Gino placed an aerosol can and the chemical-soaked cloths he'd used into a resealable plastic bag. "Sorry about those two *momos* in the front. They walked out the front just as I got us inside that place." He held up the bag with the chemical aerosol and supplies and grinned. "This stuff works like a charm. I sprayed the Russian guy in the kitchen and he just stared at me for a second and then dropped like an overcooked piece of spaghetti."

The chemical in the can was Sevoflurane, a potent anesthetic he'd taught some of the Bianchi family members how to use. It was something Levi had first encountered with some CIA operators a few years back, and ever since he'd incorporated it into his bag of tricks.

Levi motioned for Gino to follow as he walked toward the idling Cadillac, all the while, scanning the street for any signs of movement. The last thing he needed was anyone seeing a couple of limp bodies being packed into a van.

Satisfied that they were in the clear, Levi nodded to the man behind the wheel of the van and it took off, heading north on Brighton 7th Street.

Levi hoped into the back seat as Gino took his spot in the front passenger's seat.

Carmine put the Cadillac into gear and followed the white panel van.

"How far to the safe house?"

Carmine glanced into the rearview mirror and hit the accelerator. "It's right off Avenue P. We'll be there in about eight minutes."

Levi nodded. The men would likely still be unconscious.

He glanced eastward and the night's shadows fled as the horizon grew brighter, promising the beginning of a new day.

Shrugging the stiffness out of his shoulders, Levi leaned back and relaxed. It had already been a very long day for him, and it wasn't going to be ending anytime soon.

The Russian had said, *"I was expecting a visit, and you have not disappointed."* It seemed like a ridiculous thing to say, especially for someone who seemingly knew of him. *"My boss would like to gain use of your services."*

He had no idea who this so-called boss might be, and it didn't really matter. Levi would figure it out before the guy couldn't speak anymore, that much he was certain of.

CHAPTER FIVE

Levi breathed in deeply and the scent of blood and sweat permeated the safe room as he stared at the unmoving figure of Alexander Rybakov. He was slumped forward, the tight leather straps bound him to a steel chair, which in turn was bolted to the ground. The man's right eye was nearly swollen shut and blood seeped from his split lip. Levi's last smack had knocked the Russian unconscious.

The door to the room opened, and Paulie's six-foot-ten silhouette filled the entrance as he walked in and closed the soundproof door behind him. He looked down at Rybakov, his nostrils flared a bit and he shook his head. "Did you get what you needed?"

Squirting some hand sanitizer onto the palms of his hands, Levi rubbed them together, grabbed a white towel from the stack on a nearby card table, and cleaned himself up. "I got enough." He studied the large man's expression, and even though Paulie was a *capo*, a group leader within the Bianchi family, and had seen all there was to see of the dark side of mafia life, Levi could sense the man was bothered by the sight of someone nearly beaten to death.

Good. It showed his humanity.

"Paulie, what about the other two?" Levi motioned toward the closed door.

"Turns out they did speak English after all. Those two were just the muscle for this guy. It seems like one of them was the guy who snagged Jimmie from the street corner somewhere out near Flatbush, and the other was the one who interrogated him and then shoved him out of the car. That much we know." Paulie handed Levi his phone. "Frankie called and wants an update."

Levi grabbed the phone, dialed a number and put it to his ear.

"Who is it?" Frankie's voice growled on the secure line.

"It's me. I'm done here."

"Okay, fill me in. What do we know?"

"Some of it will have wait until we're face to face, but these guys work for some guy back in Russia named Yuri Popov."

"Doesn't ring a bell for me, do you know him?"

"Never heard of him. Anyway, the folks here got my name from their boss, and they wanted me for a job in Russia of all places."

"Why the hell does a Russian mobster want to hire outside help for something going on in Russia? That makes no sense, there's got to be something missing."

"I agree, it doesn't make sense. But they were willing to pay in gold, and half up front. The guy had a safety deposit key on him, which I gave to Carmine to look into. I'm wiped and need to get some sleep, so I'm heading back to the apartment."

"Vinnie's going to want to talk to you when he gets back this afternoon."

"That's fine. I've been up for over thirty-six hours straight, I need a handful of hours of sleep. After that, I'll be fine. We done?"

"Yup, tell Paulie to drive you back so you can get some shut eye. Let the crew do what they do."

"Got it."

Levi hung up and turned to Paulie. "That place over at Brighton Beach, did we—"

"Our guys emptied out the house and it's being processed in one of our warehouses. I told them to inventory everything and bring back to the Helmsley anything that looked like paperwork. You know, like contact names or records and stuff."

"Good." Levi let out a yawn. "You've got a car, right?"

Paulie nodded.

"Let's get back over to the east side, I need to get some sleep."

The big man hitched his thumb toward Rybakov. "Is there anything else you need out of this one or the others?"

"No. After what happened with Jimmie, we're done with them." Levi headed toward the door and turned back to Paulie, meeting his gaze. "I'm sure these guys won't be missed."

Paulie tilted his head as he studied Levi. "What about that boss of theirs?"

Levi snorted and shook his head. "His guys screwed up when they treated one of our own like they did. We take care of our own, I don't care who these douche bags are, you hear me?"

The big man grinned and slowly nodded. "I'll tell the cleanup crew. There's a landfill that I think needs to get filled."

———

With a full stomach, Levi sipped at his seltzer as he gazed across the travertine dining room table at Vanessa and Michael Bianchi, the Don's teenage kids, who were protesting their father's announcement.

"Dad, that's not fair. We've had this planned for two weeks already." Michael, a handsome fourteen-year-old whose blue eyes matched his mother's, complained bitterly. "You said we could go to the beach with the Ragusso's this weekend.

"Please, can we go?" Vanessa, Michael's fraternal twin, batted her eyelashes and looked back and forth between the ends of the table, hoping to win her parents over with a dimpled pout. "I'll make sure Michael doesn't get into any trouble this time."

Phyllis's voice cut through the complaints like a sword. "You heard your father, and that's final."

Vinnie sighed and focused his gaze on the kids. "I'm sorry, I'll make it up to you both, but this weekend's festivities are cancelled."

"But—"

"Enough!" Vinnie's eyes flared with the spark of anger that Levi remembered from when him and the Don were in their late teens. He motioned to the kids, "Say goodnight to our guest, shower, and get ready for bed."

Michael's shoulders slumped, any look of defiance had vanished as he and his sister got up from the table.

They both walked over to Levi and planted a kiss on his cheek. "Goodnight, Uncle Levi." they said in unison.

"Goodnight kids."

The kids trailed out of the penthouse dining room and as Phyllis began collecting the dirty dishes, she looked over at Vinnie and asked, "Is everything okay?"

"Nothing you need to worry about, baby." Vinnie blew her a kiss. "I'm just being careful."

With a dubious expression, the Don's wife grabbed

Levi's plate and said, "As long as Levi's involved, I know you aren't doing anything too crazy."

"What's that supposed to mean?" Vinnie responded with mock outrage.

"You know what I mean. You're still a hothead, and Levi's always cool as a cucumber." She turned her gaze to Levi and frowned. "But he's too cool when it comes to that Chinese girlfriend of his. Why aren't you two married and having babies yet? And if not her, I know lots of girls just as good looking and maybe a bit more eager to please her man, if you'd give them a chance."

"There you go again!" Vinnie shook his head.

Levi laughed. "Phyllis, I appreciate your concern over my love life, but I'm okay with the way things are at the moment."

Vinnie stood and motioned for Levi. "Let's get you out of here before Phyllis starts trying to book you on blind dates with her tarted up girlfriends. We'll talk in the office."

Levi stood, gave Phyllis a kiss on the cheek and said, "Dinner was great."

He followed Vinnie out of the dining room, past the foyer and entered the front office where the don veered directly to the wet bar and poured himself a drink. "You want another seltzer?"

"Nah, I'm good." Levi settled in the armchair near the large fireplace and enjoyed the warmth coming from the crackling hearth. "So, did Frankie tell you about what we learned over at Brighton Beach?"

"He did, and there's been some developments." Vinnie scooped up a small leather duffle bag that was sitting on his desk and walked over with a drink in his other hand. He dropped the gym bag at Levi's feet with a dull thud and said, "Open that up."

Levi unzipped the bag and a glint of gold peered up from what looked like a bundle of towels. He reached in and picked up one of the terry cloth bundles. From it slipped a gold bar. The markings on it were in Russian.

The markings claimed that it weighed one kilo, and was made of .999 pure gold.

Vinnie aimed his drink in Levi's direction as he sat in another arm chair facing him. "That's about sixty G's in your hand. And there's four more of them in the bag."

"Gino got this out of that Russian safety deposit box?"

"He did." Vinnie reached over to the small table next to his chair, picked up a leather-bound notebook and tossed it at Levi. "Our guys also came up with that."

Catching the notebook, Levi set aside the gold bar and flipped open the small journal to see a bunch of hand-written Cyrillic characters. He flipped through the pages and it quickly became clear it was a notebook filled with names, addresses, and phone numbers.

"It's an address book."

"I can tell." Levi grinned as he continued flipping through the pages.

"Speaking of that," Vinnie set his drink on the table and leaned forward. "Where the hell did you pick up Russian? I know years back when you first returned, there was this weird Russian thing with you and some guy—"

"Vladimir Porchenko." Levi remembered the name of every person he'd ever killed. He was a Russian politician, mobster, and indirectly responsible for the strange path Levi's life had taken. It was on that man's orders that Mary, Levi's wife had been killed.

"Yup, that guy. And I can tell by the way you're looking through that book, you're able to read that stuff, and I'd wager you can probably even speak the language. The family never did much with the Russians back in the day, so where did you pick that up?"

Levi grinned as he continued scanning through the book, looking for a name. "I don't know, to be honest. I was in Japan, China, Russia, and a few other countries for all those years after Mary died, and I just managed to pick up the languages I was hearing over the years."

"Just like that?" Vinnie snapped his fingers and shook his head, holding an incredulous expression. "That crazy memory of yours is something else."

Levi stopped halfway through the book and grinned as he spotted a familiar name. He looked across at Vinnie and asked, "Did you get anything on Yuri Popov?"

Vinnie nodded. "That's what we need to talk about. I can tell you the easy stuff: he's a former Ukrainian boxing champ. I had someone do some digging for me while you were getting some shut eye."

Levi tilted his head with anticipation as the Don paused and pressed his lips into a thin line.

"He was a known associate of that Vlad guy you had the encounter with."

"Crap… that can't be good." Levi grimaced. "Is he connected with anyone that we care about that's alive?"

"Alive? Not sure. From what I was told, this guy was one of Vlad's enforcers. Back when you took the big man out, there was a power struggle over there and this Yuri guy was on the losing end." Vinnie made a jabbing motion with his pointer finger. "Don't let that fool you, he's still got a small army of folks loyal to him over there in Russia, but word on the street is that he's trying to grow his business. He's got people in a few American cities, LA, Chicago, and here. With us taking care of a couple of his guys, we're going to have to reach out and get things squared away with him. Sort of a professional courtesy, if you know what I mean."

"Is that why you cancelled the kids' plans?"

Vinnie shrugged. "I don't like to expose a flank when I'm not sure who and what I'm dealing with."

"Makes sense." Levi grinned, turned the notebook so

that Vinnie could see it, and tapped on a name. "Well, I've got his name and a number. Want me to reach out?"

"Now?" Vinnie looked at his watch. "What time is it over there?"

"About four in the morning." Levi pulled out his phone and held down the power button to turn it back on. "If this number is any good, he shouldn't be too busy right now."

The Don motioned for Levi to go ahead, sat back against his chair, and began sipping at the amber-colored drink he'd poured himself.

Dialing the number, Levi put the phone on speaker and listened to the crackling sound of a phone ringing.

On the third ring, someone answered. "*Da?*"

Yes?

Levi responded in Russian. "Is this Popov?"

"Who wants to know?"

"The name is Yoder."

The sound of rustling broadcast through the phone's speaker. It sounded like he was getting out of bed. *"Ah, so Rybakov found you. Good. I have been trying to get ahold of you. I have a business proposition for you."*

"And that is?"

"Put Alexei on the line."

"He's not available." Levi wasn't sure who Rybakov was to this guy, so he had no idea how the man would take the news of his untimely demise.

"Fine, I assume he's given you my gift?"

Levi leaned down, unwrapped one of the other gold bars and clanked the two together. "If it's the gold you mean, then yes."

"Good, that's just a taste. I have ten times that waiting for you in a bank in Switzerland when you're done with my little mission. I have a need for your services here in Russia. When can you come?"

"Hold on." Levi frowned at the phone. "Why in the world do you need me of all people for this? You have your own people, surely they can do whatever it is you need."

Yuri chuckled for a moment and then cleared his throat. *"I have a person who I would very much like to see vanish, but none of my people can get close enough. You, on the other hand, are someone who could."*

"And what makes you think that?"

"It's very simple. The man I want eliminated is deeply indebted to you, and I know he very much wants to meet you. You may not even know him, but you surely know his former employer. In fact, he was also my employer: does the name Vladimir Porchenko stir any memories?"

"It does." Levi's frown deepened. "Who is this person you're talking about that wants to meet me?"

"Yevgeny Karpov. His father was a member of the dumas, quite a famous man. Unfortunately, dear Yevgeny is one of my country's protected ones. A friend of the Russian president. Yevgeny has an iron ring around him at all times, and none of my people could penetrate it. We've tried. But I know

that Yevgeny wants to talk with you, Lazarus Yoder. This has been true ever since Vladimir's demise. In fact, we are both indebted to you in ways that are quite complicated to explain. I've heard from very reliable sources that Yevgeny is offering a handsome reward for knowledge of your whereabouts. I'm confident that you could bypass his security and do what needs to be done if you reached out to him. Believe me, the world would be better off if Yevgeny stopped breathing."

Levi shook his head and began flipping through the leatherbound notebook once again. "If this guy is as protected as you say, it's hard for me to believe that he'd just open his door and greet me like a long-lost brother."

"If you like, I can give you his direct cell phone number."

Levi paused mid-page-turn and stared at the name "Yevgeny Karpov" with a phone number and address listing.

Yuri rattled off the number, which matched what was in the notebook. *"Did you get that?"*

"I did." Levi glanced at Vinnie who was studying him with a concerned expression. He clearly had no idea what they were talking about. Focusing on the phone, Levi took a deep breath and slowly let it out. "Yuri, I'll think about this offer of yours. But you have to also know that your people made a huge mistake when trying to reach me."

"What—"

"They killed one of mine. Don't expect Rybakov or his

two companions to be returning any phone calls you make. Do you understand?"

There was silence on the line for a full five seconds and then Yuri said, *"That is unfortunate, but I understand. Mistakes happen."*

Levi leaned closer to the phone. "To be perfectly clear, I'm able to say that there is no issue between mine and yours. We are even. Do I have the same understanding from you?"

"Agreed." Yuri's voice had a slight edge to it. *"Blood for blood. Things are currently complicated in Russia, but I can arrange for you to get across the border. Lazarus, are you in?"*

"I can't say that yet. I'll have to clear some things up first."

"I can sweeten the deal a bit." Yuri's voice held a softer tone. *"If you're interested in a new alliance, I seem to have an opening in my organization. Alexei was important to my expansion plans. Maybe we can work out details that I'm sure would be favorable as compared to your current situation. I need an answer."*

Levi grinned and Vinnie shot him a confused look. "You aren't going to get an answer from me until I've thought this through."

"A thinker, eh? Good... a week, that should be enough time for you to think." Yuri's tone had shifted slightly, and

Levi knew that weaved within Yuri's tone of voice was a level of impatience bordering on a threat.

"I'll reach out to you at this number. Good night." Levi hung up the call.

His mind raced with what Yuri had said. He'd likely have to reach out to Brice and see if they could give him some intel on what he might be getting himself into with this guy.

Vinnie stared at him with both of his hands facing upward, the fingertips squeezed together in a very Italian hand gesture. "So, what happened?"

Levi grinned. "Where do I even start?"

A man hobbled toward him, dressed in the robes of a Buddhist monk. He wore a patch over his right eye, and a wooden stump projected from under his robes. A voice in Levi's head spoke the name *Amar Van*. "The immortal one" in Hindi. As the man approached, Levi caught an overwhelming scent of cinnamon and exotic spices.

Amar Van leaned in close and flipped up his eye patch to reveal the desiccated hole where an eye had been. He breathed out, and Levi nearly choked at the scent of rot that the spices had been masking.

"You've been infected by the same curse..." the man whispered. *"You are just like me..."*

Levi lurched up from his bed with a gasp.

Breathing deeply of the air-conditioned air of his apartment, he shuddered with revulsion at the dream. It was one he'd had many times before, especially when stressed, but it had the same effect on him every time.

The man in his dream wasn't some creation from a nightmare; Levi had met the man in the remote regions of Nepal, back when Levi was running from himself—and from the memories of a dead wife. Back then the man called himself Narmer, and he claimed to be thousands of years old— though that was obviously just a tale to scare the village kids and make them behave.

"If you don't eat your porridge, old Narmer will come and take you away!"

But as the memories pulsed within him, Levi felt the same fear that always came with waking from those images.

He got out of bed, went to the sink, and splashed cold water on his face. Then he looked at the spot on his naked chest where he'd been shot. There wasn't even a blemish to remind him of the incident.

And that wasn't the only strange thing about his appearance. He looked much younger than his forty-five years. Much younger, in fact, than his friend Vinnie, who was only three months older than him. While the don now looked the part of a distinguished middle-aged head of a mafia family— a little graying at his temples, a few extra pounds here and there, a deepening of the creases in his forehead and around his mouth—none of this had happened to Levi. He seemed frozen in time.

Just as Narmer had said.

And those scientists Levi had hired when he got back to the States, they'd had no explanations for what they saw in his bloodwork, no idea what to make of the microscopic things they found swimming within him. Levi had destroyed all evidence of that examination—the bloodwork, the x-rays, the electron-scanning micrographs—but he couldn't erase his memory of the mysteries they had uncovered.

The doctors had told him he was an enigma.

Levi should have died several times over since then. He'd been poisoned. Shot. Stabbed. All these things could have—*should* have—killed him. But they didn't.

On account of a very active healing system within him.

That was what Narmer had warned him about.

It was a part of Levi's past that he tried to deny. But every time he looked in the mirror, it served as a reminder that he was lying to himself. It was only in the wee hours of the morning, like now, that he allowed himself to succumb to the accompanying fear.

What if Narmer was right?

The threat of living forever terrified him. The isolation from others. The idea of being stuck forever with his mistakes. The pain of watching his loved ones age.

He'd eventually see even his kids grow old and die.

Tearing his gaze from the mirror, he walked backed to

the bedroom and looked at the picture of his kids that sat by his bed. Lucy was in that picture, too. An important part of his life, even if they weren't a couple. Not in the traditional sense anyway.

Lucy had been abused almost all her life by the people around her—and yet had been strong enough to overcome all of it. She was the widow of a triad leader, one of the few women who held real power in the Chinese crime syndicate, and she wasn't ever going to play a secondary role to anyone. She was ruthless, but in her own way, she was very much like Levi: her intent was good.

As for her methods…

Well, her intent was good.

Levi and Lucy were two very strong-willed people who could take over the world if they joined forces. But Levi had no aspirations for greatness. His adoptive daughters were everything to him, and they came first.

He glanced at the clock. It was five a.m., and Alicia was coming for a visit. He grabbed some workout clothes and quickly got dressed.

There was only one way to relieve himself of the stress he was feeling. Down in the basement, he had an appointment with the heavy bag.

CHAPTER SIX

Levi stood in front of the apartment building as a large blacked-out SUV pulled up in front of the Park Avenue address. The front passenger's window lowered and Paulie, who was driving, looked over to him. He signaled for the big man to wait a moment as Alicia spoke into his ear piece. *"Dad, the car's navigation says I'll be there in three minutes."*

"Sounds great, baby girl. See you when you get here." He hung up and approached the idling vehicle. "Alicia's almost here."

Paulie looked past Levi and yelled, "Hey Charlie, get Joey out here right now. The fixer's daughter needs her car put away."

Charlie, one of the Bianchi family's enforcers, standing

guard outside the entrance to the building vanished, leaving just the one man guarding the front.

As a show of preparedness, Frankie had added several layers of visible security to the apartment building since they'd taken out the Russians over on Brighton Beach. Nobody was sure about how Popov would respond to having some of his guys taken out in retaliation for Jimmie's death, and it best never to underestimate a Russian mob boss, regardless of his promises that he wasn't going to escalate things.

Just as Alicia's BMW pulled up, Joey, a wiry mobster that Levi had been teaching martial arts to, walked out of the building.

Alicia put the car in park, and Joey walked around the rear of the car as she stepped out of the car.

Levi motioned to Alicia, "Give Joey the keys. He'll go park the car for you."

Alicia and the others kids had all visited him on occasion in the city, so she was comfortable with most of the extended Bianchi mob family. And even though his eldest had always been bold, Levi noticed an obvious reluctance as she handed over her car keys.

It was *her* car and giving up the keys to a relative stranger was probably challenging. Within seconds the bright-colored convertible rocketed into traffic, turned the corner and vanished into the streets of the Upper East Side.

Alicia waved at Paulie as he stepped out of the SUV. "Hey Uncle Paulie, you look like you've gained weight."

Paulie opened the door to the rear passenger compartment of the SUV and paused, looking down at his relatively flat stomach with a concerned expression.

Alicia greeted Levi with a kiss on the cheek and laughed. "Big men like Uncle Paulie are always sensitive about their weight."

The giant man wagged a beefy finger in her direction. "You know how to hurt a man, you jokester. Between your father's glare and your biting wit, it's going to take a very confident man to approach you when it comes time for courting."

"Courting?" Alicia rolled her eyes and held an amused expression. "What are you, like a million years old? Nobody says courting anymore."

"Let's leave the talk about courting to some other time. I have enough trouble thinking about my baby girl being alone around all those big-brained boys this fall." Levi grinned and motioned at the SUV. "Parking is a nightmare in the city, Paulie's going to help us out today."

Alicia jumped into the spacious back seat and Levi joined her as Paulie got behind the wheel and put the car into gear. "Where to?"

"Rosen's Sporting Goods."

"Ooh!" Alicia gushed and rapidly clapped her fingers

together, in a very girly expression of excitement. "I totally love Esther, she's awesome."

Levi grinned as the SUV accelerated and headed toward the old neighborhood.

Alicia was going to see a different side of Esther she'd never been exposed to before.

As far as his baby girl knew, Esther was the overweight owner of a sporting goods store who loved to give her candies and was the stereotypical image of the zaftig Jewish grandmother type.

Alicia would learn that Esther Rosen was anything but typical.

<hr />

A bell chimed as Levi opened the door to Rosen's Sporting Goods, and Alicia walked in with a buoyant expression, while Paulie waited outside with the car.

The store had nearly five thousand square feet of floor-space dedicated to sporting activities of all kinds, but spring was giving way to summer, and it was clear the store was in the process of rotating its seasonal stock. Gone were the snow pants and skis, and now many of the aisles advertised archery, weightlifting equipment, soccer, and things you needed for all variety of other field sports.

Levi grinned as he spotted the elderly heavy-set owner

looking through binoculars out the front of her store. "Esther?"

"Levi, hush. I'm doing something important right now!"

He looked across the street, and other than the normal morning foot traffic, he saw nothing that struck him as worthy of such attention.

"A Meyer's has opened down the street," the elderly woman explained as she continued staring through her binoculars.

Levi shifted his gaze to the store about one hundred yards down the street. It was a bagel shop. "Bagels?"

"Not just bagels, *fresh* bagels." Esther groused and suddenly her entire body tensed. "Moishe! The guy just came out with a big steaming basket, go go go!"

A dark-haired teen raced out of the sporting goods store and Esther yelled after him, "Make sure you get at least a dozen sesame and a dozen plain before the vultures swoop in and get them all!"

The lanky teen was a blur as he raced across the street, barely dodging several pedestrians, and vanished inside the small bagel shop.

"Oy!" Esther groaned as she stood up straight and set aside the binoculars. "I'm getting too old and fat for these stakeouts." She turned in Levi's direction and the gray-haired woman's eyes widened as her gaze shifted to Alicia. "*Boobaleh!*" The woman squealed a happy sound as she spread her arms wide and grabbed the tall Asian girl in a suffocating bearhug.

"I was so excited to hear that we were coming here for a visit." Alicia's muffled voice barely escaped the smothering hug.

Esther held Alicia out at arm's length and studied her from head to toe. "You've grown so much!" She finger-combed Alicia's long, straight black hair away from the girl's face and the grandmotherly figure's eyes grew misty as she whispered, "You're going to need a baseball bat to keep the boys away." Suddenly the woman gave Levi an accusatory look. "Now I know why you asked me what you did. You could have said it was for Alicia, I wouldn't have *schlepped* all the stuff I did from the warehouse. I know exactly what she needs."

"What I need?" Alicia asked.

The bell chimed as Moishe walked through the door carrying two large paper bags, one of them had hints of steam coming up from within.

"Moishe, mind your manners and say 'hi' to Alicia. You remember her, she's been to the store a bunch of times with her father."

The teenager's pimply face turned beet red, he mumbled something unintelligible, and raced to the back of the store.

Esther yelled at the receding figure of her grandson, "Don't you and Ira eat any of the sesame seeded ones! Leave those for me and our guests." She turned to Alicia and rolled her eyes. "I'm sorry he's such a *meshuggener* when it comes to pretty girls. His voice disappears and he turns tomato red. One of these days he'll get over it, but today's not that day."

Levi draped his arm over Alicia's shoulder and studied the old woman. She was in her early seventies, no more than five-foot four, wore her graying hair in a big bun, and easily weighed over two hundred pounds. Other than the amount of gray in that bun of hers, Esther hadn't changed in the last twenty years he'd known her. Hidden under that unassuming garb was a lion of a woman who was a better shot than most people who called themselves snipers, and she'd likely forgotten more about weaponry and explosives than he had ever known.

Esther walked toward the cash register, which was being manned by Ira, Moishe's twin. "Ira, I'll be in the back if you need me." She pointed at the large cardboard shipping boxes sitting in the middle of the store. "That's the tennis rackets and clothing we've been waiting for. Make sure you and your brother unpack it and put it up for the summer sports display, you hear me?"

Ira nodded and smiled in Alicia's direction. "Hey Alicia, it's been ages."

Alicia returned the smile and Esther clucked loudly at her grandson. "If you two don't have those boxes put away, I'm going to beat you with the new season's tennis rackets." She glanced at the Yoders and motioned for them to follow her. "Let's get Alicia her present. I've got a body analog for her to test against."

Alicia's eyes widened and she looked up at Levi. "Body analog?"

Levi shrugged. He had no idea what Esther had cooked up, but he grinned as he weaved past the rows of archery and weightlifting equipment. He couldn't wait to see what kind of crazy solution Esther had come up with.

They walked to the rear of the store, past the grandson who was shoving the last remnants of what looked like a seeded bagel into his mouth.

Esther led them to a long table in the far corner of a supply room, and plopped down next to it. She pointed at the two chairs next to her, and both of the Yoders took their seats.

It took her all of about thirty seconds for her to slice three bagels, schmear them with some cream cheese, and set them on the table.

Esther leaned forward in her chair, focused on Alicia, and hitched her thumb in Levi's direction. "*Nu*, did he even tell you why you're here?"

Alicia glanced at Levi and gave him that look she reserved for when she knew he was up to something. She was always the most insightful of his kids. "No, he just said we're coming for a visit."

Levi took a big bite out of the fresh bagel, which was

still warm enough to have partially-melted the cream cheese, and made a point of focusing on his snack.

Esther reached across and patted Alicia's knee. "I've known your father since he was a teenager. Always the quiet but scheming type—"

"Hey," Levi interjected. "You say that like it's a bad thing."

Esther waved dismissively at Levi. "He's a smart kid, sometimes too smart for his own good. Anyway, from what he's told me, you're going to school in New Jersey?"

"Yes…" Alicia seemed surprised by the question. "I'm going to Princeton."

Esther turned to Levi. "She's good with her hands?"

Levi nodded. "I've taught all my girls at least the basics. They're competent martial artists."

With an almost imperceptible flick of Esther's wrist, a dagger appeared in her hand and she held it up, the gleaming razor-sharp edge flashed with reflected light as the older woman turned it in her hand. "Have you trained with knives?"

"I have." Alicia took a bite from her bagel and patted Levi's shoulder. "He had us all drilling with concealable blades. But why are we talking about this? Is there something I need to know? Is there some kind of problem?"

"No, baby girl." Levi put his hand on Alicia's shoulder and gave it a light squeeze. "I'm just very careful with the things that are precious to me. At home, you're around family. There's really very little to be concerned about in our rural community. But with you being out in the real world, I want to make sure you're able to deal with anything that might come up."

"Dad, you're sounding a little paranoid."

If Alicia had a clue what kind of life Levi really led, and the enemies he might have, she'd be just as paranoid as he was.

"*Boobaleh*, that's your father's job." Esther smiled and gave Levi a wink. "And when our kids are away, it's often harder on the parents than the babies that are leaving the nest for the first time." Almost as if by magic, the knife in Esther's hand vanished. "And you're seventeen, right?"

Alicia nodded.

Esther shook her head and sighed. "Unfortunately, the laws in New Jersey are made to support the criminals. As a seventeen-year-old you aren't allowed much of anything for self-defense.

"You aren't even allowed to carry pepper spray. That's why the indecent people have it so easy. Good people who mostly comply with the laws are practically defenseless in that state. Especially younger ones, such as yourself. Nonetheless, I have something for you, my little angel." She pointed at what looked like a shoe box on the table. "Grab that box and open it."

Alicia picked up the box, rested it on her lap and

removed the top. With a perplexed expression, she removed what looked like a medium-sized metal flashlight.

Levi's eyebrows furrowed as he stared at what on first inspection looked like a Maglite-brand flashlight in Alicia's hand. But there were a few things about its construction that looked out of the ordinary. He glanced at Esther. "Is this a custom adaptation of yours?"

"Of course." Esther scooted her chair closer to Alicia.

Alicia hefted the object in her hands and said, "I don't understand. You want me to have this is in lieu of pepper spray? Why don't I just carry a billy club or something?"

"That won't work." Esther shook her head and her voice took on a serious tone. "In New Jersey, you're not allowed to carry anything that could be construed as a weapon. A billy club is undeniably a weapon. However, if you happen to be carrying a flashlight for illumination purposes, and you find yourself in a situation where you have to use it as a weapon, that's totally okay. Listen carefully, *boobaleh*.

"The line between legal and illegal when it comes to anything you use as a weapon, at least in New Jersey, is intent. Don't ever admit that you're carrying something for defense or offense. It has to be some other form of utility—"

"Like a flashlight." Alicia said as she studied the cylindrical object in her hand.

"Exactly." Esther pointed at the flashlight. "But that's not exactly what you have in your hands."

Levi smiled. With Esther, there was always a twist.

"It isn't?" Alicia frowned as her thumb passed over what looked like an on/off switch.

"Go ahead and press it." Esther nodded her approval.

Alicia pointed the flashlight at a distant set of shelves and pressed the button.

Bright light immediately bloomed from the handheld device and continued shining brightly until Alicia turned it off.

"As you can see, it works just like a regular flashlight would." Esther held out her hand and Alicia put the dull-grey metal object in her hand. "But if you notice something along the front of the light," she ran her finger along the front bezel. "This part of the bezel is made of a tungsten alloy. And I've insulated it from the rest of the light, so that if it gets hot, it won't affect the operation of the reflector or the LEDs that emit the light."

Esther flipped open a laptop that was on the table and plugged a wire into the rear of the flashlight. She connected a small box via a USB cable to the laptop and held it out for Alicia to see. "Are you right-handed or left?"

"Right-handed."

Esther flipped open the USB device and said, "Put your index finger on this scanner."

Alicia did as she was asked, the red LED on the device turned green after about two seconds and the laptop let out a single beep.

"I just programmed the flashlight to only recognize your

fingerprint." Esther removed the cable from the flashlight and pointed to a slightly darker square on the opposite side of the power button. "If you place your index finger on this capacitive square, and hold it there for two seconds, the front bezel of your flashlight will activate." She stood and motioned for Alicia to follow.

Levi walked after the two ladies as they weaved past several of the full storeroom shelves and entered an open space that held what looked like a pig carcass suspended from the rafters.

Esther handed the flashlight to Alicia and said, "When you activate the front bezel, you'll want to treat the flashlight as if it's an edged weapon."

"Activate the bezel?" Alicia held a puzzled expression as she studied the flashlight. "So, should I…"

"Go ahead and give it a try." Levi felt a surge of curiosity flood through him. "Let's see what kind of crazy thing Esther has wrought on the world."

Esther turned to Levi with one eyebrow raised. "Need I remind you that some of my crazy things have saved your *tuchus* on more than one occasion?"

Alicia extended her index finger and placed it on the off-color metal pad of the flashlight and almost right away Levi detected the scent of something burning.

Within seconds the front bezel began to glow a deep reddish color.

"Woah." Alicia's eyes widened as she focused on the glowing end of the flashlight.

"There's an induction coil wrapped within the bezel that creates an electromagnetic field. I've tuned it so that it doesn't affect the structural integrity of the bezel itself, nor will it destroy the insulating factors I've built between the bezel and the actual working end of the flashlight."

Levi sensed the heat coming from the business end of Alicia's new weapon. He motioned toward the pig carcass and said, "Go ahead and imagine the pig is someone trying to attack you, and you've got a dagger."

Alicia adjusted her grip on the torch-like device in her hand. "But can this take the impact if I hit something with it?"

Esther waved dismissively. "The majority of the flashlight is made from titanium and the circuitry inside it is designed to take heavy impacts. You're not going to be able to break it with the way it's constructed."

"Okay…" Alicia took a defensive stance, with the flashlight gripped tightly in her right hand. In a burst of movement, she launched a front kick at the pig, followed immediately by a swipe with the flashlight.

There was a searing sound and acrid smoke puffed into the air as a layer of skin was sloughed off the pig.

Alicia bared her teeth and launched herself at the porcine corpse with a ferocity that put a smile on Levi's face.

After thirty seconds of attacks, the soon-to-be college

student stepped back and made a point of lifting her finger off the flashlight's activation pad.

He'd taught her trigger discipline when handling a gun, and it pleased Levi to no end that she'd naturally applied the same principle to her new weapon.

Levi stepped up to the heavily-damaged pig and ran his finger across the deep grooves the weapon had burnt into its flesh. "This would make just about anyone wish they weren't born." He turned to Alicia and asked, "How was fighting with it?"

Alicia stared at the end of the flashlight, which no longer glowed, and the device seemed no worse for wear. "It was surprisingly easy to use. With each swipe, I made contact with the pig, but the heated end felt like it was lubed and had zero resistance."

"Actually, it *was* lubed." Levi rubbed his thumb and forefinger together, which was slick with animal fat. "With that heat, you were almost instantly rendering the fat from the skin. I'd imagine you'd have the same experience against human skin, especially since pigs are a pretty good facsimile."

Esther walked up to Alicia and tapped her finger carefully on the business end of the flashlight. "It's cool enough so that you can touch it now. Once you remove your finger, it should only take about a minute for the heat to dissipate. *Nu, boobaleh?* You think this is something you can keep on you at school?"

"I don't see why not." Alicia grinned and gave Levi an odd look. "Though I think my father is a little bit overprotective and paranoid. But I guess that's due to his job."

Esther's eyes widened and she glanced at Levi. She knew he was a part of the criminal underworld.

Alicia thought Levi was some kind of covert agent.

Levi shrugged. "I'm just looking out for my little girl."

The door to the storeroom opened and one of the twins poked their head in and raised their voice, "Grandma, the Spalding rep is here and says he has an appointment with you."

"I'll be right there." Esther yelled back. "I'm almost finished here."

Levi's phone vibrated and with a quick glance at the caller ID he stepped away from the ladies and answered the call. "Brice, I was meaning to call you. What's up?"

"We have a lead on the Russian asset our DC stooge was talking with. Mason wants you on this. You've got the Russian language skills and are mission-ready, so you're probably the right person to help follow-up on the lead. How soon can you get back here?"

Levi frowned. "You do realize that I'm not your employee. We have a sort of agreement."

Brice sighed. *"I know that, but you and I both know that this is likely something you'd want to help us with."*

Brice wasn't wrong, but not exactly for the reasons he

thought. "I can be there tomorrow if need be, but I'll need something in return."

"Like what?"

"I need to know everything there is to know about a Ukrainian-born guy named Yuri Popov as well as some oligarch over in Russia named Yevgeny Karpov."

"That seems a bit out of your normal range... I'll see what I can do. Do they have any other known associates that you're aware of?"

"Rumor has it they used to work for someone named Vladimir Porchenko."

Levi heard the clacking of keys as Brice typed.

"Got it. Oh crap... Levi, we've got a problem."

He glanced over at Esther and Alicia, and they were busy looking through a box filled with holsters, presumedly for the flashlight.

"What kind of problem?" Levi walked to the far end of the storeroom.

"Your name just popped up on an INTERPOL alert. My friend, you're wanted for the murder of a Russian citizen. Someone named Alexander Rybakov. Does that ring a bell?"

The Russian over at Brighton Beach. Popov had just landed on Levi's shit list.

"I don't know. One thing I can guarantee is that there's no evidence of me murdering some random Russian, mostly because I didn't murder anyone."

Brice was silent for a moment and then began typing. *"I'll have to look into it, but that means you probably shouldn't take any public transport for a little bit. No train or flights."*

Levi's phone buzzed with an incoming text.

"I just sent you an address for one of the Outfit's transport hubs. Bring your Outfit ID."

Levi looked at the address, it was in Harlem. "I've been to this place. Is someone going to pick me up at the destination?"

"Don't worry, I'll arrange for a pickup. When do you think you'll be heading over?"

"I assume this isn't an emergency, so probably sometime in the morning."

"Roger that, call me when you're boarding. I'll look into those names you gave me."

The phone disconnected and Levi walked back over to the ladies. He draped his arm over them both and asked, "You ladies up for a decent lunch?"

Esther shrugged out from under Levi's arm, gave his cheek a squeeze and patted Alicia on the shoulder. "You go take your daughter out and have some fun. I've got a business to run and a salesman waiting for me out front."

As Esther walked away, Levi looked at his daughter. "You up for Italian?"

Alicia snaked her arm around her father's waist as they followed Esther toward the front of the store. "Only if Uncle

Paulie comes inside with us to eat. He's pretty funny and really easy to embarrass."

Levi chuckled, and waved goodbye to Esther and her grandsons as they left the store.

He was going to take advantage of what little time he had with his eldest, but even as they got into the SUV and drove off to Sal's for a quick lunch, Levi couldn't help but dwell on what Brice had said.

"You're wanted for the murder of a Russian citizen."

CHAPTER SEVEN

The Uber pulled up to the corner of Lenox Avenue and West 127th Street in Harlem. Levi thanked the driver and hopped out. It was just before six in the morning, the streets were quiet, and even though the neighborhood was still mostly asleep, the sun was about to peek above the horizon.

Levi had lived in the city for most of his adult life, and until a few years ago, his life was uncomplicated. To normal people, he was one of the nameless, faceless pedestrians wandering the city. To those in the business, he was a Made Man. A fixer for the Bianchi crime family. But now, he felt like he was living two lives.

This morning, he wasn't the fixer, or a member of the *Cosa Nostra*. He was an agent of the Outfit. And even though Vinnie knew about this association, it felt strange to walk the city as something other than what he'd always been.

He couldn't have one of the boys drive him to this place, there'd too many opportunities for questions… questions he couldn't answer.

And only recently, this strange dichotomy of roles was further solidified with Alicia's revelation that he worked for a clandestine organization. She had no idea about the specifics, but it was better to keep her separate from the reality of his other life.

As Levi approached the unmarked nightclub, he grinned as he imagined himself donning the life of what most might think of as a Bond-like spy.

Techno music hummed through a door surrounded by purple neon lights, and the two bouncers outside stared at him as he approached.

The men were huge, probably three hundred pounds each, with a powerlifter's build and no hint of a sense of humor on either of them. It was as if these guys were drawn from central casting and the description sought someone that looked like Clubber Lang on steroids.

Levi had been wearing the contact lens that Denny had given him, and he'd begun to almost take for granted the ability for the lens to automatically highlight a person's face and give him their name. However, as he approached the men in front of the nightclub door, the contact lens overlaid a red square around the men's faces and *"unknown"* flashed under each of their faces. Not a surprise for folks associated with the Outfit. Even though he didn't know this for a fact, Levi figured it was likely that members of the Outfit were electronically scrubbed from most databases.

He walked up to them and before he could say a word, the nearest one spoke with a mild Jamaican accent. "I'll need to see some ID, Mr. Yoder."

He was obviously expected.

Levi dug the coin out of his pocket and held it out.

The bouncer grabbed the other side of it, and when the coin's eye lit up, both men stepped aside and motioned for Levi to enter.

Even though he knew that the front of the building was a façade, Levi braced himself as he opened the door, expecting an auditory onslaught.

But the moment the door opened, the sound of techno music ceased and he found himself stepping inside the building. It was utterly silent.

When the door closed behind him, the muted sound of the music started again—from the *outside*.

Or, apparently, from within the door itself.

It was one of the many ruses that the Outfit had setup, and he'd encountered others that were similarly cloaked in trickery in other parts of the world.

Levi was standing inside a wood-paneled lobby, fresh with the scent of wood polish and pipe tobacco. The reception desk stood across the room, manned by a tall, thin, white-haired gentlemen. Levi walked to the desk and grinned.

He'd met the man before.

"Mr. Yoder, it's good to see you again. You are expected." The man spoke with a very posh British accent, reminding Levi of the butler from *Downton Abbey*. "ID, please."

Levi held out the coin, and when the attendant grabbed the other side, the eye began glowing. "It's good to see you again, Watkins. Are you going to do another disappearing trick on me?"

"Sir?" the elderly man tilted his head and the slightest hint of amusement appeared on the otherwise stoic man's face.

"Never mind, I suppose I'm here to get to DC."

"Ah, yes." Watkins nodded. "Having a bit of trouble with INTERPOL, I hear."

"You hear a lot, for a simple… what did you call yourself last time? A proprietor of this location."

Watkins shrugged. "I know enough to get the mission off in good order." He motioned toward a hall on Levi's left. "Before you depart, please follow me."

Levi followed Watkins down a hallway that was lit by old-fashioned sconces with lightbulbs that flickered as if they were aflame. With his senses on high alert for anything and everything, Levi focused on every little detail.

The last time he was here, Watkins had vanished seemingly as if by magic, and the hallways in this place didn't always return to the same they place they started. This entire building had a weird haunted house vibe, what with shifting hallways and disappearing proprietors, but this time Levi was paying careful attention.

At the end of the hall a door stood slightly ajar and Watkins paused at its entrance. "Sir, as before, this is our quartermaster's domain." With a grand sweeping gesture, the proprietor motioned toward the door. "After you."

Levi pushed the door open and noticed that it was nearly half a foot thick. It must have weighed hundreds of pounds, but it moved noiselessly on well-oiled hinges.

As he stepped through the doorway, lights flickered on, revealing a room filled with individual lockers. Levi turned to Watkins and asked, "Is there a reason why we're not going directly to the train?"

Watkins shrugged. "I'm simply following instructions, Mr. Yoder." He motioned toward a pole in the center of the room. Affixed at about eye level was a visor, like one might see on a submarine's periscope. "If you will, please peer into the biometric scanner."

Levi shook his head as he approached the scanner. This was the same exact routine he'd played through some years prior, and it felt a bit odd this time around. All he needed to do was travel a few hundred miles south. He wasn't about to launch an assault on the clandestine headquarters of some former Nazis in South America. At least that wasn't currently in his plans.

Putting his eyes against the visor, Levi saw a green light flicker, followed by a series of clicks. And then nothing.

Levi stepped back and noticed that several of the lockers had popped open.

"Sir," said Watkins, gesturing at the nearest locker, "I believe you are familiar with the process. Headquarters has asked that you be properly equipped for your upcoming mission."

"Mission?" Levi frowned as he walked over to the locker. He hadn't yet signed up for a mission.

At the first locker, he picked up a handgun with a shoulder holster and several spare magazines.

"That is a Russian-made Lebedev Pistol, model PL-15K. It is a compact nine-millimeter pistol with a fourteen-round magazine, and it already had a round in the chamber. It has a single-action trigger with a lightweight trigger pull and short length."

Levi turned to Watkins, holding up the gun. "I already have two guns on me, why this one?"

"Sir, I believe that management has their reasons."

Levi removed his suit jacket, shrugged into the leather shoulder harness and seated the Russian pistol into the holster.

The next locker held a wallet with a military-issue ID called a CAC, a common access card. There was a yellow sticky note on it that read, *"To be turned in after arrival to HQ."*

Levi pocketed the ID, figuring that it was only needed since he was going to be appearing in the middle Joint Base Andrews.

He walked up to the remaining open locker and retrieved a palm-sized red booklet. It was covered with Cyrillic writing and was clearly a Russian passport.

He flipped it open and found his face staring back at him. The passport was under the name Maxim Volkov.

Between the Russian semi-automatic pistol and the passport, the Outfit clearly had something in mind for him, and it involved travel to Russia.

Something he hadn't yet agreed to do.

His mind drifted back to what the Russian mob boss had said when he told him that some of his people wouldn't ever be returning his calls.

"That is unfortunate, but I understand. Mistakes happen."

Mistakes happen…

The Russian mobster was the only one who'd have known to get INTERPOL on his butt. Evidently the man had his own plans when it came to Lazarus Yoder.

If Popov had plans for his elimination, regardless of what the man had said, Levi needed to take care of that threat. Vinnie would feel obligated to help, since it was a beef that occurred while on mob business.

A mob war was something the Bianchi family didn't need.

Watkins motioned toward the door they'd entered through. "Mr. Yoder, I believe you said you needed to travel."

Levi nodded. He definitely had to have a conversation with Brice. Maybe a trip to Russia was something that actually did make sense. "Let's go."

The white-haired man smiled and motioned for Levi to follow him.

They went back down the same hall through which they entered, but like last time, the lobby was no longer there. Somehow, despite his focus on the details, the hallways had been switched. Instead, they'd arrived in a small room with a set of stairs going down.

Levi looked at Watkins. "What's with the hallways changing where they start and end? Where's the lobby?"

"Sir, you know as well as I that you don't need to go to the lobby." Watkins gave him a sympathetic look and motioned toward the stairs. "The train is waiting for you."

Knowing that just like last time, there was no point in arguing with the man, Levi walked down the steps.

In the small subterranean chamber, Levi spied a sleek railway car waiting for him, its doors open.

The chamber was dimly lit by a few LED floodlights embedded in the ceiling, and other than the faint smell of dampness, likely coming from the bedrock, there was nothing else for him to do but get on the train.

Levi stepped on board.

A disembodied voice announced, *"The train will be leaving in ten seconds. Please hold on to a rail or you will likely be thrown backward. This is your only warning."*

Levi took a seat and gripped one of the poles.

"Five seconds. Four. Three. Two. One."

Levi slid backward as the train accelerated at a pace rivaling that of a race car. Within seconds, the wind was keening wildly as the train flew through the darkness.

Unlike the first time he'd traveled on this train, he knew a bit more about the Outfit and its history. This was just one example of the hidden resources at the centuries-old organization and one that was hard to imagine having been built without others knowing about it.

After all, it had to have taken many years to dig through all of this bedrock to create this tunnel.

Levi traveled at break-neck speed for nearly forty minutes before the train began to decelerate.

The disembodied voice returned. *"We will be arriving at Joint Base Andrews in approximately five minutes. Please disembark only after the train has come to a complete stop."*

Within the span of an hour, Levi figured they'd gone over two-hundred miles along the eastern sea board—a pace that rivaled that of Japan's bullet train.

The train pulled into a well-lit chamber and coasted to a smooth stop.

The doors opened and Levi stepped out. A young military officer greeted him. "Mr. Yoder, can I please see your cack?"

Levi retrieved the laminated military ID, the so-called Common Access Card, and handed it to the Lieutenant.

She inserted the card into a reader, an LED flashed yellow several times and finally gave off a solid green light. Lieutenant Humphries handed the ID back and hitched her thumb toward the stairs to her left. "Mr. Yoder, there's a car waiting for you on the tarmac to take you to your destination."

"Thank you, lieutenant."

Levi bounded up the stairs and squinted at the bright sunlight as he emerged on a large airfield.

The last time he was here, it was the middle of night, just in time for the start of a dangerous mission.

A blacked-out SUV with a flashing blue light pulled up beside him and the driver's side window lowered, revealing Director Mason at the wheel. "Levi, hop in, we've got to talk."

Levi looked up from the surveillance reports he was poring over when the door to the conference room opened and

Mason walked in. Brice entered right behind him, followed by a middle-aged olive-skinned man and a tall, distinguished-looking pale gentleman with dark hair and gray streaks along his temples, neither of which he'd ever met before.

As the door closed, the conference room's glass windows turned milky white, ensuring privacy as everyone took their seats, with Mason at the head of the conference room table.

Mason, the director of OCID, motioned in the direction of the darker-skinned man and said, "Levi, this is Giuseppe Russo. You may or may not have seen him flitting about here in DC, he's former DIA and has been surveilling a few of our suspected congressmen."

He stood, leaned across the table and shook hands with Levi. "Just call me Joe."

"The person to your right is Gregor Manheim. He's here for the week, so I asked him to attend this meeting so you two can meet. He's the DI for Europe and Eurasia and normally works out of the German offices."

"DI?" Levi asked as he shook hands with the man.

"Director of Intelligence. He's the eyes and ears for the Outfit in that part of the world. He's probably going to help us with logistics regarding your upcoming mission."

"Hold up," Levi tapped on the stack of papers that Mason had left with him. "I haven't gone through all of this yet, but what mission are we talking about?"

"There's a string of events that have led us to this place."

Mason's unblinking gaze focused on Levi, he had an almost imperceptible grin and shifted his attention to the Italian. "Joe, fill Levi in on what's happened so far, and then we can talk about next steps."

Joe cleared his throat and held a pensive expression, as if trying to gather his thoughts. "Well, we've had several members of Congress under surveillance along with certain key staffers." He motioned in Levi's direction. "After you gave one of those staffers, specifically Tony Banks, a set of compromising photos of a particular congressman's wife, we cranked up the surveillance on that public servant and his wife, knowing that there was a better than average chance at something happening.

"We were right.

"It turns out that the congressman in question had a rip-roaring fight with his wife, and we have the full audio of it.

"Clearly the staffer who you'd passed the photos to had somehow managed to talk with the congressman and that was the gist of the screaming match between the couple."

Joe frowned. "We clearly had a hole in our surveillance, because we know the staffer talked with the congressman, because part of the argument mentioned something about photographs. We don't know how the staffer reached out to the congressman, because we thought we had all communications monitored and didn't catch that dialog. Anyway, we analyzed the driving patterns of both the congressman and the staffer."

"You had their cars tagged with some kind of GPS tracker?" Levi asked.

Brice nodded. "Yup, we've got tracking devices on just about every elected official's personal vehicle along with all of the congressional limos and official transports."

Joe hitched a thumb in Brice's direction. "With agent Brice's help, we have a record of the staffer and the congressman both being in the same supermarket parking lot in Bethesda. They were there for only five minutes and then they both left."

"That could explain how the congressman learned about the photos." Levi furrowed his brow. "But that doesn't explain how they knew to meet at that supermarket."

"Correct." Joe nodded. "Again, with agent Brice's help we had a long history of where the staffer had been driving. We looked for patterns and didn't really find any, except we got lucky…

"It was only by chance that I happened to be at a pizza parlor in Arlington, of all places. It's less than half a mile from my apartment. I remembered seeing the staffer walk in and nearly choked on the slice of pizza I was eating at the time, since I had only just been assigned to keep tabs on him and I was off duty. I didn't focus too much on him, because I didn't want to draw his attention, but now that I think about that time I saw him, the encounter was a bit weird."

"How so?" Levi asked.

"Well, he came in, had a whispered conversation with

someone behind the counter, and went into the back. The bathrooms are near the back of the restaurant, so I figured that's what he was up to. Soon after, he left the restaurant and drove off, empty-handed."

Brice grinned. "But our guy has visited that pizza parlor seven times in the last three weeks. Each time he was there for not much more than five minutes." He motioned in Joe's direction. "And when he told me what he'd seen, my *spidey-senses* began tingling."

Levi grinned. Brice had a lot of hard skills that made him good at being the glorified quartermaster and technology *guru* of the Outfit, but one thing he'd learned since meeting him—he had very good instincts as well.

"I did some digging into that pizza shop," Brice continued, "and wouldn't you know it… it's owned by a naturalized citizen. A former green card holder who immigrated to the States about eight years ago."

"Let me guess," Levi felt the Russian-made Lebedev Pistol weighing heavily in his shoulder holster. "The owner's from Russia?"

"Correct." Brice nodded. "And after learning that little tidbit, I dug deeper. That property has three active phone lines going into it. I did some searching around and it seems like two of them are listed for the business and were being actively used for it. One voice line and the other for faxed in orders. The third line is not used in any of the advertising the store does.

"I tapped all three of those lines and confirmed that the two seem to be used for legitimate restaurant business. The third rang all sorts of alarm bells for me. The data we extracted from the few times that third line was activated was complete garbage. It has some advanced point-to-point encryption on the line and I can't tell what it's being used for."

"I'm not sure I follow you." Levi leaned forward in his chair. "You said you have the line tapped, can't you just tell whether it's a voice or something else on it?"

Brice shook his head. "That's not how it works. When I'm tapping a phone line, I'm doing it at the central office where the phone calls and information are going across the wires on the telephone network. On a normal unencrypted line, I can translate whatever is going across the connection from its source, whether voice or data. But the encryption puts a kink in what I can do."

"Can't you unencrypt it?"

"I tried, believe me, I tried." Brice grinned. "I did some analysis on the data patterns and I suspect the method they're using is some combination of the double ratchet algorithm with an extended triple Diffie-Hellman handshake. It wouldn't surprise me if they're using Curve25519 for the asymmetric cryptographic operations. In other words, we need to get someone inside that place and get a simple audio bug in there."

Levi raised an eyebrow. "And is that where I come in?"

"Yes and no." Mason interjected. "We have reason to believe that this staffer is communicating with someone in Russia – but we need to be sure, and we need to know who it is before we go off half-cocked."

"We do know that the encrypted line is being used by that staffer you met." Brice interjected. "The line seems to be used several times a week, and about half of those time coincides with when our Mr. Banks is visiting the pizza shop."

Mason nodded. "I have some ideas on how you might be able to help with gathering more info for us. But before we go into that, let's talk about those names you gave Brice. Popov and Karpov." He turned to the man on Levi's right and said, "Gregor, why don't you fill us in on who those two characters are."

Gregor turned slightly toward Levi and spoke with a mild German accent. "Yuri Popov is a leading member of the rather infamous Wagner group. It's a Russian paramilitary organization operating out of the disputed regions of the Ukraine. We know with absolute certainty that the Wagner group has connections to the Kremlin, and with the on-again off-again border hostilities between Russia and Ukraine, we believe Popov and his associates are trying to win favor with the Russian state by destabilizing the Ukraine. From what I've been able to dig up, he's an unpleasant character who is well connected with the Russian leadership. His daily activities are something that are not well known."

Levi clenched his jaw as he recalled what Popov had told him about a rival of his:

"Unfortunately, dear Yevgeny is one of my country's protected ones. A friend of the Russian president. Yevgeny has an iron ring around him at all times, and none of my people could penetrate it.

Believe me, the world would be better off if Yevgeny stopped breathing."

If Popov was part of a group that was beholden to the Kremlin, and the Kremlin nowadays *was* the Russian president, the foundation upon which Popov had built his story was beginning to crack.

"And Karpov?" Levi asked.

Gregor rubbed the back of his neck. "Yevgeny Karpov is an interesting one. The man's father was a member of the Russian State Duma, think of him simply as the equivalent of a US congressman.

"Much like his father, Yevgeny runs in political circles, but it seems like his interests lay more in post-Soviet wealth creation activities. His business primarily has to do with commodities trading under the name of his company, the Vostok Group."

"Remember though that even such activities are sanctioned by the Russian government and in itself quite suspect," Mason noted with a grimace. "Almost all of the political circles in Russia nowadays are tainted with some form of corruption."

Gregor nodded. "That's a fair assessment. Especially in today's climate with the active hostilities on the Russian border. The West's sanctions on Russia's access to SWIFT—"

"Swift?" Levi asked.

"I forget what exactly the letters stand for, but it's how payments are processed by banks. Part of the sanctions on Russia have hampered their ability to pay for or get paid for things via the worldwide banking system. We have many reports coming out of Russia that this has caused a lot of turmoil amongst the elites. For those most closely associated with the Kremlin power structure, their foreign assets are being frozen and property is being confiscated. Financially, Russia has become a pariah state. And the troubles are not just for the upper echelon, there's a huge amount of internal strife with the common people. Much of it coming from the brutal crackdown on the media and free speech within Russia. The Russian people's access to foreign media has been completely cut off, and the Kremlin is of course blaming everything on Western forces, especially the NATO members."

Levi wasn't big on watching the news, but even he had seen reports about a hellish landscape in the Ukraine and parts of Russia. How much of it was true was always up for debate, but what Gregor had described seemed like the media was watering down the troubles within Russia. In his mind, he was picturing a nightmarish landscape for the Russian people.

"And this is what I'm getting myself into?" Levi thought to himself.

"As to my information regarding Karpov, I have to preface this with a word of caution. The data I have about him is accurate and from prior to the start of the difficulties Russia has had with the West. That being said, things could have changed drastically since then.

"The last we knew; Karpov was certainly a wealthy man. We don't have any records of him being directly or indirectly responsible for any criminal enterprises. Everything seems to indicate that Yevgeny Karpov is as legitimate as a Russian oligarch can be, and as director Mason indicated, you should take that with a large spoonful of salt—if you know what I mean."

Levi nodded.

"However," Gregor motioned in Brice's direction, "with the help of agent Brice, I did try and anticipate why you might have asked about these two men. I came up with no clear link between you and Popov, but there's a very strange thing that came up in the search having to do with Karpov." He looked over at Brice. "Maybe you can explain what you found?"

"Sure." Brice pulled out a folded-up sheet of paper from his shirt pocket and unfolded it. "I did a basic search trying to link your name and those two names you gave us, and like

Gregor said, nothing came up for Popov, but I found something very odd in the search through the Russia media. It was in Pravda of all places."

"Isn't that the Soviet newspaper that was basically the propaganda arm for the USSR?" Levi asked.

"Actually, yes. And believe it or not, they still exist, and in post-Soviet Russia it's run by the Communist Party of the Russian Federation. Your name actually appeared in it a few years back in a want ad."

"What? How..." and Levi recalled what Popov had said.

"But I know that Yevgeny wants to talk with you, Lazarus Yoder."

"Let me guess, looking for Lazarus Yoder?"

"Yes!" Brice's eyes widened and looked down at the paper. It's a strange want ad, it says the following, I apologize for the Google translation of this, *"Long lost brother, Lazarus Yoder, being looked for. Will pay for information that leads to his safe return to his family."*

"That is a bit bizarre, especially since I have no brothers." Levi pressed his lips together as his mind raced, trying to make sense of what seemed like a message that might be hiding some alternate meaning. "I'm assuming you're telling me about it because you've somehow linked that to Karpov?"

"Correct. There was a number and a mailing address associated with the paid ad, and I even hacked into Pravda's database and confirmed the source of the payment for the ad. It came from a shell company that Karpov owns."

"Well, Mr. Yoder." Mason focused his intense gaze on Levi. "It looks like you have some unsolved mysteries awaiting you having to do with a Russian oligarch, but let's set that aside for now. It's a distraction. Let's talk about the pizza shop."

Levi shifted his gaze to Brice. "Brice, I assume you have some tiny gadgets you'd want to be placed in and around that restaurant and wherever that third phone line is?"

The techno-wizard nodded. "I have a bag of them ready for you to deploy."

"And this place is in Arlington?" Levi asked.

Joe nodded. "It is."

"Okay, I'll need your bugs to plant." Levi panned his gaze across table and then focused on Mason. "I'll also need some of the Outfit's cash, without too many questions."

The edge of Mason's lip curled up in a half-smile. "How much money are you talking about?"

"About ten thousand dollars should cover it. Don't expect it back."

Everyone in the room looked at the frozen image of Mason, the man didn't even blink for nearly ten seconds and finally he nodded. "Okay. I'll get it to you in twenty minutes. What do you have in mind?"

Levi grinned. "It's best we not discuss the details. I'll do what I can to arrange for planting Brice's little toys and that'll be that. I'll have to make a few phone calls, but let's assume I'll reach out to the pizza shop tomorrow night."

Mason stood and pointed to the stack of papers in front of Levi. "Study those while you're here, on site. They'll come in handy if and when I think this goes in the direction I think it might."

As the others stood and began walking out of the conference room, Levi knew who he needed to reach out to.

Dino Minelli would be able to help with what he was planning. Any operation in Virginia needed the approval of Don Marino, the head of the Marino crime family, and regardless of what he did for the Outfit, there were protocols that had to be followed in that world.

Especially with what he had planned for this pizza shop.

CHAPTER EIGHT

Levi walked into Ma Kelly's Bistro, a place no self-respecting New York member of the Mafia would find himself in. It was an old Irish pub converted to serve food to folks that didn't care about what kind of animal the meat was coming from. The place was dingy and smelled of stale beer and rancid fryer oil. Not surprisingly, it was nearly empty. His shoes were sticking to the floor as he walked into the dingy joint.

Levi scanned the room and recognized the tall, barrel-chested man getting up from one of the tables.

The contact lens immediately drew a yellow rectangle around the man's face and flashed *"Dino Minelli"* under it.

Additional text began scrolling under the superimposed rectangle:

"Known member of the Marino crime family.

No active warrants."

He walked over to Levi and they kissed each other's cheeks. A greeting of equals.

As Denny's lens accurately stated, it was Dino Minelli, one of the *capos* for the Marino crime family out of Virginia.

"Levi my friend, it's good to see you again." Dino motioned to the two men who'd been sitting with him and were now standing on either side of the *capo*. "On my left is Joey Pelosi, and on my right is Victor Romano. They're friends of ours."

Denny's contact lens agreed.

Levi shook hands with both men, knowing exactly what they were without having ever needing to hear it outright.

Being friends in *La Cosa Nostra* has a special meaning and there was a code that all members followed. When introducing someone to another member of the Mafia, you'd introduce them in one of two ways, they were either *my* friend, which meant the person you were introducing was a connected guy, and business wouldn't be discussed in front of that person, or you'd introduce them as *our* friend, which meant they were a *made* guy, a person of mutual respect, and someone who could be trusted with business. A person who'd taken the oath.

Joey and Victor were two big men. *Made* men. Easily two hundred and fifty pounds each, built like concrete blocks, a few inches shorter than Levi's six-foot frame.

Levi shifted his gaze back to Dino and shook his head.

"What's with you and this crappy place we keep meeting at?"

Dino grinned as they walked out of the dingy bar, his arm draped over Levi's shoulder. "You know me, I just wanted to make sure nobody saw us talking, and the last place they'd think to find Dino Minelli is at some two-bit Irish bar." He motioned to the black Cadillac XTS parked on the side of the street, pressed the car's remote, and the car beeped twice, unlocking its doors. "Levi, you take the front passenger seat and navigate us to this place you've got a beef with."

Even though Levi had never been to the pizza shop Joe had talked about, he'd used Google Maps and gotten a visual of what it looked like and its exact location. As Dino drove east on Wilson Blvd, Levi pointed ahead and to the right, "Just past Emerson, you'll see the place. It's called Pirrone's Pizza, it's the building with the brown roof."

"Got it." Dino slowed the car and turned into the far end of the parking lot, on the other side of two large dumpsters.

It was late in the evening, the sun had gone down, and there were a few customers in the pizza shop.

Dino switched off the headlights, but left the car idling.

Levi turned in his seat to face Joey and Victor. "You guys ready?"

"Hold up," Dino shifted in his seat. "Let's get a few things cleared up. This guy you're after was up in your neck of the woods and crossed a line with the sister of one of Don Bianchi's *made* guys. I would have put a bullet in his forehead and called it done, if it were me, but you want to put the squeeze on this guy, and that's it? Joey and Victor are just backup muscle in case things go sideways?"

Levi nodded. "I'll take the lead into the restaurant, Joey and Victor just hang back. I'll take the owner in the back and convince him that he's made some bad decisions in life and he needs to make amends. Whatever I get, you guys earned it. I don't need a taste. If it takes more than ten minutes, there's probably people coming out in a body bags."

Dino grinned. "Sounds good to me." He looked over at his two companions. "Any questions from you two?"

Joey leaned forward and spoke in a whisper, "So neither of us do anything unless Levi gets in trouble, right?"

Dino pats Levi on the shoulder and says, "In there, whatever he says goes, you *capisce*?"

Both men nodded.

"Fine." Dino motioned in the direction of the pizza shop. "You guys go and I'll keep the car running. If it's more than fifteen minutes, I'm leaving all of you in there."

Levi patted his left shoulder holster and felt the reassuring weight of the Glock 19 he normally carried. On the other shoulder holster, he had the Russian gun, although he still didn't have a good idea why the Outfit had given it to him. He hopped out of the car and the two men silently followed him as he walked toward the restaurant's entrance.

The front door's bell jingled as Levi pushed it open, and he surveyed the inside of the restaurant. Immediately ahead of him was the main counter, set up like an old-style diner, with several empty seats and behind it were the pizza ovens and prep areas.

To his left were a smattering of table with four chairs each, and in the back was a sign for the restrooms and an unmarked door that he presumed would be the back office.

There were five customers at two tables, eating their pizzas.

Behind the counter was one college-aged kid kneading dough, another person of a similar age was manning the counter and cash register, and in the back was a middle-aged guy with a pizza peel who had just taken a pizza out of the oven and deposited it into a takeout box.

Levi glanced over his shoulder as Joey and Victor entered the restaurant. "Hang out near the entrance for now. Let's keep things quiet."

He walked up to the kid at the cash register and leaned over the counter. "Hey kid, is that the manager of the store?" Levi nodded in the direction of the man running a pizza cutter over the freshly-baked pie.

The kid nodded. "Did you have some problem with one of our pizzas? Maybe I can help."

As Levi leaned closer to the kid, he surreptitiously

slipped one of Brice's listening devices under the counter and said, "No, this is something I need to talk to the manager about."

The kid turned and called out to the man boxing up the freshly-sliced pizza. "Carlo, we've got someone who needs to talk to you."

Levi took a few steps to the far-right hand side of the counter as the manager walked toward him, glancing in Joey and Victor's direction with a concerned expression. Levi could only imagine what he was thinking: two large men in suits standing at the entrance to the restaurant, while another man in a suit wants to talk. Either the FBI or something worse.

Carlo pasted on a smile and stood on the opposite side of the counter from where Levi was standing and spoke with a muddled accent that clearly wasn't Italian. "Yes sir? How can I help you?"

A yellow rectangle appeared around the man's face and the name *"Carlo Ingenoso"* appeared below the rectangle.

Scrolling below the name additional information appeared:

"Born: Sergei Romanov.
Active FBI file.
Under surveillance by FBI, approved via FISA court.
No active warrants."

Levi secretly placed another of the listening devices

under the counter, leaned forward and motioned for the man to get closer.

He did.

"Sergei, you have something of mine."

The man's brow furrowed; he opened his mouth but no sound came from it.

Levi purposefully shifted his suit jacket, briefly exposing one of his holstered handguns.

The manager's eyes widened and for a moment he looked unsteady on his feet, almost as if he was about to pass out.

The old-fashioned phone on the wall, with a stretched-out coiled connection to its handset suddenly rang, and Levi immediately pulled the phone from the wall with a single yank.

The cashier yelled, "Hey—"

The manager immediately turned to the kid at the cash register and snarled, "Mind your business!" He turned to Levi and spoke with a hushed tone. "I'm sorry, but I think you're mistaken." He glanced nervously at the restaurant's entrance. "What is it you think I have, Mister…"

"I was told a package was mailed here to someone named Ribikov from our friends overseas." Levi motioned to the back of the store. "I'll find it myself, you come with me."

"But—"

Levi's voice took on a gravelly tone as he grabbed the

man's shirt collar and squeezed. "I'm starting to think you're purposefully hiding something from me. I'll make this simple: you and I go in the back, look for my package and then I leave, or my two friends and I will burn this place to the ground. Which is it going to be?"

"Okay, okay!" The man nodded rapidly and motioned to the back. "Come, I'll unlock the storeroom. I have nothing to hide."

The manager slowly walked along the counter, the cashier tried to say something and the man nearly back-handed him for his trouble.

As Levi passed his guys, he whispered, "Joey, come with me and make sure nobody disturbs us in the back room. Victor, just make sure things stay peaceful. It won't be long."

Levi walked past the tables and the customers who were focused on their own conversations and had barely noticed the disturbance.

With shaking hands, "Carlo" unlocked the door at the back of the store. He looked over his shoulder and saw Levi and the Marino family soldier right behind him.

He opened the door and a light automatically flickered to life in what was clearly a storeroom of sorts. Levi put his hand on Sergei's shoulder and guided the man forward into the room while Joey turned around and stood at the store-room's entrance.

"Sergei, lock the door." Levi said it in Russian.

And as the man closed the door and fumbled with his key, Levi panned his gaze across the room. In the far corner, he spotted a plain, unadorned desk with a modern-looking phone. Very new school for a place filled with nothing that looked newer than thirty years old.

Levi heard the metal snick of the deadbolt sliding into the doorframe, pulled out his Glock and aimed it at the manager's head. "Drop the keys right where you're standing, take three steps back, and raise your hands."

The man trembled and began praying in Russian as he did what he was told.

Levi grabbed the keys and led Sergei to the far corner of the storeroom, a place on the opposite wall from where the desk was located. "Get on your knees and face the wall."

As the man slowly lowered himself, he begged in Russian, "Please, please. I've done nothing wrong. I swear to you, there's been no shipment. I get all the mail. I see everything. I don't make mistakes like that. Please, I beg of you, I have a wife and children."

Levi motioned toward the wall. "Lean forward with your forehead against the wall."

The man began sobbing, but did as he was told.

"Now put your hands behind your back."

Again, he listened.

"You move from this position while I'm looking for my package, and I swear to you, I'll make sure your wife and children see your dismembered body before they too are killed. If I finish my search and I'm satisfied you aren't lying, then I will leave you and your family unharmed. Do you understand."

"I, I do." Sergei pulled in a shuddering breath and closed his eyes.

Levi holstered his weapon and walked over to a pile of boxes, began ripping them open, all the while placing Brice's listening devices in unobtrusive hiding spots.

One bag of semolina flour accidentally ripped open and poured its contents across the floor.

Levi made a show of searching for something as he worked his way toward the desk with the phone. He glanced at Sergei, and even though he was sagging a bit from exhaustion, he was very focused on the wall in front of him.

Levi stuck a listening device to the bottom of the phone, and seeing that the receiver was held together with a screw, he quickly retrieved a tiny Philips-head screwdriver from his suit pocket, opened it and placed a wire-thin listening device into the listening end of the phone's receiver.

He quickly reassembled the phone, made a few more loud kicks at some boxes, hid the last of the listening devices, and cursed loud enough so only Sergei could hear it.

The entire process had taken about four minutes, with another couple of minutes in the front of the store, he didn't have any more time.

Levi had completed what he needed to do, walked over to Sergei and growled in Russian, "Get up."

The man was pale and his face streaked with tears. "Did you find it?"

Levi pulled an envelope from his suit pocket and handed it to Sergei. "This is for the mess and the trouble I've caused you. Clearly, I was given some bad information."

Sergei accepted the envelope with shaking hands and a confused expression.

"Go ahead, you can open it. I'm leaving now. You will not see me again, and for that, be thankful."

Levi unlocked the door and heard a gasp behind him. He turned to see Sergei's eyes wide with shock as he held a fistful of one-hundred-dollar bills. He dropped the keys on the floor, looked at Joey and said, "Let's go."

The three of them left the store largely the way they'd found it.

Levi got into the Cadillac's passenger's seat, and Dino slowly drove out of the parking lot.

He turned to Levi as he stopped at a red light. "Well? Did you get what you were looking for?"

Levi pulled another envelope out of his suit jacket pocket and handed it to Dino with a lop-sided grin. "There's a mutual understanding and I don't think he'll repeat his mistake."

Dino hefted the thick envelope and glanced at Levi as he continued driving. "And this is?"

"Five thousand bucks. It was pretty much all the guy had in his safe."

Dino snorted and tossed the envelope to Joey in the back seat. "You two split that and give the Don his cut."

Victor chuckled. "Two-and-a-half G's for just standing around for ten minutes works for me."

Joey opened the envelope and whistled. "Dino, you should have seen it. Smooth as silk, Levi had that guy eating out of his hands in less than a minute, and the only thing that got hurt was a wall phone."

"A wall phone?" Dino gave Levi another sidelong glance and nodded. "That doesn't surprise me in the least."

Levi leaned his head back against the headrest, feeling satisfied with the night's activities.

His mind drifted back to Sergei and how shaken the man was. Would he be calling somebody in Russia right now, or just changing his shorts and closing up early?

With the number of listening devices he planted, Brice was hopefully going to start getting answers to a bunch of questions being formed in his mind. Maybe his next stop wouldn't be bed in his hotel room, but headquarters instead.

"Levi, I'm meeting up with some of my Virginia Beach crew, you up for some late dinner?"

It wasn't often that members of different families socialized in this way. Despite his curiosity about what might have happened after he left the restaurant, Levi knew he was being extended a courtesy by a representative of the Marino family.

He looked over at Dino and nodded. "Sure, who needs

sleep when there's hopefully a decent bowl of pasta fagioli to be had."

Levi yawned as he entered Brice's office, which was dominated by a large workbench filled with soldering irons, gadgets, and other things the electronics whiz was working on for the Outfit. It was three a.m.

The bespectacled head of all gadget-like things turned in his chair and motioned impatiently for him to take a seat. "What took you so long to respond? I texted you five hours ago."

Levi plopped himself onto the chair and rolled it closer to Brice. "I was busy with some of my other associates. Tell me, do you *ever* sleep? What's so urgent you needed me here now? You couldn't possibly have anything from the listening devices yet, or do you?"

"You'd be surprised." Brice tapped on his computer's keyboard and pulled up what looked like audio analysis software. "I swear to you, I was having kittens while you were in that pizza shop and I couldn't warn you, do you want to know why?"

Levi leaned forward. "Why, what happened?"

Brice turned to Levi and said, "It could have been a total nightmare, but we got lucky. You know that staffer you met over at Lincoln Park? I'm not sure how you missed each other at the pizza shop, because I swear, he parked in that restaurant's parking lot probably thirty seconds after you left the store."

Levi's eyes widened. "How do you know when I left?"

Brice turned to the screen and pulled up an audio file. "You deposited nine different transmitters, not including the one in the phone. I was able to map out the interior of the restaurant and figure out what was going on by which transmitter was picking up the sound of your voice and footsteps." He clicked on the *play* button.

Levi looked up at the monitor and noticed that Brice had a rudimentary outline of the restaurant's inner wall structure, and nine red dots, which he presumed were each of the listening devices.

"Sergei, you have something of mine."

The red dot on the bottom right of the map blinked as Levi's words broadcast through the room.

"Hey—"

Levi nodded. That was the cashier being picked up by another listening device, and another red dot.

"Mind your business! I'm sorry, but I think you're mistaken. What is it you think I have, Mister…"

"I was told a package was mailed here to someone named Ribikov from our friends overseas. I'll find it myself, you come with me."

He turned to Brice and patted him on the shoulder. "Those listening devices do the trick."

"Right. Let me fast forward a bit." Brice clicked a few times and hit play.

Levi listened to the sound of footsteps from the red dot near the cash register, then the jingle of the bell as the front door opened and then shut.

There was a pause and then a faint voice said, *"You going to check on Carlo?"*

But before anyone responded, the jingle of the bell announced the opening of the front door.

More footsteps and a voice Levi recognized as the staffer's said, *"Where's Carlo?"*

"He's in the back, but—"

"Stop talking at me and mind your pizzas."

Levi shook his head. "You're right, that encounter could have turned pretty sour pretty quickly." A surge of adrenaline rushed through him as he realized what had just happened. "Oh crap, so did you get what you needed? Did he call his contact?"

Brice fast forwarded and hit play again.

There was a muffled sound as the phone's receiver was picked up. The staffer made a sucking noise through his teeth as he tapped on the keypad.

The phone rang once… twice… *"Banks?"*

The man had a Russian accent.

"Yup it's me. I'm very close to getting the votes needed for loosening up the restrictions on the NordStream 2."

"It helps when a congressman's wife is a drug addict, doesn't it?"

The staffer gasped. *"How—"*

"Mr. Banks, there is not a thing you do that I am not aware of. Remember that, you're indebted to me, and I expect faithfulness in your execution of my needs. Doveryay, no proveryay.

"I'm sorry, I don't understand Russian."

"It's a phrase your American president stole from us. Trust, but verify. You've been a good worker, and have been compensated. What else can I do to help with this vote of yours?"

"I think if we played this as a humanitarian cause, it would sway some to vote against their party's wishes. Russian people starving, Europe freezing during the winter, those kinds of things."

The Russian let out a warm chuckle. *"I'll make some calls and see what I can have my people do. I've been hearing rumors about talk regarding the NordStream 1. What can you tell me?"*

Banks breathed heavily into the phone. *"There are some firebrands in the House and Senate that are talking about embargoing the gas coming through that pipeline. I think the humanitarian story is strengthened by those threats. Germany and most of the EU is dependent on what you're supplying. And with the anti-fossil fuels movement here in the US, that's easy enough to keep us from helping. I'm not too worried about the shutdown of number 1."*

The Russian sniffed. *"Let's not leave anything to chance. I want for you to get me a list of people in your House and Senate who you think are problems, those who will never be sympathetic to our cause. I'll work on influencing them in other ways."*

There was an awkward moment of silence and Banks said, *"I'll get you that list."*

"I'll do what I need to from my end. You get me what I need and let me know if there's any trouble."

"Understood."

The line went dead and Levi heard the sound of the receiver being put back on its cradle.

"Infl...like...Sa....z."

"What did he just say?" Levi asked.

"I had the same question, so I ran the audio enhancer on it." Brice picked up a notepad from his desk. "Banks said, 'Influence like Sanchez.'"

"Sanchez? Any idea who that is?"

Brice shrugged. "I can't be certain, but I did find a congressional candidate who ended up having a heart attack on the campaign trail. He campaigned on getting tough with Russia and China."

"How old was he?" Levi asked.

"Thirty-five, with no history of heart issues whatsoever."

"Holy crap... that's not just a *little* suspicious." Levi

replayed in his head the conversation he'd just heard and felt a surge of anger. "This Banks is as dirty as it gets. Why don't you guys lock him up?"

"We've talked about that, and that's the plan, eventually. But this guy is playing with some others who are clearly pulling the strings. We need to know who else is involved."

Levi frowned. "Not only pulling the strings, it sounds like they're willing to do just about anything to get their way. What's the deal with this NordStream thing? I know it's come up in the news, it's some kind oil or gas pipeline from Russia to Europe?"

"Actually, it's two pipelines. Each is worth about ten billion dollars a year to the Russian state. The second one is held up due to sanctions-based red tape and there's talk of shutting down the NordStream 1 pipeline as well, all because of the political conflicts with Ukraine."

Levi leaned against the back of his chair. "Do you know who the Russian is?"

Brice nodded. "It took the computers a while to get an approximate match, especially since the guy was speaking English and lots of the voice data the computers had to search through was mostly in Russian. But we got lucky. His name is Konstantin Porchenko."

"Porchenko?" Levi felt a chill race up his spine.

"Yes, he's the head of a Russian State energy company. A rich man, without a doubt, and one who has enough resources to likely get whatever he needs done."

"And has a tight grip on the short hairs of lots of folks in DC, it seems." Levi frowned. The possible loss of ten billion a year in revenue would be a strong motivator to almost anyone. "This Porchenko guy, is he by chance related to someone named Vladimir Porchenko?"

"Wait a minute, you'd asked me about him before…"

"Right, but that was also when I appeared on INTERPOL's most wanted and we went off on a tangent."

"Right!" Brice turned back to the computer and banged several commands on the keyboard. It took less than a minute for him to nod at what was scrolling on the screen. "Looks like Konstantin is well-connected, as you might expect, and yes, he has an uncle named Vladimir. Or should I say he had one, it seems like he's recently deceased."

Levi pressed his lips together and his mind raced. He had a thing or two to do with Vladimir's demise.

Brice flipped a page on his notebook and tapped on the sheet of paper he'd scribbled on. "This is where it gets interesting. Remember that name you gave us, Yevgeny Karpov?"

Levi nodded.

"Well, it seems like Karpov and Porchenko are direct competitors. They've competed on nearly every energy resource acquisition since the breakup of the Soviet Union."

Levi opened his suit jacket and showed Brice the Russian handgun in the shoulder holster. "This is all interesting, but why did you guys give me a Russian gun and a

Russian passport. How am I going to help with this, you guys have people like that Black Widow chick who seems to get off on killing people. What are you and Mason and whoever else is making decisions thinking I'm going to do?"

Brice grinned. "First of all, Annie, the so-called Black Widow, is pregnant, retired, and we're getting married in a few weeks."

Levi blinked as he tried to imagine the short pudgy engineer with the sadistic black beauty who would likely had dozens of kills to her name. "Congrats, I guess."

"Anyway, it's pretty simple. We've verified that the phone Porchenko used with the staffer has made a bunch of incoming calls to the US. Folks in DC seem to be a favorite of his, even inside the Pentagon. We have to assume the worst, and that he's the puppet master of a bunch of people we don't have a clear identity for."

"So you want the head of the snake to be chopped off?" Levi asked.

"Well, in not so many words, yes. It's impossible to tell how much damage this guy can do. Hell, he's got the chief of staff of one of the senior Congressman as his lapdog. Maybe he has a few generals in his back pocket? Even some FBI agents... put it this way, we could try and send an assassination force in, but from what we've been able to gather, this Porchenko guy is already at war with others inside the Russian State. He's going to be hard to get to. But you have an in."

"I do? Oh, you mean through this Karpov guy who is supposedly looking for me? Let me guess, you're going to assume he's looking for me because he wants to be best friends, and he'll help us out in trying to kill his business rival, is that where you're going with this?"

Brice almost looked embarrassed for a moment and then snapped out of it. "I did research on Karpov with the resources we have in the Russian State. He's legitimately known as a straight shooter and as honest as honest gets in Russia. You have to realize, in the swamp that is DC, sell-outs are as common as fleas on a mutt. As soon as we start trying putting the fleas behind bars, this Porchenko guy will realize what's going on and who knows what'll happen?

"The best course of action seems to be to not let on that we have some idea of what's going on, let it continue—"

"While I go to Russia, suck up to some oligarch I don't know and see about braining this Porchenko guy for interfering with our government operations."

Brice smiled. "I couldn't have said it better myself. So, is that a yes?"

Levi closed his eyes and felt the weariness wash over him. He took a deep breath, let it out slowly, and focused his gaze on Brice. "Have you taken care of the INTERPOL thing yet?"

Brice shook his head. "I talked to Mason about that and he thinks it's a bad idea to do anything yet. It might tip folks off that we know something is up and we don't want to show our hand if we can avoid it. At least for now."

"So, how am I supposed to get there?"

"If you're a 'go' on this, then Mason will pull some strings, you take a military transport to Incirlik over in Turkey. From there, we have an office that can transport you across the border and you'll be in spitting distance of the Kremlin within ten hours of landing in Turkey."

Levi leaned back in his chair and massaged his temples. "I must be crazy to say yes to this. Go ahead, rev up the jet engines.

"I guess I've got some borscht in my future."

CHAPTER NINE

With his cell phone buzzing on the nightstand, Levi reached out and answered the call. "Who is it?" he said, followed by a loud yawn.

"Levi, I've gotten the Air Force to cough up a C-37B for your flight." Mason's gruff voice broadcast loudly through the connection. *"You've got a driver waiting for you downstairs to take you to Andrews right now."*

Levi flung aside the bedsheet and glanced at the clock. It was five a.m., and it was still dark outside. "You guys don't really believe in sleep, do you?"

"You'll have ten hours or so to get some sleep on the trip over there. The driver will hand you a briefcase that has your mission brief that you can read through. It has all the background data on your targets and gives you a list of your contacts in-country."

Levi switched the phone into speaker mode, tossed it on the bed so he could slip into his slacks and finish getting dressed. "Did Brice get the stuff—"

"Everything you asked for and a bit more will be on the plane at Joint Base Andrews. And before you race downstairs, just realize that we've got your back the entire way. Our people at Incirlik will meet you as your plane touches down and help ferry you into enemy territory. One thing you'll need to understand. Whatever you've got that has any identifying markers such as a serial number will have to be left behind. That means any sidearm you have that isn't Russian-made gets set aside. Our folks will help equip you with anything else you need."

Levi shrugged into his bullet-proof vest. "What about my suit and clothes? Let's just say they're all custom-made, have no labels on them and shouldn't be traceable."

"Even your underwear? Socks?"

"Well, I guess I have some off-the-shelf stuff." Levi frowned as he slipped into his loafers and realized that he wasn't wearing the right clothes for any kind of physical mission.

"You'll meet a Mr. Osman in our offices. He'll handle your on-site mission needs."

Levi grabbed the phone, took it off speaker and headed for the door. "If you say so. Okay, I'm heading downstairs."

"Roger that. Remember, if you've got any emergencies,

Brice is your main point of contact. He'll arrange for what-ever is needed. Good luck, Levi."

The phone went dead and Levi took the stairs to the first floor, walked through the lobby and out the front door. He was immediately greeted by a dark minivan with police lights parked twenty feet from the hotel's entrance. On the front passenger door was a logo with *"Security Police"* and *"Department of the Air Force"* emblazoned on it.

Levi heard the doors to the minivan unlock and the front passenger's door cracked open a bit. He opened the door and was greeted by a driver in an Air Force uniform.

"Mr. Yoder, the jet's fueled up and ready to go."

Levi hopped into the front passenger seat, closed the door and as he wrapped the seatbelt around him, the Airman turned in his seat and showed one half of a silver coin to him. Exposed on the face of the coin was a familiar pyramid with the Eye of Providence. One of the Outfit's IDs. He grabbed the exposed half and within a second a light emanated from the eye.

The Airman pocketed the coin, put the car into gear, and they lurched away from the hotel, heading east. He glanced at Levi and held out a military ID, which he took. "That's to get you past the main gate and onto the plane." He also hitched his thumb toward the back seat. "There's a briefcase in the back you need to take with you. It's an Outfit-secured package."

Levi reached into the back, grabbed the briefcase and set

it between his knees as he looked down at the CAC with his face on it. The military ID noted that his name had suddenly become "Warren Jennings" and he was a First Lieutenant in the Air Force. He looked at the driver's uniform, caught the name and rank and asked, "So, Airman Weaver, you obviously know my real name. Do you know why the ID has a different one listed?"

"Sir, I don't know for certain, but I was briefed on a few things that might pertain and I can speculate, if you like."

"I would like."

"I was told that there may be higher ups in my military chain of command who are compromised—"

"Ah, and our people don't want anyone to know that I'm the one taking a little trip."

"Yes sir. In fact, I know that the C-37B that's been fueled up for Incirlik is officially registered as being used to facilitate a meeting for an American and a Turkish VIP. It's being treated as a black bag operation, which isn't that unusual. The Deputy Chief of Mission will meet you on the plane, he's one of our guys. On paper, you are flying over to act as a technical advisor and translator for this meeting."

As the minivan turned right off of Dower House Road, they passed a sign that read, *"Pearl Harbor Gate Hours 0500 – 2100"* and within moments they'd arrived at a well-lit security outpost.

The airman lowered his driver's side window and as they pulled to a stop, they both handed their IDs to the guard.

After a quick check, the guard handed the IDs back and they were quickly driving through the base, past the East Perimeter Road and within moments, the minivan was slowing as it approached a mid-sized jet, a US flag on its tail, Air Force logo on its engine, blue and white paint scheme, and "United States of America" painted just above the passenger windows.

Levi had been on military jets before, but they were almost always gray and largely unmarked. This was a bit different.

The lights flickered brightly on the wings, and a staircase yawned open as he stepped out of the minivan with the brief-case in his hand and the CAC clipped to his lapel.

A woman stood in silhouette at the top of the stairs and motioned for him to come.

Levi hopped up the stairs and was greeted by one of the crew members, who was also wearing an Air Force uniform.

"Sir, can I see your ID to confirm."

Levi unclipped his ID and handed it to Airman Garcia.

Upon looking at it, his face, and then at the CAC once again, she handed the ID back, saluted and motioned for him to enter. "Lieutenant Jennings, there's a secured crate in the back section of the plane waiting for you. If you can please buckle in, we're taking off as soon as I pull up the stairs."

Levi's gaze fell across the interior cabin. It was clearly an executive jet. One probably used mostly for people like the Speaker of the House and other so-called VIPs. It easily sat six in the first section of the plane, and the was another section further in the back that he could see past an open door.

A tall man approached, who wore a suit and they shook hands. "Good to have you onboard, Jennings. I'm Frank Luck, the number two at the Turkish embassy. We'll talk a bit more in the air, but…" he motioned toward the leather-upholstered seats. "Grab a seat and buckle up, because these fly boys aren't much into waiting."

It was a bit odd there being only two passengers on the plane other than the pilots, who he didn't see, and at least one other Airman who had her hand mashed down on a button.

Levi took a seat somewhere in the middle of the cabin as the sound of hydraulics echoed through the plane.

The Deputy Chief of Mission for Turkey sat at one of the front chairs, unfolded a newspaper, and buried his nose in it.

From Levi's vantage point he saw the stairs folding up and within a handful of seconds, there was a thud and Airman Garcia disappeared toward the front of the plane.

The air pressure changed and the speaker crackled overhead.

"This is Captain John Wunderlich, and I'll be the pilot for this flight to Incirlik.

"We are first in line for takeoff. We will be cruising at an altitude of 48,000 feet at an airspeed of approximately 500

knots. Flight time is expected to be approximately eleven hours from wheels up to wheels down.

"This will be the only communication until we land at our destination."

Levi grinned. "The military guys weren't much for the niceties that the FAA forced on the commercial airlines. He looked at the briefcase, which had no obvious key nor way of opening it, except for one familiar logo.

The pyramid with the Eye of Providence was engraved on a metal plaque at the top of the briefcase.

Levi pressed his thumb on the logo, and within seconds felt something inside the suitcase click and it popped open a quarter-inch.

The plane veered to the right and its engines whined as the pilot revved up the RPMs.

He peered inside the suitcase and found a stack of papers, photos, and maps.

There was one red piece of paper that immediately caught his eye. He opened the briefcase just a bit and glanced at the paper.

"Before departing the plane, ensure that all the contents are back in the case. The locking mechanism is engaged by the same method used to open the case.

"Upon engaging the locking mechanism, the contents will be safely incinerated. The case and its contents will be rendered safe for disposal."

Levi felt himself being pushed against his seat as the

pilot released the brakes and the jet launched itself down the runway.

Within seconds, they were airborne, and climbing up to altitude at a much steeper rate of ascent than any commercial aircraft normally would.

Eleven hours.

If he was lucky, he'd be able to go through this data dump of mission briefings and grab a few hours of sleep before they landed.

Levi put his head against the headrest, waiting for the plane to level off.

As they rocketed into the sky, he couldn't help but wonder what the next leg of his journey would be like. Russia was locked down... yet the Outfit didn't seem to think that was a problem.

It wouldn't be long before that hypothesis would be tested.

As the plane banked for a final approach to Incirlik, Levi pressed his thumb against the Eye of Providence and heard the lock on the briefcase engage.

Within seconds he detected the faint smell of something burning, and even though the briefcase immediately felt warm to the touch, it never got uncomfortably hot.

The plane landed with a thud, and the engines roared as

Levi lurched forward due to the heavy application of brakes and thrust reversers.

Levi unbuckled his seatbelt as the plane coasted to a stop near a set of hangars emblazoned with the US Air Force logo. He stood, hefted the backpack he'd retrieved from the crate in the back, and the diplomat motioned for him as the stairs unfurled from the body of the aircraft.

"I'll walk you to your connection, Lieutenant."

Levi followed the diplomat off the plane and noticed a Mercedes limousine waiting nearby with a small American flag sticking up from the front right quarter panel of the limo, and the red crescent and star flag of Turkey waved from the limo's front left quarter panel.

The diplomat waved at the Airman standing by the car and yelled over the sounds of the nearby taxiing jets, "I'll be right back." Frank motioned for Levi to continue following as he walked toward the hangar.

Levi caught up to the man and asked, "Where are we going?"

"Where are *you* going is the better question. I'm not briefed on the details of your mission, just that I'm to help you get to the office."

They entered the large hangar and veered into a hallway that led to plainly-appointed offices and Levi followed him down a set of concrete steps into what looked like a bomb shelter.

In the tight hallway, lit by hanging LED lamps, there

were signs that had a logo with three yellow triangles, labeled "Fallout Shelter" painted all along the network of concrete halls. The diplomat paused and pointed down a dimly-lit hallway that seemed to lead to a dead end. "The entrance is that way. It's biometrically keyed, so you should be fine. Any questions before I go back up top-side?"

Levi frowned, "Um, isn't someone going to wonder where I am, why I didn't go back up with you?"

The diplomat shook his head. "Don't worry about it. The crew from the plane that brought us has likely already departed for its hangar, and nobody was expecting you at the embassy anyway."

Levi shook hands with the diplomat and walked toward the end of the hallway.

Posted near the ceiling was an old painted logo of the Eye of Providence, and on the concrete wall was a plain metal panel with no obvious markings or any indication this was an entrance of any kind.

It looked like a dead end.

Levi glanced over his shoulder, saw nobody, and pressed his splayed hand against the metal plate.

The plate was warm to the touch and almost immediately he heard a click. The wall in front of him lowered into the ground, revealing a dark corridor.

He stepped across the threshold, and the wall immediately sprang up and shut with a whoosh as bright lights blinked on, illuminating the hallway.

"Mr. Yoder, welcome to Turkey."

The disembodied voice had a warm tone with an accent that was hard to place. It was possibly Middle Eastern.

"Please walk to the end of the hallway, place your feet on the tiles located in front of the inner door. Look straight ahead with your arms at your sides."

Levi walked the length of the fifty-foot corridor, placed his feet on the tiles and stood in front of a metal door. A set of spotlights immediately beamed onto him, forcing him to squint at the sudden brightness.

"Identity confirmed."

The metal door lowered before him, revealing a middle-aged gentleman with black hair and a thick black beard. The man motioned for him to approach. "Welcome to our office. I believe this is your first time in Turkey, is it not?"

Levi stepped through the doorway into a lobby, and just as before, the door behind him whooshed upward. "It is." He panned his gaze across the richly-appointed lobby filled with leather chairs and hallways exiting the room on both the left and right-hand sides.

They shook hands. "I am Mr. Osman, the office manager. I believe you have a mission to complete, and time is of the essence. Please, follow me." He motioned for Levi to follow and walked to the left, past a set of empty leather chairs gathered around a coffee table and entered the hallway.

Lights turned on and off automatically as they traversed

the maze of hallways in this complex. "Mr. Osman, I was wondering if you have some Russian clothes that—"

"We are heading to the supply closet, don't you worry. I believe all your requests have been anticipated. And if they haven't, we should be able to accommodate your needs in short order."

As they walked along the hallway, past several intersections, Levi quickly realized that this place was massive. "How did this place even come to be? It had to have taken years to dig all this out from the bedrock."

Mr. Osman glanced in his direction and smiled; the lights reflecting off his dark eyes. "Many of these tunnels existed long before the birth of the Outfit. Whether they were built by the Romans, or later by those in the Ottoman Empire, it's uncertain. The exact history of these tunnels has been obscured, lost in time so-to-speak. But it *is* an engineering marvel."

They both entered a large chamber and Levi grinned at the familiar sight. All along the edges were lockers, very much like in the New York office, and not much different than you'd what expect in any high school.

The proprietor pointed at an unmarked metal plate on the wall and said, "Please, place your hand on there, and we shall start equipping you for your mission."

Levi pressed his hand on the warm metal panel, and almost immediately heard a series of clicks across the room as several lockers popped open.

"Sir," said Mr. Osman, gesturing, "let's start with this side of the room, shall we?"

Levi walked up to the first set of open lockers and spied several pairs of underwear, white t-shirts, dress socks, and some jeans and pullover shirts. He looked at the first pair and grinned at the Russian-branded labels.

"Please, Mr. Yoder." Osman motioned at the clothes. "I was told you should leave behind any items with any American markings, including any clothing, your wallet, the military ID, and anything that indicates where you're from."

Holding up a pair of underwear, Levi knew that he was wearing some Hanes labeled underclothes. "In other words, change out of my clothes."

"Please." Mr. Osman nodded and held up a medium-sized cloth bag. "This is for your discards."

Levi quickly stripped down, changed underwear, socks, and t-shirt.

As he got dressed, Mr. Osman produced a small, unmarked leather duffel bag. "This is for you to stow your mission items if they aren't to go into your backpack."

Levi opted to remain in his suit and packed the rest of the Russian-made clothes into the duffel.

Mr. Osman pointed to the next locker.

Levi walked over to the next locker and spotted a set of black fatigues, which he stowed into his bag, and continued through the remainder of the open lockers.

The next several lockers contained a soldier's kit,

including combat boots, a battle vest with ballistic inserts, load distribution system, and inserts to help protect against small-arms fire as well as side ballistic inserts. All of them were Russian-made and conspicuously dark in color, which would make him stand out in a snow-covered field, but Levi imagined that they'd work really well to maintain cover at night.

One locker contained a thick walking stick, which Levi appreciated, and had several good ideas on how he might use it.

And from the last open locker, Levi retrieved a wallet filled with Russian money and holding one Visa platinum card issued by a Russian bank, all of which he pocketed.

Opening the cloth sack, Levi deposited his old wallet, his two Glocks, and the underwear and socks he changed out of. The rest of his stuff was completely custom-made, and had no obvious identifying marking. He handed Mr. Osman the bag and said, "I hope to retrieve this when I return."

"Don't worry." Mr. Osman nodded. "I will keep these items safe." The middle-aged man motioned for Levi to follow him. "It's time for your next leg of the journey."

They went down the same hall through which they'd entered, but unlike the odd loopbacks to other rooms in the New York office, this place seemed to make more sense. They passed through the lobby he'd entered from and walked through it, into another hallway and within one hundred yards of the lobby they turned into a room with a set of stars going down.

Mr. Osman motioned toward the stairs and said, "Very much like other outposts, we have several underground passages to other locations."

Several passages to other locations?

Did that mean the New York City office had tunnels to places other than DC? Was each office a sort of Grand Central Station for underground travel?

"Below, you will find a train that will take you across the border, under the Black Sea, and into Russian territory. You will arrive in Moscow, and will be greeted by Ms. Petrova. She will arrange for your needs in Russia." He handed Levi a paper bag. "This is for you on the trip. It will take some time, and you may get hungry."

Levi glanced into the bag and grinned at what he saw. It looked like a school lunch any parent might pack for their kid: a sandwich, an apple, a small bag of mixed nuts, and a sealed package of Turkish dates. He held up the bag and turned to thank Mr. Osman.

His eyes opened wide as Levi stepped outside the room and looked down the hallway.

No Mr. Osman. The man had vanished into thin air.

Staring with his mouth agape for a moment, he couldn't fathom how the unassuming man had managed to vanish in the few seconds he'd inventoried his meal. Levi held up the bag and said "thank you" to the empty air, feeling a bit foolish and walked down the stairs with his pack slung over his shoulder, the walking stick tied to it, and the duffle in his left hand.

A sleek railway car was waiting at the bottom of the stairs, its doors open. It looked identical to the one he'd boarded in New York City. Levi stepped on board.

A disembodied voice announced, *"Welcome. The train will be departing Incirlik for Red Square station. The trip will be approximately twelve-hundred miles, two hundred of which will be traveling under the Black Sea, and the train will arrive in approximately six hours.*

"You have ten seconds to cancel the launch of this railway car. Once en-route, there will be no stops. Please hold on to a rail or you will likely be thrown backward. This is your only warning."

Levi took a seat and gripped one of the poles.

"Five seconds. Four. Three. Two. One."

Levi slid backward as the train accelerated at a pace not unlike what he'd expect from a formula one race car. Within seconds, the wind was keening wildly as the train flew through the darkness.

The lights were dim in the cabin, but unlike the train he'd taken in New York City, this seat had buttons whose illustrations implied they had the ability to recline.

Levi pressed a button and his chair slowly adjusted into a rather comfortable position. Setting an alarm on his phone, he closed his eyes and tried to get some rest.

He was going to be in enemy territory when he woke up.

———————

It was midday as Brice sat at his computer, pulled up his spreadsheet where the latest alerts had been logged, and scanned through the hundreds of alerts he'd received from his transmitters.

As his eyes darted across the rows and columns of data, he noticed a new transmission from the Pizza parlor and clicked on its link.

The system pulled up the recorded audio and broadcast through the monitor's speakers.

"Banks, you have an issue." It was Porchenko's voice. Brice had listened to enough tapes of the man speaking where he no longer needed computerized voice analysis to ID the man with certainty.

"What issue?"

The staffer sounded nervous.

"I sent you a link to the security video from the shop you're in. A man visited a couple days ago, caused some trouble, and left. I need to have him identified."

Brice's eyes widened as he listened to the conversation. Was Porchenko talking about Levi?

"I can have a friend in the FBI try and run it through the computers. One second, let me look at what you sent... oh

crap, I know this guy. That's Lazarus Yoder. He's a local mobster... I've met him before."

"I can't have people poking their nose into my business. Get me his location."

"Um, that might be a problem." Banks's tone of voice suddenly gained a tremor. He was nervous. "The FBI has a file on him several inches thick. I've seen it. He's a ghost of sorts. They don't seem to know his whereabouts. If they need to contact him, there's a drop box they use that—"

"Not acceptable. I need his location." Porchenko's voice had a menacing edge to it. *"I need to know why he came to the pizza shop, and what he was looking for."*

"Well, I might know the whereabout of his daughter."

Brice's heart began racing, and he wrote the timecode down for the audio track. "Oh crap, this isn't good!"

"He has a daughter?"

"I think so. Evidently Alicia Yoder is attending college this fall. I was asked to go through names of the recent admissions to some of the country's top schools with an eye toward recruiting them for internships. I noticed her last name, made a few calls, and it turns out the name of Alicia's father is Lazarus. Her address was left empty for some reason, but it's listed as being in New York City, which I know is where the mobster is supposed to be based out of."

"Good."

Brice could almost hear the smile on Porchenko's face as he frantically took notes of what was being said.

"I want you to get me Yoder's address... or maybe... what school is the girl going to?"

"I'll have to double check," Banks sounded very nervous. *"But I think it was Princeton."*

Brice shook his head and began dialing Mason's number. The Outfit needed to do something about this, and this was way above his pay grade.

"Okay, get me Yoder's address and verify the girl's school. Get me the information I've asked for, and I expect a response in hours, not days. Do you understand?"

"I-I do." Banks stammered a response.

The audio ended and Brice put his phone to his ear as Mason picked up. *"What's up?"*

"Boss, we've got a problem."

CHAPTER TEN

Levi felt the train decelerate and the disembodied voice returned. *"We will be arriving at Red Square station in one minute. Please disembark only after the train has come to a complete stop."*

The train doors opened and Levi stepped out. The dimly lit station was empty. Painted on the concrete wall was a faint message in Russian, which loosely translated said, *"An uninvited guest is worse than a Tatar."*

He wasn't exactly sure what that meant, but it seemed like an ominous warning of sorts. Somewhat like, "If you're here and unexpected, turn around and go away."

It seemed odd that there was nobody here to greet him, but then again, he might not be expected. His briefing paperwork didn't really cover much about the Outfit's office structure in Russia.

Panning his gaze across the barren concrete station and seeing no other way to go, Levi walked toward the far end of the station where he'd spied a darkened hallway.

As he approached, lights flickered in the stone tunnel and Levi caught an oddly familiar scent as he walked into the hallway.

The hallway led to a set of stairs and he quickly climbed up them as the scent of food grew stronger.

The peanut butter and jelly sandwich that he'd eaten somewhere under the Black Sea had quelled his hunger pangs, but the ever-stronger aromas wafting down the stairs made Levi's stomach gurgle in anticipation.

As he exited the stairway, Levi found himself in a makeshift kitchen of sorts.

It was a large room with a hallway door to the right and on the opposite end was a bank of ovens, a kitchen island with open-flame burners next to a flat wood-topped area where an old woman was busily chopping a large pile of mushrooms. She looked up, their eyes met, and she didn't seem surprised to see a strange man come up from the station below.

She waved him forward and yelled something he couldn't quite make out.

Levi approached and the old woman, who had to be at least seventy years old, pointed abruptly with a thick wrinkled finger at the stool next to the island and gruffly said with a strong Russian accent, "Sit."

With a growing sense of amusement, Levi shrugged himself out of his backpack, set the duffel bag down and sat on the stool. "Ms. Petrova?"

The old woman waved dismissively and with some padded gloves picked up a tray of roasted chickens, and drained the fat into a large sauté pan that was bubbling with some concoction that smelled very familiar.

"What is it that you're making?" Levi asked. "It smells delicious."

The woman took a handful of sliced mushrooms, tossed them into the pan, and then began roughly tossing the contents back and forth, somehow managing not to spill even a drop. "You're hungry. I can see it in your eyes. *Kasha* will fill you up."

Levi smiled. Kasha. He should have known. It was something his grandmother used to make ages ago. It was a buckwheat porridge of sorts, but he'd eaten it as a breakfast cereal with milk and honey. This was *not* that.

It took only a few minutes for the liquid and chicken juices to be absorbed by the brown grains and from another pot, the old woman tossed in some bow-tie noodles, and with a large serving spoon, filled a wooden bowl with the steaming food and placed it in front of Levi.

"Eat." She commanded as she placed a tablespoon next to the bowl.

Levi scooped up the brown grains, making sure to catch a piece of mushroom and one of the noodles. He held up the first spoon, looked at the old woman and nodded. "Thank you, Miss…"

The old woman's face scrunched up as she stared at him. "I'm a *babushka*, that's who I am, that's what you call me."

Babushka was Russian for grandmother.

Breathing quickly through his mouth, he tried cooling the too-hot spoonful of food he'd shoved into his mouth, chewed quickly, and swallowed.

Even though he felt the searing heat from the lump of food traveling to his stomach, Levi grabbed another spoonful, and this time spent a bit more time blowing on it before eating. He looked up at the gnarled old woman and smiled.

She wasn't paying any attention to him or looking for a compliment. She knew the food was good, and the woman had shifted her attention to a grapefruit-sized ball of dough, which she was busily kneading.

The door on the far side of the room opened and a woman walked in, spied Levi and grinned from ear-to-ear as she walked toward him. "Mr. Yoder, I see you've met my *babushka*."

"Ms. Petrova?"

The woman nodded and spoke with a breathy voice, colored with a thick Russian accent. "In the flesh."

"Nadia!" The old woman's voice was like the crack of a whip. The woman switched to Russian as she addressed her granddaughter. "Don't you flirt with this man."

Nadia motioned dismissively at the old woman who'd

picked up her walking stick and waved it in a threatening manner. The woman shifted her attention back to Levi and extended her hand. "Nadia Petrova, I'm the proprietor of this little place we have hidden under Red Square."

Levi noticed the coin gripped between her thumb and forefinger, grabbed the offered half, and the light from the coin flashed brightly. Nadia looked like she was in her thirties with dark hair gathered under a gray newsboy cap, which gave her a somewhat retro look, but it was the scar that caught his attention. She had white, pencil-thin scar that ran from her hairline, down her temple, across her left cheek and ended at the base of her chin. He switched to Russian and said, "It's good to meet you. Considering the other proprietors that I've met, I was expecting someone older…" he smiled, "and less attractive."

"You speak Russian!" Nadia smiled brightly as the old woman smacked the pile of dough down onto the table with a loud thud. She grumbled something unintelligible, and continued kneading furiously.

Nadia hitched her thumb at the old woman. "Don't mind her, she's very protective of me." The woman trailed her pointer finger down the side of her face, tracing her scar. "Especially after I got this from my husband."

"Your husband did that?" Levi stared at the woman, unsure how to react.

Nadia put her hand on his shoulder and gave it a squeeze. "It turned out he was an informant for the FSB. I hadn't known that when we'd gotten married. Personally, I have a problem with anyone close to me helping the current government. And of course, he had a problem with me not sharing where I went during the day."

The FSB was the modern-day version of the Soviet KGB, more commonly known as the secret police.

"He gave this to me just before I stabbed him in the…" She paused mid-word and laughed. "Well, I didn't mean for that unpleasant topic to jump out as we first meet." Nadia looked over at her grandmother and asked, "Are you making dumplings?"

"Of course. If I don't, you'd only eat the garbage up on the streets. Today is chicken and kasha with mushrooms."

"We'll be back soon for dinner." Nadia motioned for Levi to follow her. "I have a room where you can temporarily put your supplies, and we can discuss some of your mission's next steps."

Levi hopped off his stool and gathered his belongings.

The old woman looked up from her kneading and focused on him. "Be careful on the streets. Strangers tend to disappear, do you hear me?"

Levi nodded. "Thank you for the warning."

As they walked out of the kitchen area, Nadia lowered her voice. "I was given some names of people you are trying to reach, and I did a little bit of research ahead of your arrival. I think one of them might be dead."

"Which one?"

Nadia shook her head. "No more words until we're settled in the quiet room."

After passing through a few intersecting hallways, she turned into a room that was no bigger than a large coat closet, about five feet by five feet.

He followed her lead and stepped into the room, turned as she had to face the door, and Nadia warned, "Get ready." She pressed her hand against a waist-high metal panel to the left of the doorway.

Suddenly the room shot upward, plunging them into darkness as the sound of whooshing air surrounded them.

And just as quickly, their upward trajectory stopped, Levi felt himself go nearly weightless as the room-turned-elevator slowed and then stopped at a new level.

Nadia turned to him and did a bad job at suppressing her amused expression. "Are you okay?"

Levi's stomach wasn't so sure about the unexpected acceleration and deceleration, but he grinned. "That was fun. We should do it again."

With a wink, she motioned for him to follow her. "We're about fifty feet below the street level. Let's get your stuff settled and get down to business."

The conference room was in what Nadia had called "the quiet wing" of the Outfit's offices. Levi couldn't necessarily tell the difference between this room and any other, but he had noted how thick the conference room door was… it was almost certainly soundproof. In fact, the only sound in the room was that of his own heart beating and Nadia's quiet breaths as she sat across the conference room table from him and sorted through stacks of photos and printouts.

Levi focused on the gruesome photos arrayed on the table in front of him. From their fatigues, it looked like Russian soldiers. They were all dead, all bloodied and in some cases mutilated, as if an animal had chewed on their hands and faces. Some had clearly been burnt, and others had huge tears in their uniforms, and some even had missing limbs… possibly from an explosion.

"Ah, found it." Nadia picked up one of the papers and began reading. *"The Russian command hadn't accounted for the challenges they'd face in the Izyum woods. It led to catastrophic losses in the 64th and 38th Separate Guard Motor Rifle Brigades.*

"Their numbers are now estimated to be less than 100 able-bodied servicemen in total.

"It seems like the Russian commanders failed to provide proper equipment to their fighting units in the wooded terrain. Much of their heavy artillery was non-functional. And it seemed like the troops had ineffective electronic communication with their command, relying on messengers to get word back and forth, likely due to a lack of encrypted phones.

"Ukrainian forces struck the Russian advanced positions with drones, keeping their people out of harm's way. The Russian guns for hire, the Wagner folks, they refused to participate in combat, leading to a lack of advances on the Izyum axis.

"Several drone strikes were launched by the Ukrainians at a well-armed group that was hanging back, away from the wooded terrain. It is believed that some key members of the Wagner Group may have been killed.

"Identities cannot be confirmed by their physical appearances or possessions, we are awaiting DNA analysis to help identify the dead."

Nadia leaned across the table and tapped her finger on one of the photos in front of him. "We believe this is Yuri Popov. His last known whereabouts were somewhere outside of Slovyansk, which is between Donbas and Izyum."

Levi stared at the image of the man. Half of his face was shredded from what he presumed might have been shrapnel. On the man's shoulder he saw a mutilated patch whose center had a skull, and the word "group" was legible. Whoever this was, he was wearing a Wagner group patch, a Russian paramilitary organization known to operate out of Ukraine.

Nadia pulled out another photo from her pile and slid it toward Levi. "That's the only picture we have of Popov taken within the last three years."

As Levi studied the image, his contact, which he was

still wearing, didn't activate. In fact, it hadn't activated since getting on the train in Turkey. It was likely due to how far underground he was, and his Bluetooth-connected cell phone was next to useless down here.

He compared the image of the living man to the dead one that Nadia had pointed to and it was hard to be certain. The dead man's face was thinner, more haggard, and the scraggly salt and pepper beard obscured much of the face that wasn't destroyed by the drone attack.

The door to the conference room opened and in hobbled the old woman. One hand on her walking stick, the other holding a plate piled high with pan-fried dumplings, smothered with glistening fried onions.

Levi's eyes widened as his mind inventoried all of the sensitive information scattered across the table. It seemed to him like a huge breech of security to have someone's grandmother in this room. He looked back and forth between the old woman and Nadia.

"You two are taking too long, the dumplings will get cold." The grandmother placed the plate, which had two forks on it, on the table amidst the gruesome photos and various reports. She settled onto a chair at the end of the conference room table, and motioned toward the food. "You two can work and eat at the same time."

Nadia blew her grandmother a kiss and grinned in Levi's direction. "You're thinking I'm crazy for letting my grandmother see this stuff."

It wasn't a question.

The old woman shifted her attention to Levi and gave him a gap-toothed grin. "I was working for the same organization you work for before you were even born, young man."

Grabbing a fork, Nadia stabbed one of the dumplings, popped it into her mouth and said, "My grandmother was the proprietor of this place during the fall of the Soviet Union."

Levi reached across the table and sampled one of the dumplings. The noodle was succulent, with crispy pan-fried edges, and as he bit down on the dumpling, the warm filling filled his mouth with the buckwheat grains, perfectly fried onions, mushrooms and pieces of chicken. It was delicious.

The grandmother nodded. "It was a strange time back then. So many years under communist dictatorship, with the KGB watching everything and everyone. And then *perestroika* happened, the reforms began. It was the beginning of the end for the Soviet Union. Many of us cheered its demise, myself included.

"But things changed. We saw a Western prosperity that seemed almost unimaginable just a handful of years earlier. And eventually things began to settle into a new normal." The old woman held a grim expression.

"It didn't last long until the men who run things now began to shift things in their way. A way that resembled the old ways."

The woman's voice had a sad tone to it. Levi asked, "In

what way have things changed? I was in Russia a few years ago, but I have nothing to compare it to."

Nadia made a clicking noise with her tongue and shook her head. "Even in just the last handful of years, things have changed a lot."

"Ay, they have." The old woman glanced at her grand-daughter. "Nadia, these changes… they're going in a bad direction, and my darling Nadia, you have no idea how terrible that direction truly is. I was too young to remember what was going on back in the 50's, but my mother's tales of Stalin's reign should terrify anyone within Russia today.

"Stalin used the secret police as his own personal force within the Soviet Union." She held up her hand with her thumb and forefinger pressed together. "People who said even *this* much against Stalin vanished, never to be seen again. Millions disappeared from the streets.

"And we're seeing this all happen again.

"Our so-called leaders are making our beautiful country a pariah in the world. Those who wish to leave are forbidden passage. Those who speak against the reforms that are happening fifty feet above us, they too are vanishing, just like in the days of our Great Leader… it makes an old woman sad." She turned to Nadia and blew her a kiss. "I'm not sad for myself, but for what my poor Nadia has to deal with. I just hope her training is enough."

Levi looked over at Nadia who'd reached across the table and held her grandmother's hand. This was an emotional moment he wasn't expecting to encounter in the Outfit's clandestine office under Red Square, but it was a good warning for him. "Training?" He focused on Nadia. "I know very little about how these offices are run. Is there some specific training involved in being a proprietor?"

Nadia grinned and tilted her head in her grandmother's direction. "She taught me everything I know about spy craft and hand-to-hand combat. It's hard to imagine now, but my grandmother was a third-degree black belt in judo."

"Bah!" The old woman grumped at Nadia, grabbed her walking stick and got up from her chair. "I still am, Nadia! I still am." A sheepish expression grew on the old woman's wrinkled face and she sighed. "But I suppose age has begun to catch up with me." She motioned with a sweeping gesture to the both of them and said, "I'm going to bed."

And with that announcement the old woman hobbled her way out of the room, the door closed silently behind her.

Levi grinned at the closed door and turned to Nadia. "You're lucky to have her."

Nadia nodded and pointed at the photos in front of him. "As to Popov, he's a bad character, certainly has his fingers involved in various elements of organized crime both here in Russia as well as in the US and Canada. But as a friend of the Russian leadership, he exists because he's a useful tool, nothing more. If he's dead, I'd wager that much of his loosely tied organization will unwind, especially due to the strained local situation. Nonetheless, I'll keep monitoring the intelligence coming out of that region and confirm if the DNA test results prove anything. I'd counsel you to for now ignore him.

"As to the other names I was provided, I did some digging into their past. Talked with a few people who know their situation better than most, and I learned that Konstantin Porchenko and Yevgeny Karpov both worked for Vladimir Porchenko as his lieutenants."

Levi nodded.

"Vladimir was a very powerful man in post-Soviet Russia. Ex-KGB and like a brother to the current Russian president. He was wealthy beyond comprehension, and with the help of several key accidents and friendship of the government, he'd acquired ownership of almost all of the energy business within Russia. He's dead now, and even though the official cause of death was listed as a heart attack, there are several reports claiming that he'd been assassinated."

Levi maintained a bland expression, not wanting to unnecessarily give away things that only he knew. He was in the room when Vladimir had his so-called heart attack.

"When Vladimir died, his two lieutenants fought over the controlling interests and ended up splitting it, with the larger share going to Porchenko." Nadia shifted through her stack of papers and scanned through one that caught her attention. "I've gotten a copy of some of the investigative results of Vladimir's death, commissioned by Karpov." She looked at Levi with an amused expression and tapped her index finger on the paper. "It says here that there was security footage of someone entering the building a few hours before someone found Vladimir's dead body. Evidently, whoever Karpov had commissioned to investigate the death ended up running the security footage through some facial recognition software and identified a person by the name of Lazarus Yoder."

Levi shrugged. "You don't say."

"I do say." Nadia grinned. "And oddly enough, there was no record of a Lazarus Yoder ever entering Russia, at least through normal means. I suppose that might be why I found a mention of your name in a newspaper want ad, soon after Vladimir's demise."

Levi sighed. "So, this Karpov guy likely thinks I killed his former boss and wants to get a bit of revenge?"

Nadia leaned back in her chair and frowned. "I don't think so. Karpov has a reputation of being scrupulously honest, which is ridiculously rare in today's Russian society, especially amongst that class of people. And to be honest, if you hadn't killed Vladimir—"

"I never said I killed him." Levi interjected.

"Of course, of course." Nadia patted the air and grinned knowingly. "I'm sure it was all a coincidence. Anyway, if Vladimir hadn't died, Karpov likely wouldn't be alive today. The Porchenkos have a nasty habit of having people die around them when they're displeased in some way, or their use had waned. Vladimir was infamous for having climbed a bloodstained ladder to get to where he was. To be honest, I can't say why Karpov would want to meet you, but I'd say with certainty that he's not upset with Vladimir's demise." She wagged a finger in Levi's direction. "But Konstantin Porchenko is another story. He's known as a madman. There's talk on the street that he even killed his own twin brother over a girl they were both attracted to back when they were kids."

"Great." Levi sighed. "And that's the guy I'm really trying to get to."

Nadia shook her head. "That's not a healthy goal, in my opinion. He's protected by the secret police at all times. His offices are in the Lubyanka Building, do you know of it?"

"I do." The last time Levi was in Russia, he'd seen the building, from the outside. He could hardly imagine the thousands of tortured souls that had died there. "The home of the Soviet-era KGB and today's FSB."

"Correct. What is your ultimate goal?"

Levi had been asking himself that same question ever since taking on the mission. "To be absolutely honest, we believe that Porchenko has no care whatsoever who gets killed as long as he gets his oil and gas through his pipelines. And to accomplish that he's been leveraging compromised resources within the US government. Although the Outfit would prefer that justice prevail—"

"Justice!" Nadia snorted with derision. "In Russia?"

"The Outfit's management it seems have idealistic goals at times." He shrugged. "Well, since justice isn't likely to be available, the problem still needs to be solved."

"You're here to cut off the head of the snake?"

Levi grinned. "Very well put."

Nadia's expression turned serious. "Then you need to pray to whatever God you worship, because that's a task that might be beyond our ability to accomplish."

"This isn't *our* problem, it's mine." Levi met her unwavering gaze. "We shall see how things turn out." He glanced at his watch. It was late in the evening.

Nadia stood and motioned toward the items strewn across the table. "I'll secure this room so that we can leave all of this where it sits for now. It's getting late, and now that I realize what you're trying to do, I'll talk with my brother, who is also an agent for our common employer. He should be coming back from his assignment at any moment, and I'll talk to him about this problem of yours. I'll see if we can come up with some non-suicidal options for you in the morning."

Levi stood, stretched his arms above his head and heard the pops of his vertebra as he twisted his torso. "You don't by chance have a gym and showers around here, do you?"

"Actually, we do." With the conference room door open, Nadia motioned for him to follow. "But I suggest waiting until the morning. This office is still dependent on the state's resources for electricity, and due to evening rationing, we may not be able to syphon enough power to run all the lights and equipment you'd like."

Levi nodded. None of the intelligence he'd read had talked about Russia having in-country rationing of power. It *was* sounding a lot like some of the stories he'd read about the Soviet Union.

As he followed Nadia out of the conference room and down the dim hallway, he asked, "What time will the power be restored?"

"It will be six a.m. We'll pass the gym on the way to your room. Workout, shower, and we can meet in the conference room at seven. I'll hopefully have some options we can consider."

"Lucy, it's been a while since we last talked."

Lucy Chen's grip tightened on the wheel as she drove down Flatbush Avenue. She hadn't expected to hear Doug Mason's voice broadcasting through her car's speakers. "It has. I thought we weren't speaking anymore."

"That wasn't because of me. You wanted to distance yourself from the Outfit, and even though you're a member, I've tried to honor your request."

"But… there's always a *but* with you, Doug."

"This is a bit complicated, but you know Alicia Yoder, right?"

"Of course I do." Lucy felt a chill race up her spine and she pulled her car off to the side of the street to focus on the conversation. For someone in the Outfit to mention a civilian's name was never a good thing, and even though Levi was who he was, the kids were innocent. Her voice developed an edge as she said, "I knew her before Levi had ever scooped her up from the streets. What makes you bring up her name?"

"Calm down dragon lady, I'm trying to help." Mason sighed and the line grew silent for a moment. *"Levi is overseas right now on an assignment. He doesn't know about this and it would jeopardize the mission he's on if he knew. There are elements of the Russian mob that are trying to get to Levi, and to make a long story short, they've learned about Alicia going to Princeton."*

"But that's in the fall."

"Unfortunately, she's been invited to attend some special orientation at the dorms, and she's leaving her grandmother's farm tomorrow."

"How do you know that?"

"We just do. Our undercover resources that could help with this are sparse, and already committed to other things. Right now, I have agents watching the farm, and we can follow her up to the point of getting to school, but after that, things get dicey."

Lucy frowned. "If you have Levi's mom's house bugged,

and I wouldn't put it past you guys, you know he's going to flip out."

"Anyway, do you think you can help?"

"And how the hell did Russian mobsters find out about Alicia?"

"You know I can't say.

"How credible is this threat?"

"Sadly, we believe it's very credible. I wouldn't otherwise be calling."

Lucy imagined Alicia's happy face from when she last saw her at the farm. She was ecstatic about going to that school. And she was so damned innocent… she had no idea who her father really was. Feeling a growing sense of frustration, she blurted out, "What do you have in mind? What do you want me to do about this? Is she in danger of maybe being kidnapped to get to Levi or is this some assassination thing?"

"Kidnapping is the primary concern. The girl is going into Whitman College, it's one of the dorms on the Princeton campus. I can adjust a few things in the system and maybe get you a spot in the orientation. Be her roommate?"

Lucy snorted derisively. "We may not have seen each other in a couple years, but I can guarantee you that I won't pass for a coed at a university. I'm the wrong person, but I have an idea…"

"Realize the kind of people we might be dealing with—"

"Doug, to not put too fine a point on it, I'm a killer, and I know what Alicia needs for protection. I'll get you the details of what I'm thinking of once I've set some things up."

"Perfect."

Lucy's gaze narrowed as she stared out the car's windshield. She'd grown to despise Mason over the years. In a way, she blamed him for some of her difficulties with Levi. Yet, the man had never truly gone against his word. "You said she's driving to school tomorrow?"

"Yes, as of right now, the Yoders are eating dinner, and will be getting to bed soon. First thing in the morning, Alicia's going to leave the farm and start heading for Princeton."

"I swear, if Levi doesn't kick your ass for bugging his mother's home, you're one lucky son of a bitch. Because I can assure you, that I'm going to tell him."

Mason's sigh broadcast loudly across the car's speakers. *"Send me the details as soon as possible, because I have some miracles to conjure up in the next twelve hours or so."*

Lucy shifted the car into gear, pulled into the late rush hour traffic and headed toward the Upper East Side. "You'll get it within the hour." Her voice took on a threatening tone. "Watch over that girl, she's precious to more than just her adoptive father."

CHAPTER ELEVEN

Even though the below ground rooms that the Outfit maintained were kept much colder than he was used to, Levi had managed to get some decent sleep. There were several sets of street clothes in the room, and even one pair of sweat pants, which he'd donned along with a white, sleeveless t-shirt. As he walked into the gym, he was surprised at how well stocked it was, considering it was fifty feet underground.

The gym had floor-to-ceiling mirrors mounted on the walls, and state-of-the-art workout equipment ranging from stationary bikes to treadmills to a series of weightlifting stations.

Levi's attention turned to the man on the lone weight bench as he pushed up what looked like at least 350 pounds of free weights. After ten reps, the man easily set the bar back onto the metal bracket, sat up, gave Levi a nod and moved on to a rack of heavy dumbbells.

He presumed the man was Nadia's brother, and he looked strong enough to be a formidable opponent on the streets.

Shifting his attention to the far side of the room, Levi spied a heavy bag hanging by a chain from the ceiling and smiled.

He approached the bag and began his warm up, with a few flurries of punches and kicks.

After about five minutes of warming up, he felt the blood rushing to his muscles, and beads of sweat had accumulated on his forehead. Levi grunted as he performed a series of snap kicks, the heavy thwacks of his shin against the canvas echoing loudly across the room and sending the heavy bag whirling in random directions.

Nadia's brother pointed to the bag and asked in broken English, "Does you want me to hold it?"

Levi gave him a nod, and the big man grabbed the bag, steadying its gyrations.

With an ever-increasing pace, Levi sent a barrage of jabs, kicks, and punches at the now-steadied target. His hits grew in intensity, forcing the man to brace himself against the onslaught.

After nearly two minutes of nonstop attacks, Levi finished with a spinning back kick that knocked Nadia's brother two steps backward and left Levi breathing heavily.

"Nicely done, Levi." Nadia remarked as she walked into the gym. "I see that you and my brother Ivan have become acquainted."

Ivan fist-bumped Levi and he turned to Nadia and said, in Russian, "I'm going to shower. Anything else you need from me before I go up?"

Nadia shook her head and the man walked out of the gym. She approached Levi with a grin, wiped her finger across his sweat-slicked arm and tasted it. "You're not what I expected either, Mr. Yoder." She pointed toward the door and said, "Assuming you're done, go shower and I'll meet you in the conference room. You might want to wear your suit; it has the right look you'll need."

"My suit? So, you have an idea on how to approach Porchenko?"

Nadia shrugged. "Let's talk in the conference room."

The woman turned and walked out of the room, leaving Levi's mind racing.

What in the world did she mean by *"it has the right look you'll need."*

Under Nadia's direction, Levi placed his finger on the stained concrete wall.

"Two centimeters to the right and one down from the crack."

Levi frowned as he spied the hair-like crack in the concrete. "If I'm having so much trouble finding the biometric scanner with you showing me where it is, how am I going to find it when trying to come back in?"

Nadia patted him on the back and spoke with a soothing tone. "The crack isn't real. It's a pattern in the concrete, and you'll see the exact same markings on the outside wall. We also have motion detectors all along the alley to prevent the door from opening if there are others outside a ten-foot radius of the door."

He gave her a look and she grinned.

"It's unlikely people will just randomly be hanging out in this alley. You'll know why I said that in a minute." She motioned toward the concrete wall. "Go ahead…"

Levi followed the crack, measured off two centimeters, which was just about the width of his index finger, and one centimeter down from that, he pressed his finger onto the cool concrete surface.

It took almost a second, but there was a loud click and Nadia whispered, "Go ahead and push."

Levi pushed and the wall swung open on oiled hinges.

The intense smell of ammonia slammed into him as he stepped through the doorway.

His eyes were watering from the acrid smell of urine and the moment Nadia stepped through the doorway, the door automatically sealed itself shut.

"Let's go." Nadia turned to the left and hurried past him.

Without hesitating, Levi followed her, all the while trying to figure out where the intense smell of urine was coming from.

She glanced at him and whispered, "The smell is pumped in from the sewers."

As they approached the end of the alley, the smell practically vanished, only to be replaced with a faint aroma of mildew from the humid streets.

They stepped out onto a wide sidewalk and Nadia turned to the right. "We're on Myasnitskaya Ulitsa. It's an old road here in Moscow. Some trivia for you about this road: Myaso, as you know, is Russian for meat, and about five hundred years ago, this street was filled with butcher shops. And even to this day, we can find shops and tea merchants all along this road."

Levi panned his gaze across the street and it seemed odd to him. One side of the street had various stores, while the other side of the street had the back of buildings. He'd never seen such a thing in all the cities around the world he'd been, the street was usually where the so-called front of any building faced. Not on this street. There was graffiti on the backs of the buildings, many of which had lazily been scrubbed over with white paint, and someone later painted more graffiti over the sloppy cleanup attempt. He pointed at a storefront that they were approaching and asked, "Is that where your brother said Karpov gets his tea and pastries?"

Nadia nodded and slowed to a halt.

It was still early in the morning, at least thirty minutes before the oligarch made his daily walk from his luxury apartment a few blocks away.

She looked at him with a furrowed brow. "Are you sure you want to do this?"

Levi studied the storefront and then shifted his gaze to the empty benches across the street. He nodded. "I'm doing this."

Nadia touched the back of his arm and gave it a squeeze. "Okay, I have to go. I can't be seen loitering around you, just in case. Is there anything else I can do?"

He shook his head and she continued walking down the sidewalk.

Levi pulled out a pen from inside his suit jacket and began scribbling a message on a square piece of paper as he walked across the street to the Perlov Tea House.

He entered the store and was immediately hit with the scent of freshly-baked pastries. The scent of sugar hung heavily in the air.

He approached a serving counter and despite the garishly colorful storefront and somewhat rundown state of the buildings across the street, this place was clearly a high-end shop. The myriad of baked offerings put most of New York's bakeries to shame.

And despite the high-end look of everything, the prices were relatively modest. Certainly they were priced lower than what most people paid for equivalent treats in Manhattan.

An older gentleman standing behind the counter looked over at him and asked, "Can I help you?"

Levi's contact lens kicked into action and a green rectangle formed around the man's face. His name was Mikhail Polyudov.

Levi pulled out a 1000-ruble banknote and a slip of paper. "Mikhail, I believe Yevgeny Karpov comes here regularly, is that true?"

The man's lips pressed thinly together and he immediately gained a suspicious expression.

With a warm smile, Levi spoke with a soft tone and said, "I believe he was looking for me long ago, and I just learned of this." He handed the man the cash and the slip of paper. "When you see him, can you give him this? The money is for your trouble."

The old man took both items and held them as if they were coated in pee. "I don't know... this doesn't seem right."

Levi pulled out a five-thousand-ruble note and ripped it in half.

The man's eyes widened with shock.

Five thousand rubles represented nearly a week's salary to the average Russian.

Levi placed one of the torn halves on the counter and slid

it toward the man. "If you give him that slip of paper, I will learn of it, and I will return with the other half."

As soon as the man took the torn half of the bill, Levi turned and walked out the door.

This would either work or it would backfire.

Levi walked across the street, approached one of the empty wooden benches and sat down to wait.

Alicia felt a surge of excitement as she walked down the third-floor hallway in the Whitman dorms. She had her student ID, which also served as her keycard to just about everywhere she'd go on campus, including her dorm room.

She'd been assigned a quad, meaning she'd be sharing a room with three other girls. The idea of having roommates was kind of exciting, but terrifying nonetheless. Having spent her teen years in an Amish community, she worried about how uncool she might come off. Despite her browsing the internet at the library in Lancaster, researching what kids her age normally did, Alicia knew that she was going to be the country girl who didn't know the first thing about video games, yet knew all about milking cows, making cheese, and was pretty good at mending fences when the two-thousand-pound bull scratched his rear against a fence post, inevitably knocking it over.

Scanning the numbers on the door, Alicia got her

keycard ready and as she reached her room, swiped her card on the electronic lock.

It immediately clicked and she opened the door to the sound of laughter.

The bedroom was small, had just enough room for the two single beds and a set of dressers, but to her left was a doorway to a larger room and a girl came over with a large toothy smile.

She was Asian! What a cool coincidence.

The girl was tall and lanky, with long black hair and a thin face. She extended her hand and spoke English with a thick Chinese accent, "Hi, I'm Liu Ruxia, but my English name is Ruth." She pointed at the bed that had a pink teddy bear on it. "I'm your roommate."

Alicia slid her wheeled suitcase toward her bed, shook Ruth's hand and began speaking rapidly in Mandarin. "Hi, I'm Alicia. Where are you from?"

"Oh!" The girl's face lit up and she began speaking in Mandarin. "I was born in Taiyuan." Ruth motioned for Alicia to follow her into the other room. "This is so cool that you're Chinese!"

Alicia walked into the larger room, which was dominated by a futon, several chairs and two desks. Two other Asian girls hopped up from where they were sitting as Ruth clapped with a child-like exuberance.

Ruth pointed to a tall, athletically-built girl with a long, braided ponytail. "Feng Min, this Alicia, our roommate."

Alicia shook hands with the girl, who immediately averted her eyes and blushed.

"And this is Ye Ting."

A petite girl approached Alicia and gave her a hug. "That's weird how they put the Chinese people together."

Alicia grinned. "To be honest, I'm from Hong Kong."

"No way!" The three other girls exclaimed in both Mandarin and Cantonese, the dialect spoken in Hong Kong. "Us too!"

"Woah, are you living in the US or—"

"Only recently." Ruth motioned to the other two girls and said, "We came to the same host family, but the Chinese government sponsored us to come and study. What's your major?"

"My focus will be on neuroscience. What about you guys?"

Ruth glanced at the other two and shrugged. "The government is paying for us to focus on civil engineering."

Alicia nodded even though she had no idea what that really meant, other than maybe it having to do with building things, which made sense for the Chinese government to invest in.

She looked at her watch it was almost noon. "Our orientation is supposed to start at three o'clock, do you guys want to get something to eat ahead of that?"

All three nodded and Ting asked, "Do you know where

the cafeteria is? We were talking about needing to get a campus map or something."

"Oh, no worries." Alicia swiped on her phone and brought up a map that she'd bookmarked. "I've got one right here."

Ruth grabbed a backpack, as did the other two, and she motioned toward the door with her toothy smile. "The one with the map leads."

———

Panning his gaze up and down the street, Levi sat up straight as he noticed three well-dressed men turn the corner onto his street. They were heading south on Myasnitskaya Ulitsa, and even though he couldn't make out their faces from this distance, he noticed that the man in the front was focused on whatever was ahead of him, while the other two kept their heads on a swivel.

Those two were bodyguards, Levi had no doubt about it. He glanced at his watch.

Right on time.

All three of them entered the Perlov Tea House.

That had to be Karpov and his men.

Levi waited.

Would the old man be waiting for Karpov's arrival and immediately hand him the note, knowing that almost a week's worth of extra pay was hanging in the balance? Or maybe he wouldn't risk possibly getting in trouble.

Counting the seconds since the men entered the store, it took only half a minute for someone to step out of the store, holding something in his hand.

Levi smiled.

Almost immediately the man made eye contact with him as his two companions also exited the store.

Levi lifted his hand and gave a small wave.

Karpov nodded as his two bodyguards followed him across the street, walking directly toward Levi.

Levi's contact lens snapped awake as it painted a yellow rectangle onto Karpov's face. It immediately printed below the rectangle the information he needed.

Yevgeny Karpov.

As they stepped onto the sidewalk, not more than fifteen feet away, Karpov motioned for his men to wait and he continued forward, stopping just outside of arm's reach.

Levi paid careful attention to Karpov's men.

They had their hands forward, holding onto the front of their suit coats, very much like the US Secret Service does for protection details.

The two men were strategically positioned so they had a clear angle of attack if they needed to shoot him.

Karpov tilted his head and said, "You're either a very brave or very stupid man."

Levi shrugged. "Maybe a little of both."

The oligarch held up the piece of paper and read aloud, *"You were looking for Lazarus Yoder. I know where he is. See me across the street on the bench. I am armed, but I intend you no harm whatsoever."* He crumpled up the paper, flung it aside and sat on the far end of the wooden bench.

There was about three feet between them.

The man shifted so that he was facing Levi and asked, "How do you know of this name and how do you know I have interest in such a person?"

Levi faced the man and noticed the brilliant blue eyes hidden within the wrinkled face of a man well into his sixties. "How do I know that name? The answer is simple… my mother and father gave it to me when I was born."

A smile grew on Karpov's face and he let out of low chuckle. "Interesting. If that's the case, tell me why I care about who you are." The oligarch glanced at his men and gave a quick nod.

Both men pulled out their pistols and held them aimed directly at Levi. Their fingers were in the trigger well. They were ready to shoot.

Despite the tension in the air, Levi felt a sense of calm as he said, "You had worked for a man named Porchenko. Vladimir, to be specific. Vladimir died, and you wanted to know the truth of his death. You hired investigators and learned that there had been a visitor to Porchenko's building who had never checked out of the building.

"Yet, you didn't get fooled by the name that had been left in the log book—"

"What was the name of that person in the log book?" Karpov asked, his eyes growing wider.

"Ronald Warren was the name in the front desk's log book."

Karpov's mouth dropped open and he motioned for Levi to continue.

"I know the investigators weren't fooled by the false name. They used security footage and facial recognition software and they provided to you another name. Lazarus Yoder. He was the one in the building.

"*I* was the one in the building. And yes, I was there when Vladimir passed away, but not from the heart attack that was reported in the news." Levi paused and smiled at Karpov. "You wanted to know the truth. I can tell you what really happened. But I need something in return."

Karpov made a downward motion toward his men and they immediately put their guns away and went back to their ready position. "How much do you want?"

Levi shook his head. "I don't want money. I need some information."

"Really?" Karpov's eyebrows shot up and he leaned closer to Levi. "I took you for an assassin. A man for hire."

"I've been called many things, and yes, I have an employer, but it isn't money that I need, I need information."

"What kind of information?"

Levi leaned in and whispered, "I need help with getting access to Konstantin Porchenko."

Karpov breathed in through his teeth and shook his head. "I can easily tell from your accent you aren't from this country, so I must warn you. I'm not sure you understand what you're asking. He's a protected man in this country. He has the ear and protection of the Russian president."

"I understand that. I also understand that his offices are in the Lubyanka building. I seriously doubt I'll be able to get in there—"

"Why would you want to?"

Levi sighed. "The man is responsible for the deaths of many innocent people. He's a risk to international stability. I've been contracted to eliminate that risk."

Karpov shook his head. "You misunderstand me. Why do you want to go to his offices in Lubyanka? Those offices are just for show. It's a Russian thing… the reputation of Lubyanka and having one's 'official' offices there is to seem intimidating to others. His office is at his home in Rublyovka, about an hour away."

"Really?"

The oligarch nodded. "Why do you want to get to his office?

"I need to understand the threat he poses to those who have hired me."

"Killing him is insufficient?"

Levi nodded. "There are those who have worked with

Porchenko. I need to know who they are. Either through questioning him, or through searching his records."

Karpov scratched at his chin. "And once you know who he has worked with, then what?"

"All threats to my employer must be eliminated."

"So... you *are* an assassin." Karpov grinned.

Levi shrugged. "I eliminate threats, that is all."

Karpov leaned closer, his voice barely qualified as a whisper, "I owe you a debt already for Vladimir. If you manage to take care of Konstantin, then doubly so." He extended his hand and spoke in a more normal tone. "A deal then. I give you the information you seek, you take care of a mutual problem. Fair?"

Levi shook hands with the oligarch and nodded. "Fair."

Karpov stood, handed Levi a business card, and said, "Meet me tomorrow morning at this address. I will have what you need, and you will help me with some history lessons."

Levi handed Karpov the torn half of the five-thousand-ruble banknote and said, "If you're going back to the tea shop, can you give the man—"

"No need." Karpov pulled out from his pocket the other torn half of the banknote and handed them both to Levi. "Mikhail told me what you did, and I replaced the half you gave him with a whole note." The man turned and walked back across the street; his bodyguards close behind.

Levi watched as Karpov disappeared back into the tea shop and grinned.

He looked down at the business card and his mind raced, wondering what kind of business were they going to transact at a place called Rasputin.

CHAPTER TWELVE

Alicia lurched up into a sitting position, her heart racing as she stared frantically into the darkness of her dorm. She glanced at the digital clock on her roommate's dresser. It was three a.m.

Swinging her feet out from under her covers, Ruth shifted in her bed and whispered, "Where are you going?"

"Nowhere, just to the bathroom."

Ruth flung her sheet to the side, grabbed her toiletry bag and said, "I have to go as well."

Alicia yawned as she donned her slippers and heard Ting's voice from the common room. "What are you up to?"

Ruth turned to the voice in the other room and waved the question away as Alicia poked her head into the adjoining room.

Ting was sitting up on the futon, her phone in her hands and she was putting on a pair of flip-flops.

"Why are you even awake?" Alicia asked.

Ting shrugged. "It's a new place. I have trouble sleeping in new places. Where are you guys going? Can I join you?"

Alicia laughed and pointed at herself. "*I* am going to the bathroom. You guys should probably be asleep."

"Now that you mention it, I think I have to go as well." Ting reached for her toiletry bag and it slipped from the futon, hitting the floor with a heavy metallic thud.

"What in the world do you have in there?" Alicia asked.

Ting's face turned red and she shook her head. "Just some toiletries," she muttered softly.

Based on her quad-mate's look of embarrassment, Ting was obviously lying.

Alicia felt her face getting warm as she tried *not* to imagine what might be hidden in the zipper-topped bag. This Amish girl *so* didn't need that kind of image in her head. She walked out the door, heard Ruth whisper something and then her roommate raced after her.

As the taxi slowed in front of the KFC, Levi tapped the driver's shoulder. "This is good enough. Stop here."

The driver pulled over to the side of the road, stopped

next to the sidewalk and looked over his shoulder at Levi. "Do you need me to wait? I *can* wait."

Levi shook his head. "Thanks, but I'm here for lunch and will have a friend picking me up." He flipped a few bills at the driver, it was nearly double the cost of the cab fare, and he hopped out of the taxi.

Nadia had warned him that the cab drivers weren't to be trusted with anything. Many of them would try and cheat their customers… it was a desperate time in Russia. And a good percentage of them reported in to the secret police anything they found to be unusual, with the hopes of getting some small remuneration.

After nearly a minute of waiting, the cab driver put his car into gear, swerved into the midday traffic heading east on Zubovsky Boulevard, and eventually merged onto the highway.

Levi breathed in the familiar scent of fried chicken and began walking west to his destination.

This was a commercial area with small shops and every-thing was well-maintained and modern.

He walked past a bank on his left and felt a sense of amusement as he spotted his destination.

In America, it wasn't very often you'd find a bank and a strip club sitting next to each other, yet there it was: above the red-framed entrance the name, Rasputin, had been written with a garish red font—the Cyrillic characters spelled out the name of the infamous mystic from the early twentieth century.

With a quick glance in all directions, he sensed nobody looking in his direction and entered the club.

Likely because it was the middle of the day, the place seemed pretty tame for what it was. The club reminded Levi of a Las Vegas lounge, with several areas where food and drinks would be served, a center stage with smaller tables arrayed around it, and lots of nooks and crannies that were deep in shadowy areas where other things might happen.

At the moment, he caught sight of several waitresses, all wearing normal, albeit skimpy attire, and a couple dozen patrons eating at their tables.

There were two large men strategically positioned near the entrance who eyeballed him as he stood at the hostess' stand where the sign told him to wait.

A beautiful blonde woman with a skin-tight dress and an hourglass figure approached, bearing what looking like a genuine smile. "Welcome, sir. Is it just you for lunch?"

A red rectangle framed the woman's face and Levi's attention was immediately drawn to what the contact lens was showing him.

Katarina Pavlova
  Member of the Russian FSB.
  Assigned to counterintelligence.

· · ·

Interesting.

Having been in the mafia for most of his life, it was second nature for him to not say anything that could incriminate him, but around this woman—doubly so.

Levi returned the woman's smile and held up the business card Karpov had given him. "Mr. Karpov and I have a meeting."

The woman nodded. "Your name, please?"

"Yoder."

She picked up a phone behind the hostess' stand, held it to her ear for a moment, and said, "Mr. Yoder is here to see Mr. Karpov. Shall I have him wait in the lounge?" Her eyes widened. "Oh, okay. I'll tell him." The woman hung up the phone and turned to Levi. "Mr. Karpov is just now getting off the phone and is coming down." The blonde motioned toward the bar. "Can I get you a drink, Mr. Yoder?"

Levi shook his head. "I'm fine."

The woman leaned closer and spoke with a soft voice. "You have an interesting accent. I can tell you're foreign-born. Where are you from?"

"Moscow." Levi responded with a grin. He pointed at the empty stage and then at the mostly empty nightclub. "Is this normal during the day? For it to be... not so busy?"

A look of discomfort flashed on her face and her voice took on a cheerful tone. "It's been a bit slower than the past, but it gives us all a rest for the evening rush, which keeps us all quite busy."

"I can imagine you guys get very busy. Especially if everyone who works here looks like you." Levi winked.

The woman laughed and shook her head. "You're too kind, and I suspect you need to have your eyes checked. The other girls are absolutely gorgeous, you should come here in the evening and see them." A door opened near the far end of the club and Katarina pointed in its direction. "There's Mr. Karpov. I hope you and he have a productive meeting." She patted him on the back and whispered, "If you have time afterwards, it would be nice to talk to someone from… Moscow." She gave him a stunning smile and a bit of red bloomed in her cheeks.

"I am very glad to see you." Karpov exclaimed loudly, grabbing Levi by the shoulders and giving him a kiss on both cheeks. He draped his arm over Levi's shoulders and they walked toward the back of the club, the same body-guards Levi had seen yesterday trailed closely behind them.

As soon as they walked past a heavy door that closed with a thud, Karpov said, "Lazarus, I'm very—"

"One second." Levi stopped mid-stride and removed his suit jacket.

The bodyguards immediately pulled their weapons and Karpov yelled "Nyet! Nyet!" at them both.

One of them pointed at Levi, whose weapons were now clear for them all to see.

Karpov's eyes flashed angrily and he turned to Levi. "What are you doing?"

Levi ran his hands across the back of his jacket and felt it before he saw it.

It was a fingernail-sized patch of cloth, or so it seemed as he peeled it off his suit. Its color perfectly matched what he was wearing. Levi squeezed it and there was something hard woven inside the patch.

Levi motioned for silence as he knelt, putting the cloth patch on the floor, he extracted one of his daggers and slammed its hilt onto the patch.

A loud metallic crack echoed loudly in the hallway.

Sheathing his throwing knife, Levi held up the dark-color item and rubbed it between his fingers. It crunched as the broken pieces moved against each other.

Levi hitched his thumb back toward the front of the club. "What do you know of that hostess of yours?"

Karpov grinned wider than it seemed possible. "You are very very good, Mr. Yoder." He held out his hand. "Let me see that."

Levi shrugged his suit jacket back on, handed Karpov the ruined device, and the oligarch motioned for them to continue down the hall.

After passing through another door, the bodyguards remained outside as another man ran a wand over Levi. He paused at Levi's suit pocket. "A phone?"

Levi nodded and pulled out his phone.

"Please turn it off."

He did as he was told, and the man finished his inspection.

Karpov handed over the patch, and the short man examined it closely and then nodded. He extracted a small metal box from his pants pocket, placed the patch inside, and left the room.

Levi panned his gaze across the spacious office and noticed many of the books on his shelves were technical in nature. Engineering and physics books, along with three-ring binders labeled with various topics such as geological studies of Siberian permafrost regions, geothermal studies from Novosibirsk, and many others. This man was not just some random government stooge who lucked into some energy contracts. He might have earned his way into this position. Nonetheless, Karpov might not be the bureaucrat he'd initially taken him for.

The oligarch motioned to one of two armchairs. "Please, have a seat."

As Levi settled into the chair, the older man poured an amber liquid into an etched old fashioned glass.

He offered the drink to Levi. "It's an American whiskey. It's over a quarter century old, and I have to admit that I've grown quite fond of it."

Levi shook his head. "No, thank you. I don't drink."

"Very well, that would leave more for me." Karpov smiled, and took a sip. He motioned at the door to his office. "Yes, I know all about Katarina. She's a plant. They think they'll somehow get something on me, to incriminate me, or somehow figure out what my next moves are so they can cut me off."

"They being…"

"Those in power. Whether it's Porchenko and his cronies, the government itself sending its people to spy on me. It's actually somewhat fun, but at times it's a bit insulting. After all, I've been playing this cat and mouse game all my life."

Levi studied Karpov's demeanor. He liked the man's self-assured attitude, and he was impressed that the man kept known spies within reach. That was something Levi probably wouldn't do, no matter how in control he felt he was. It was too easy to make a mistake. "Let me guess, you're former KGB?"

Karpov winked. "Among other things, young man. Among other things." He clapped his hands together with a meaty thwack and nodded in Levi's direction. "As a professional courtesy, can you tell me what really happened with Vladimir? That's a mystery that I've been longing to resolve."

"I can do more than that." Levi held an amused expression as he unsheathed one of his throwing knives and laid it on the end table between them. "That's the knife that killed him."

A look of surprised flashed across the oligarch's face as he retrieved the knife and studied it.

Levi went over the details of what had happened a handful of years ago. Even though it was actually Levi's weapon that produced the killing blow, that blow hadn't landed until after Levi had been shot and during the ensuing melee, a fatal blow was struck.

Karpov's eyes were wide as he studied the knife, turning it end over end as he seemed to replay the path the knife had taken across the room and into his former boss. For a moment, the man seemed to be living in another world, another time, but he suddenly snapped out of it, his eyes focused on Levi as he held up the knife. "May I keep this?"

Levi nodded. "I have others, but I thought that one might be particularly special to you." He no longer had any idea which of his four throwing knives it was that landed the killing blow, but Karpov didn't need to know. And Levi's gift would hopefully return its investment.

The man turned in his chair, lay the knife on the desk behind him, and focused again on Levi. "Thank you for this. Now, let's move on to Konstantin, the other Porchenko.

"You say you need access to his files. I've given this some thought, and you have one distinct problem: those files reside in Porchenko's home. That home is an absolute fortress, and gaining access to it would require a small army. And even if you had this small army, remember that this man is protected. A friend of the Russian president. You would have almost every law enforcement officer converging on your location in almost no time whatsoever."

Levi frowned. "Do you know anything about the security? I have some experience bypassing alarm systems and other such things."

"I'm sure you do, Mr. Yoder." Karpov grinned. "Believe me when I say that Konstantin spared no expense in securing his home. Remember, this is where he does all of his business. That office in Lubyanka is a false front."

Levi sighed. "You're not painting a very pretty picture, Mr. Karpov."

"Yes, well… like I said, I've been giving this matter a lot of thought." A smile bloomed on the man's face. "Konstantin's security has one weakness. And now that I've met you, you might be able to exploit that weakness."

"What weakness is that?"

Karpov turned his gaze toward the wall clock. "Konstantin has a daughter, and I've arranged for her to win a rather valuable prize. A radio station has notified her that she's won a 'presidential-level' party for her and her friends to have a lady's night out. The young lady has confirmed with the radio station manager and the limousine is picking her up in about six hours."

Levi's mind raced as he processed what the man had just said. "I'm not sure I follow your logic. What good does Porchenko having a daughter do? Are you suggesting I try to… actually, I have no idea what you're aiming for."

The oligarch leaned against the back of his chair and drummed his fingers on the leather-upholstered arm. "Let's just say her father will do just about anything to save his little girl. I have some ideas about how you'll gain access to his compound, and that's through daddy's little girl. As to some of your other goals, those I think you and I may need to put our heads together. I have some things that may help." Karpov's steely gray eyes flashed brightly, the man's geared were turning quickly. "I'm very motivated for you to be successful in your goals, but for completely different reasons than those who have acquired your services. I'm sure whatever contract you are trying to complete would allow others to gain some fringe benefits, no?"

Levi stared at the man and recalled Brice's words about Karpov.

He's legitimately known as a straight shooter and as honest as honest gets in Russia.

He may very well be honest, but that didn't mean the man wasn't a ruthless psychopath either. The idea of messing with someone's family didn't sit well with Levi, but he didn't yet really know what the man had in mind. And even if it was as bad as he imagined it could be, if it saved lives in the long run, that may ultimately be the only thing that truly mattered.

The only thing left for him was to figure out which was the lesser of two evils.

He nodded at Karpov. "I have only my goals, if others benefit, then so be it."

The oligarch reached behind him and pressed a button on his desk.

Almost immediately the door opened and his bodyguards peered into the office.

Karpov motioned to them. "Tell Grigori to bring my equipment to the security room."

One of the men disappeared as the oligarch stood and motioned for Levi. "Come, let's go plan some mischief."

Levi sat in Rasputin's security office with a bank of monitors that flickered to various locations throughout the club. The security people had been cleared out of the room and it was just him with Karpov and Grigori, the oligarch's tech guy. It was now the evening and he felt the hum of music through the floorboards.

Karpov was on the phone and had walked away from the table.

Grigori slid what looked like a metal cigar box in front of him. On top of it was the USB dongle that contained a computer virus. Levi picked them up and the box was heavy for its size. "That's 750 grams of Semtex with a cellphone trigger." He pointed at the strip of double-stick tape running across the box. "The number you've memorized will not be capable of receiving a signal until you remove the foil strip and stick the device to something."

Semtex was a type of plastic explosive Levi had used before. It was safe to carry around, similar to the US military's C4, and wouldn't blow up unless using a specially-made triggering mechanism. "What's this thing's lethal range?"

The engineer frowned as Levi slid the box into the inside pocket of his suit. "The steel case is built to create lethal shards, very much like a traditional grenade. I'd say anything within a three to four-meter radius would be torn apart from the concussion and shrapnel."

"So, about ten feet."

"It's been a long day." Karpov walked over and put his hand on Levi's shoulder. "And for some, the day is only beginning." He looked over at Grigori and asked, "Are we all set?"

The engineer nodded. "I think so."

There was a knock on the security room's door and Karpov motion to it. "Grigori, please get the door. I've asked for food to be brought here."

The engineer opened the door, and loud music poured into the room. He let the nervous-looking brunette carrying a large tray of food enter the room, and he departed through the same door.

Karpov pointed to the table, which had been cleared off. "Please, my dear. The table is fine."

Levi looked at the woman and a green rectangle framed her face.

Natasha Lubov.

He studied the woman's face and even though she had perfectly applied makeup, and wore a near-see-through gown that showed her fantastic figure, she didn't look much older than nineteen or twenty.

She laid the first dish on the table and with a velvety voice that purred with sex appeal, she described the first dish. "We have a smoked salmon roulade with cream cheese and topped with red caviar." She laid another plate on the table. "Salmon tartare with chopped avocado, shallots, and salmon caviar."

Most of the dishes consisted of assorted pickles, salads, and other relatively light fare.

The last dish off of her tray she described as, "Freshly-picked forest berries dusted with powdered sugar and a drizzle of thick sweetened cream."

Levi looked up at the girl and smiled. "Natasha, it's all almost as beautiful as you."

Her neck and cheeks almost immediately turned crimson

and she stammered a thanks as she bowed her head and backed out of the security room with her empty tray.

Levi scooped a spoonful of the salmon tartare and placed it on a toast point as Karpov took his seat at the table.

The man stared at Levi with an amused expression. "You're quite a man of mystery, Mr. Yoder."

"How is that?"

Karpov popped a pickled cherry tomato into his mouth and chewed slowly. He waved in the general direction of the door and said, "I'm wondering how you knew that young lady's name. She's only worked here a week. Katarina was different, she's been here a long time, and you could have done your research on her. But Natasha? Interesting…"

Levi shrugged. "I need to practice with my flirting. How old did you say Porchenko's daughter is?"

"She's thirty-one. And I have faith our little plan will work." Karpov's eyes darted to one of the monitors, he popped another tomato into his mouth and pointed. "There's our girl."

Levi looked over at the monitor the oligarch had pointed to. It displayed an image of the entrance to the club. A large limo had pulled up and its chauffeur was opening the rear door. A half dozen ladies spilled out of the vehicle. They were all dressed up with shimmering outfits and one of the girls was wearing a tiara. Even through the security camera, he could see the flash of diamonds on the tiara. He glanced at Karpov. "The girl with the tiara is her?"

"Yes, that's Anya Porchenko." Karpov nodded as the girls were escorted into the club. "The bartender has the drugs ready for her, but like you asked, he's waiting for you to separate her from the others." The oligarch shifted his gaze from the monitor to Levi. "How are you planning on doing that?"

"Doing what?"

"Getting her away from her friends."

Levi popped a piece of the salmon roulade into his mouth, chewed quickly and swallowed. During their planning stage, Karpov had posed several options that to Levi seemed unnecessarily dangerous and they'd settled on his method for gaining control over the oligarch's daughter. He stood and adjusted his tie. "I suppose I'll show you in a couple minutes."

"I've got a girl who's looking for when you come out of this room. She'll lead you to an empty table near one of the darker alcoves. It'll make things easier… the rest is up to you, Mr. Yoder."

He glanced at his reflection in the mirror, brushed back his hair and shrugged. No time better than the present.

Levi opened the door and a wave of techno music assaulted his ears.

Levi sipped at his seltzer as the club pulsed with activity. To his left was the main stage where a group of women were in the middle of doing a strip-tease in front of a man hand-cuffed to a chair. There was cheering as clothes were removed and all variety of naked distractions kept the crowd engaged. But for him, his eyes were focused on the six ladies standing by the bar.

The girl with the tiara was noticeably thin, not quite anorexic, but Levi strongly suspected that if she removed her dress, he'd easily be able to count her ribs from afar. None-theless, the ladies had attracted a gaggle of studs to ply them with drinks and flirt, as most young men did.

Some things were universal.

Draining his seltzer, Levi walked across the club zoning in on his target. Taking a large bill from his pocket, he walked right up to Anya.

Just as their eyes met, he placed the one-thousand-ruble note in her hand, and said, "Can you please get me another seltzer?"

Levi turned and walked back to his table, unsure how this little game of his would play out.

"Hey!"

The woman called out, and he hurried toward his table, reclaiming his empty seat.

Levi looked in the direction of the bar and maintained a stone-faced expression as the dark-haired girl with the tiara stomped toward him, a look of ever-increasing anger etched on her face.

As soon as she was within speaking distance, she threw the crumpled bill at him and snarled. "I'm not one of the waitresses, you idiot!"

Just as she turned on her heel to leave, Levi blurted out, "I know."

"You knew?" The woman looked back at him, her angry expression softening a bit as Levi scooped up the crumpled bill and stood. "Then why in the hell—"

"How else was I going to get you away from all those people so I could buy you a drink and talk privately with the most beautiful girl in the club?" Levi spoke in as warm and sincere a tone as he could muster. He waved for the waitress, who'd been waiting for this moment.

The waitress rushed over and asked, "What can I get you?"

Levi looked in Anya's direction and motioned toward the waitress. "What can I have her get you?"

The woman's angry expression melted away and she smiled. A pretty smile. She looked at the waitress. "A vodka and cranberry."

The waitress turned to Levi and he handed her his glass. "Just a refill."

Levi motioned to the empty seat next to him and smiled. "I'm sorry if my approach was a bit rude, but it was the best I could think of at the time."

The girl extended her hand and said, "My name's Anya."

"Levi," he smiled as they shook hands and took their seats.

The waitress arrived with their drinks, she placed the pink-colored drink in front of Anya and the seltzer in front of Levi. The waitress turned to the woman. "The bartender asked me to make sure that the vodka he used is acceptable. It's a new premium brand from just outside of Moscow."

Anya took a big swig of the drink, closed her eyes and nodded. "Oh, it's strong… but quite nice." She opened her eyes and smiled. "Tell him to prepare another. I don't think this one will last long."

"As you will." The waitress scurried off in the direction of the bar.

"Levi," the girl said it loud enough for the next table to hear. She leaned forward and stared at him. "Do you know who I am?"

"I'd like to get to know you, but right now I just have the first name a girl who caught my eye from across the room." He smiled. "And besides, I'm not from around here, so I really don't know anyone. *Should* I know you?"

Anya took another gulp from her glass and her eyes became glassy as she leaned toward him and put her hand on Levi's knee. "You don't kn-know me."

Her words were a bit slurred.

Levi scooted his chair closer and he held out his hand.

She drained her glass, grabbing his hand to steady herself.

"Are you okay?" Levi asked as he spotted several people coming closer from his periphery.

Anya stared at him with a sloppy smile. "You have beau-beautiful bl-blue eyes, Levi. Did an… Did anyone ever…"

Her eyelids began to droop.

Whatever sedative and Ambien-like concoction they'd spiked her drink with, it was working at an alarmingly fast rate.

Levi held onto both of Anya's arms just as her head drooped and two of Karpov's men quickly escorted the semi-conscious girl away.

Sipping at his seltzer, it was only moments later that Grigori came by, handed Levi a plastic card and whispered in his ear, "That's the girl's keycard. Mr. Karpov's driver is waiting for you in front of the club, he will take you where you need to go."

Levi pocketed the card, dropped the crumpled note on the table and walked to the front of the club.

CHAPTER THIRTEEN

It was late in the evening as Alicia walked out of the dorms with her three quad-mates, heading toward the campus library. They'd just started talking about dinner and she couldn't believe the reaction she'd gotten from them when she'd suggested that they grab some pizza.

"How can you eat that?" Min held a sour expression as they walked along the sidewalk toward Elm Drive. "That cheese they put on it, it's made from spoiled milk, isn't it? It can't be healthy for you."

Alicia laughed. "I guess you could say the milk spoiled, but not really. Either way, it tastes great." She looked at Ruth and Ting. "None of you have had cheese before?"

They all shook their heads.

"We're definitely picking up some pizza. You're in America now, I'll introduce you—"

"Why is it so dark?" Ting asked, her voice held a tinge of concern.

As they passed the decorative metal sculpture in front of Whitman, Alicia noticed that the nearby street lamps were all out.

"Hey, Alicia?" The man's voice came from a shadowy figure near the metal structure.

Alicia turned toward the voice and suddenly everything seemed to move in slow motion.

The shadowy figure stepped closer, the glint of metal in his right hand.

Min launched herself at the figure, her kick slamming into the man's arm with a heavy thwack that sent whatever had been in his hand flying.

A car on Elm Drive gunned its engine, its headlights turned on.

Ruth grabbed Alicia by the upper arm and yelled, "Follow me," as she pulled her back toward the dorms.

Mid-stride, Alicia hesitated. "What about—"

"They can take care of this." Ruth pulled ever-harder as the sound of a gunshot erupted.

Alicia's heart raced as she pulled out her flashlight, knowing that it was already too late to be useful as she ran toward the dorms.

It took no more than thirty seconds for them to swipe into the dorms, and into the safety of the building.

Alicia grabbed for her phone to call the cops, but as she

patted her pocket, her heart sank. "I must have dropped my phone out there."

They'd approached the nearest set of stairs when Ruth's phone vibrated, and she put it to her ear. "Yes?"

The thin girl nodded several times with a repeated grunt of affirmation. "You got the license plate?"

Another two grunts.

Alicia's mind raced as she replayed what had happened.

That metal glint… she hated to think it was possible, but it was probably a gun. If it had been keys, they would have made some kind of jingling noise when Min had kicked them out of his hand.

And the man's voice… it wasn't a student's voice. He sounded older. He had a Russian accent.

She didn't know anyone who was Russian. Who could that have been? And how did they know her name?

The door leading into the North Hall opened and Ting walked in.

Alicia's heart sank as the girl jogged toward them. "Where's Min?"

Ting gave Alicia a hug and asked, "Are you okay?"

"Where's Min!" Alicia wiped tears from her eyes as her heart thudded loudly in her chest.

"She's okay, she's talking to the police, giving them the license plate number to the car." She dug a cellphone out of her pocket and handed it to Alicia. "Here, I found this in the grass."

"What happened to the man with…"

"The man by the sculpture ran to the car and they escaped."

"I heard a gunshot."

"I don't think so." Ting's expression remained calm, despite what had happened. Almost as if this was all a normal thing. "Maybe you heard the getaway car's exhaust backfire and it sounded different during the chaos, but I don't think so."

"Come on," Ruth put her arms around them both. "Let's go back into the room and just relax for a bit. Min was the one who called me and she's taking care of a few things. When she's done, we can maybe order some of that pizza you want us to try."

Alicia's heart was still racing, and her hands shook as she climbed up the steps.

Why would someone be after her?

Doug Mason's phone vibrated and he tapped on his earbud. "Yes?"

"Doug," it was Lucy Chen's voice on the line. *"We had an attempted contact with Levi's daughter."*

The director of operations sat up straighter. "Is she okay?"

"She's safe in the dorms with my people. I need a

cleanup crew for one body, and it's going to have to be quick. We don't need some kids going into the bushes to make out and find some dead guy. I also have a license plate for the car that the getaway driver used. And yes, he got away."

"Are there any other witnesses?"

"My people don't believe so. We got lucky. I think Alicia is spooked, but we evac'd her from the scene as soon as it went down. I don't think she suspects anything other than it was a random event."

Mason frowned. "I'm sure she suspects more than she lets on."

"Maybe, but my people will handle Alicia's mental state. I need you to bat cleanup for this."

"Fine, send me the GPS coordinates of where you've stashed the body as well as the license plate. I'll take care of those things on my side. Do you need any other help locally? I can get a team down there."

"No. My people are with Alicia 24/7 until she heads back to Pennsylvania. We've got two more days. When is Levi getting back? He's going to want to get involved with this, and I'm not playing your games. He's going to hear about it from me regardless of what you say."

"Levi is still on his mission. If things go as I hope, he'll be heading back roughly when Alicia's ready to leave for home. I'll talk to you in a couple days."

The line went dead and Mason leaned back in his chair,

stared up at the ceiling and said to nobody in particular, "Levi is going to go on a rampage when he hears about this."

Konstantin got up from the computer, removed the heating blanket from his sore shoulder and was about to head to his bedroom when the phone rang.

Nobody called this line, especially at this time of the night. He shifted his gaze to the digital readout. It was some business called Sleeping Systems. Clearly some automated junk call. He grumbled, "It should be illegal to do such things."

He waited for the four rings and the ringing stopped, likely answered by the digital answering machine somewhere at the phone company.

Almost immediately the phone rang again.

It was the same place, and Konstantin's anger shot through the roof as he grabbed the phone and yelled, "I don't want whatever it is you're selling."

"Sir! Sir! I'm sorry for the call, but this is the mattress store security, and I have someone here who gave me this number. She's drunk or maybe on drugs, and I think someone robbed her. She threw her purse at me, and the only thing in it was her driver's license."

A chill ran up his spine as he walked purposefully

toward Anya's wing of the house. "Who gave you this number?"

"The girl did. Her license says her name is Anya Porchenko."

The man continued talking as Konstantin walked past the main kitchen and down the hallway. He slammed open the door to her suite and he called out, "Anya!"

Clothes were everywhere, like always. The maids cleaned daily, yet somehow his daughter was incapable of keeping a tidy room. He left the bedroom, heading back to his office.

"Let me talk to her."

"Sir, she's passed out again on one of our floor displays. She doesn't smell too strongly of alcohol, but she's not right. She was crying about some lost tiara. She's very combative when I try to wake her."

Konstantin pulled in a deep breath and slowly let it out. It certainly sounded like his daughter. "I'll send somebody to get her."

"I'm sorry sir, but in her condition, I can't just release her to any stranger. She's probably safest with the police. I just called because she'd insisted that I do so before she passed out again."

"You are not going to call the police."

"Sir, I have to. I don't know what else to do, but she's broken into the store, and I don't know what kind of damage she might have been done yet. I'm the only one here at the

moment, and I can't be responsible for her or the damage she may have caused by breaking into the store."

"I will come get her myself."

"Sir, who are you to her? And are you nearby?"

"I'm her father." Konstantin sat at his desk, typed in the name of the company he'd seen on the Caller ID display, and pulled it up on the map. "You are at Universitetskiy Prospekt?"

"Yes."

"I'll be there in forty-five minutes."

"Sir, I have to call someone—"

"What's your name?"

"Boris."

"Listen to me, Boris. My name is Konstantin Porchenko, I'm the head of the Russian State Energy consortium. I am personal friends with the head of the FSB as well as the President of our great nation. You have two choices right now, and they are as follows: you will wait for me to arrive and get compensated for your patience and silence, or you will do what you feel is necessary and suffer whatever consequences may occur. Which will it be, Boris?"

"Uh... s-sorry Mr. Porchenko. I didn't know—"

"What's your answer?" he yelled into the phone, any semblance of patience having just vanished.

"I'll w-wait. Sir, I'll watch over her and m-make sure she's safe."

"I'm leaving now." Konstantin hung up, grabbed his car keys, and walked out of the office.

As the oligarch walked out of the house, he turned to one of the members of his home security and said, "I'm going downtown for a bit. I'll be back in a couple hours."

The guard pulled a walkie-talkie from his belt. "Sir, "I'll wake your driver and—"

"No." Konstantin waved away the suggestion. "I'm going alone."

The last thing he needed was to have more people see what Anya had done to herself—again.

Levi stared at the privacy barriers all along the Rublyovo-Uspenskoye Highway as the sedan slowed. There was no such thing in the US, but this neighborhood had very obvious corrugated barriers along the road that curved partially outward, making it nearly impossible to climb. Occasionally, he spotted a break in the barriers, and despite the lack of street lights, he spotted the silhouettes of mansions with their lights twinkling peacefully past the barriers.

If there was such a thing as oligarch alley, this had to be the place. It was probably beautiful during the day, but at night, it was one lonely dark stretch of road that seemed more ominous than attractive.

Karpov had provided him with blueprints of the original building of Porchenko's home as well as satellite views from above, thanks to Google Earth.

It was the satellite images that helped Levi formulate his plan. And after one of Karpov's men was sent out and confirmed the accuracy of the images, the method for his entry had been set.

Despite all of the Outfit's planning and Levi's insistence on being prepared, he found himself within a quarter mile of his objective without any of his normal gear. A tactical penetration into an unfriendly area was not normally done in a suit and tie, yet here he was.

And he was somewhat counting on a quiet penetration, retrieval of data, and depending on whether they could get Porchenko out of the house or not, either an assassination or laying the groundwork for such a thing.

The driver pulled to the side of the road and motioned ahead. "The home is to the left. I will wait in the gas station a quarter mile down the road, past the Porchenko home." He turned in his seat and offered Levi a hand-sized flat box. "Mr. Karpov asked me to give this to you as a gift. You might find need for it in there."

Levi took the box, removed its lid and found a small handgun.

"Mr. Karpov was concerned with your having the Lebedev as the gun you carried. This is a PSS-2, silenced pistol. It's used by today's FSB in wet operations."

Wet operations was the old Soviet term for assassinations. Activities that could lead to things getting bloody.

"It has six 7.62x43mm sub-sonic rounds and believe it or not, the sound of the falling casings will likely be louder than the gun's action."

Levi checked the magazine, it was full. He racked the slide, chambering a bullet and tucked the snub-nosed gun in his suit pocket. "Okay—"

"One second!" The driver pulled up a paper map to block his view of the road ahead and turned to Levi. "Someone is leaving the Porchenko home."

Levi ducked low in the back seat and within thirty seconds a car drove past.

The driver tossed aside the map. "It is clear. The gate has shut once again."

He patted the back of the driver's seat and hopped out of the dark sedan into the blackness of the lonely road.

The driver pulled away and Levi walked nonchalantly past the entrance to Porchenko's home without even giving it a second's glance.

The property itself bordered nearly one-thousand feet of the road, with metal barriers and concertina wire draped along the top.

There was a hum of a generator somewhere nearby, and it wouldn't surprise him in the least that even the razor wire was electrified.

Levi crossed the road as he entered what turned out to be

a construction site for the lot adjacent to Porchenko's. From the moon shining above, he made out the nearest parts of the neighbor's poured foundation.

There was ivy growing from some of the equipment, and he got the distinct feeling that the completion of this home was in no means imminent. Maybe due to the strife within the country, the neighbor hadn't been able to finish building the home. Maybe he got killed by the secret police, or just made the wrong business decision and got clobbered by one of the bigger fish.

Regardless of why construction had clearly stopped a long while ago, Levi stepped carefully across the grounds and spotted what he was looking for.

There was a large piece of heavy equipment parked right next to Porchenko's wall. Just like it showed on the satellite imagery.

Levi retrieved a thin nylon rope from his pocket, and hopped onto the tracks of the large dirt-moving equipment. Within moments, he'd climb up on top of the cab, tied one end of his rope to a metal loop and flung the remainder of the rope over the security wall.

He crouched down and surveyed the property from the top of the cab.

There was a guard outpost stationed near the gated entrance and on the side that Levi was located was the second entrance into the home.

The entrance Anya used.

After about five minutes of watching the grounds, and seeing no movement whatsoever. Levi leaped from the top of the cab, and landed with practiced efficiency as he tucked and rolled up onto his feet. He was fifty feet from the side entrance of the home.

Retrieving the keycard from his suit jacket, Levi crept forward and swiped at the panel next to the ornately carved door.

There was a loud click and Levi pushed his way into the home.

With the silenced weapon in hand, Levi crept along the white marble tiles, all the while remembering the layout of the home he'd seen in the blueprints.

So far, things matched well.

He'd walked through the guest foyer, past Anya's bedroom and through her own living, dining and cooking area, before getting to the door that was supposed to lead into the main portion of the house.

Levi reached for the doorknob when the door swung open.

A large man with a stone-chiseled face walked through the doorway, and time almost seemed to stop as his eyes widened.

The man reached for something inside his suit jacket

when Levi squeezed the trigger, blowing the back of the man's skull against the wall.

The guard collapsed like a marionette whose strings had been snipped, making more noise as he fell to the ground than the pistol had.

He had no idea how many people were in the house, but the last thing he needed was to leave a bloody trail to alert everyone that something was amiss.

Levi closed the door, and with the swipe of a few kitchen towels, cleaned up the blood that had begun to pool on the ground, shoved the towels into a new kitchen garbage bag and put it over the man's head. He then dragged the guard by his shirt collar down the hall, and into a hallway bathroom.

Patting him down, he retrieved a phone, which he crushed under his heel, and a German-made SIG P365 9mm handgun, which he pocketed.

He stepped out into the hallway and closed the bathroom door.

Breathing slowly, Levi sensed no sounds in the house. He continued onward. There were no obvious trailed of blood on the marble tiles, and he ignored the bloodstained wall where the security guard had died, and entered a lavish kitchen.

The kitchen alone was easily the size of his apartment, and despite Porchenko's reputation as a recluse, the man certainly had the kitchen to prepare a feast for a huge quantity of people.

Levi spotted a lot of American brands as he looked past the pair of 60" Viking ranges, and the commercial-grade SubZero refrigerator. Following the map in his mind, he walked past the kitchen and then the beige-colored travertine dining table that had seating for twenty-four around it.

He passed through a corridor, into an open area for entertaining guests, and eventually found himself climbing upstairs to the end of a long hallway.

Karpov's intel was solid.

The double-door entrance to Porchenko's office was wide open and the large room lay before him. It was particularly well-maintained. Not a paperclip out of place, but oddly enough, a heating blanket that was still plugged into the wall lay draped across the arm of a leather wingback chair.

It sure seemed like Porchenko may have left in a hurry. It might have even been that car that they'd spied leaving the compound.

Levi smiled as he spied the desktop computer. The monitor was on, and so was the computer.

Retrieving the USB dongle that Grigori had given him, he plugged it into the back of the computer and a green LED flickered, followed by red, followed by a solid green. That was supposed to be all he needed to do to install the virus.

"The case containing the explosive has a cellphone receiver. In fact, the entire thing is an antenna that's activated the moment you pull the foil off and stick the case to

something. All you need to do is install the virus and when someone logs into the computer, it will automatically reach out to a service that will call the case's number and boom."

Levi retrieved another dongle from his front pocket. This one was one of Brice's specialties.

He pressed the USB device into one of the computer's empty slots. A red LED flashed once and went silent, just as his briefing paperwork had described.

It was yet another virus being installed, but this one was different.

"The virus will reach out to one of my public servers and through a private key exchange, establish a secure connection with one of the Outfit's workstations. The moment that happens, my scripts will automatically begin sucking down all the data that I can access from it."

Taking the as-of-yet inert bomb out of his suit jacket pocket, Levi removed the foil, exposing the sticky side of the tape and placed the Semtex directly underneath the computer.

The bomb was activated.

Levi glanced at his watch. He'd promised himself no more than ten minutes in this place.

On the desk was a photograph of a man and a woman holding hands. Having met Anya, he saw her in the woman's eyes and smile. And the man next to her also held a resemblance to the young woman. Levi wondered where the wife was, and felt a sudden sense of urgency to get out of this place.

He pulled open one of the desk drawers, and it was completely empty. He inspected the rest of the desk's drawers and only found pens, pencils, and a stash of mints.

Opening what looked like an address book, Levi flipped through the pages, being careful to focus on the details.

Hovering over the desk, Levi studied the phone and pressed the up arrow on the digital display. He grinned as the digital readout on the phone displayed a list of both incoming and outgoing numbers. He pressed the up and down arrows and began scrolling through the list.

He scrolled all the way back to as far as the memory on the phone allowed, which was about two weeks' worth of calls.

Levi panned his gaze across the room, and then looked at his watch. He had to leave.

He retrieved the dongles, backed away from the desk and compared what he was seeing now to when he'd first walked in. Everything was still in its place.

With the gun in his hand, and his senses tingling with anticipation, he strode purposefully out of the office, across the house, and toward Anya's entryway.

Brice rushed back into his office, he tossed the bag of hastily collected half-eaten food onto his workbench, sat down at his computer and began typing.

The alerts he'd received on his phone told him one thing, but as he reached across the internet, attaching a local process to the exposed network port somewhere in Moscow, he began to smile.

A remote drive was mounted on his local machine and he shook his head. "Holy crap, Levi. You did it."

Files had been transferring for the last twenty minutes out of the machine that had been infected with Brice's back-door virus.

His phone buzzed and he tapped the speaker phone as his fingers blurred over the keyboard. "What's up?"

"Did he make contact?" It was Mason calling.

"It looks like it. One second, let me see if I can confirm something." Brice scanned the directories that had already been transferred, looking for a .PST file. He found one, ran it through his cracking software and pulled it up in an Outlook viewer. "Alrighty then." He scrolled through the list of e-mails and the automatic translation filter was having trouble keeping up. He selected one of the subjects that looked interesting. "Let's see. I'm currently staring at an e-mail from a Konstantin Porchenko to some deputy minister of some department nobody's heard of in the Kremlin. Wow, Levi actually did it. How the hell he managed it; I have no idea. But we're in. And I'm pulling the data as quickly as Porchenko's outbound internet spigot will let me."

"Okay. Make sure you get everything you can, this will be one very large set of arrests, but it needs to be air tight. I'll reach out to our person in Russia and expedite Levi's way out of there. Him and I have a talk that needs to happen."

Brice winced at the idea of how that conversation with Levi might go. This was way beyond his measly pay grade. People get unpredictable when it comes to their family being endangered by their job. "Well, it's about 10 p.m. over there, so they're probably still doing something."

Konstantin maintained a death grip on his steering wheel as he drove home. His entire body ached with the anger he was feeling toward Anya for having done this to herself. Tomorrow would be a new day, but tonight, he needed to take care of his little girl. Maybe hire full time help to watch over her. He glanced over and cringed as her head lolled from side to side. His only daughter had been babbling in a semi-coherent state for most of the way home.

She'd said something about an award. A prize of some type.

She couldn't remember where she'd been. Who she'd been with, and to his chagrin, how she'd ended up being found, asleep, by some security guard at a bedding supply store.

His baby girl had the same gene that had killed her mother. The temptation to drink and or do other things was too much, and a sense of desperation washed over him as he realized that he was watching the only thing that kept him sane slowly kill herself.

He pressed the button in the car and the gate yawned open.

The guard nodded as Konstantin drove up to the main entrance of the house.

He parked the car, ran to the passenger's side and he ignored his shoulder pain as he lifted his baby girl up into his arms.

Anya laid her head against his chest and she whimpered. "Daddy, I miss when you and mommy would throw parties."

"Me too, baby girl." He kissed the top of her head as one of the security guards rushed to open the front door for him.

As Konstantin approached the door, the guard opened his mouth to say something, thought better of it and averted his eyes. "Yuri, whatever it is, it can wait until tomorrow."

He walked over to his bedroom, laid Anya on top of his blankets and kissed her on the forehead. "I'll be right back."

He closed the door to his bedroom and jogged upstairs.

He sat on his office chair, picked up the phone and pressed one of the speed-dial buttons.

The line rang once and a man speaking with a perfect American accent picked up. *"Yes?"*

Konstantin's voice cracked as he heard the man's voice, and he spoke rapidly in Russian. "Alex, she's just like Anna. She's going to die, I can feel it. It's going to happen again and then what will I do? I can't do this for much longer, she needs me."

"Stop it! Get control of yourself. This will be your undoing, and I need you to remain with the program."

Alex continued speaking in English, never dropping out of his adopted identity, never thinking that the Soviet's failure would be his own.

Konstantin breathed deeply and let out a shuddering breath. "You're right. I know you're right. We're almost at the end, aren't we?"

"Yes. Things are lining up the way we need them. I've sent you the contacts for what I believe will be five more influencers. The last set I sent you have been persuaded, and those votes are ours. We need five more in the House, and two more in the Senate."

"I miss you. It's been forty years."

"Did you hear me? We're very close. Do what needs to be done."

The phone line went dead, and Konstantin sighed.

Setting the phone back down, he turned to the computer, typed in his screensaver password, and—

The world flashed white.

CHAPTER FOURTEEN

Climbing up the stairs from Incirlik's underground bunker, Levi breathed in the scent of jet fumes as he walked onto the tarmac of the Turkish airport. As he squinted from the bright sunlight, he breathed in deeply and smiled. It was freedom that he was breathing into his lungs. Stuffed into his duffel was his suit, that smelled of sweat and urine, and instead he wore his dark fatigues as he panned his gaze across the tarmac. Someone in uniform was running toward him with something clutched in his hand.

"Lieutenant Jennings, your ID, sir." The man held out Levi's military ID.

"Thank you, airman." Levi clipped the ID onto his fatigues and asked, "Do you know when my stateside transport is arriving?"

The airman pointed northeast. "That big gray bird that's

heading this way. It's going directly to Andrews with nothing in it but you."

Levi shook his head. "I wonder how bad the pilot screwed up to get that assignment? Probably some variation of the 'you'll be flying a cargo plane full of rubber dog shit out of Hong Kong.' But instead of dog shit, he's just got me."

"Sir?" The airman held a confused expression.

"Never mind, airman. Someone once said it in a movie from before your time."

"Sir, I was told for you to reach back to HQ as soon as possible."

Levi pulled out his phone, it finally had signal again, and he dialed Brice's number. Almost instantly, the phone picked up. *"Levi, did you talk to Mason yet?"*

"Well, that's a fine 'how do you do?' I'm in Turkey right now, and no, I didn't talk to Mason. I was told to call HQ, and he's not who I normally talk to, that would be you my good sir. Why, what's going on?"

There was silence on the line, which never boded well.

"Hold on, I'm trying to get Mason on—"

"Goddamn, Brice, just tell me what's going on. Did you get through to the computer?"

"Oh, yeah. I'm analyzing the stuff that's streamed off of there. Unfortunately, I didn't get a full download before the signal got cut off. I'm guessing someone detected my snooping is what I can figure."

Levi frowned. "How long was the signal up before you lost it?"

"About two hours and fifteen minutes."

Karpov's men were supposed to setup Anya's pickup in downtown Moscow. About an hour's drive from Porchenko's home.

Levi grinned. "Well, you may want to check through the grapevine if a head of some energy concern in Russia suddenly got blown up."

"No! You're kidding. How did you—nope, never mind. I don't know anything about that. But I'll check into things on my end."

A large unmarked cargo jet taxi'd within a couple hundred yards from him and slowed to a stop.

"Listen Brice, I'm about to board a plane to Andrews. Was that what Mason was going to say to me?"

"Damn it, I can't seem to get Mason on the line. I've been trying the entire time I've been talking with you. I'll go ahead and tell you, because I'd want to know, and I don't want you to be pissed at me for not telling you when I first had a chance."

Levi's heart began to thud more loudly in his chest.

"Let me start with saying that everyone is okay. And I mean it. Totally okay. But you might be glad that you may or may not have taken care of Porchenko, because sometime after you went dark on us, I caught a transmission from him to our friendly staffer in the pizza parlor. He really wanted to

know how to reach you, and our staffer somehow knew about Alicia going to Princeton."

"He knew *what!*" Levi yelled into the phone as a set of stairs were wheeled up to the large jet. "What happened? Tell me everything."

"*Well, it started with Mason calling Lucy Chen...*"

"*Hey, no problem, Levi,*" said Dino. Levi pressed the phone to his ear to better hear the man's voice over the sound of the jet engines throttling up for takeoff. "*I'd do the same thing if I were you. Tell me when you get in town. We'll make a party of it.*"

"Thanks, Dino."

Levi was pressed hard against the seats of the C-5 heavy transport jet tilted up into the sky. He looked back at the huge empty space in the cargo hold. His was the lone seat slapped down onto the cargo tracks.

He had a lot of people to talk to when he got stateside. The right thing to do was to stop off at HQ. Debriefing needed to happen, and he needed to know more about what had happened with Alicia before talking to her. He knew she wasn't harmed, but until he talked to her himself, he wouldn't rest easy.

He closed his eyes and focused on his breathing.

He had ten hours before they landed.

He'd need that time to recharge.

Levi had no windows in the cargo hold to tell him what was going on, but it had been over nine hours since takeoff and he'd felt his ears pop several times as the plane lost altitude.

Almost home.

Suddenly his phone vibrated, telling him that he must be low enough to be getting signal. He retrieved the phone from his pocket and saw several texts scroll past.

Unlocking the phone, he opened the texts and focused on the one that had come from Lucy.

She almost never texted.

"Levi, I know you're up in the air. Call me the minute you land. It's important."

His back stiffened as he dialed her number.

The phone rang once... twice... and suddenly Lucy's voice echoed loudly in his ear. *"Levi, are you back in the States?"*

"I'm in the back of a military transport, and I think I'm landing at Andrews in about twenty minutes, give or take. Before anything else, is Alicia okay?"

"She is. She's fine, and I believe she's literally just arrived at your mom's place in the last thirty minutes or so."

Levi breathed a sigh of relief. "Thank God. With what you said in your text you had me—"

"But you need to hear what happened! A Russian—"

"Brice already filled me in, but I want to verify a few things before I call Alicia. Tell me what she knows and what she's seen."

"Okay, it's pretty simple. Three of my girls were Alicia roommates in that orientation she attended. As far as Alicia knows, they're students from China and that cover was never really compromised. When one of the Russian mobsters tried to pull something, one of them was able to disarm him as Alicia was quickly escorted out of sight."

"And the mobster?"

"Eliminated from the equation. The Outfit helped with cleanup on that. There was a getaway car, and with Denny's help, I got tracking data on the car, and even an ID on the driver. The Russian safe house had an unfortunate fire, and anyone who tried to escape didn't make it. A tragedy, really. My people took care of the cleanup operations for that. I didn't want to put Mason into a difficult situation for him and his mysterious bosses."

Levi nodded as he felt the jet banking to the left, likely lining up for approach.

"Alicia thinks the Russian was a common mugger, and thinks that one of the girls had filed a police report. Evidently she was pretty cool about it. She's a tough cookie. The girl's seen much worse before you took her from the streets. The last report I got was earlier today as they'd packed up and left the dorms. Mason's folks took over watching from afar as she drove home. Brice texted me that she arrived safely. That's about it."

With a warm feeling in his chest, Levi smiled. "Lucy, I owe you."

"Of course you do, and I expect you to visit me at my place when you get done with your debrief. It's been way too long. I miss your pretty face."

He laughed. "Isn't that what the guy is supposed to say?"

"You're not the top in this relationship, and I'll prove it later when you come over. Go call Alicia, I know you're dying to do that. I'll see you soon."

The connection ended and Levi did exactly as Lucy had predicted.

Just as Levi heard the first ring, Alicia's excited voice came on the line, *"Ahbah! I tried calling you for a while, but your phone wouldn't ever pick up."*

"I've been out of the country, and just now getting back. How was your orientation thing that you went to?"

"You know…"

"I know what?"

"Come on, Dad. I'm not stupid. Three older Asian girls as my roommates? You set that up, you had to have. I'm pretty sure they were all armed as well."

"Wait, what are you talking about? Armed?"

"Well, one of the girls dropped their toiletry bag and it made a big thunk like a gun was in it. It was either that or the heaviest vibrator ever made."

"What, what do you know about… never mind." Levi's mind was racing. Unlike what Lucy believed, Alicia was obviously very suspicious about what had happened. "I don't want to know. You didn't answer my question. How was the orientation?"

"It was cool. I think this coming year is going to be awesome. I can't thank you enough for being able to go. I know this is expensive—"

"Baby girl, it's fine. If it weren't, I'd tell you. So, things are good. Did you just get home?"

"I did. And you can tell your friends they can stop following me around. I don't know about Ruth, Ting and Min, but those guys in the Cadillac that followed me the entire way from Princeton. They kind of suck if they thought I couldn't see them tailing me a few cars behind."

"I'm not sure I know—"

"Dad, come on… give me a little credit, will you?"

With a sense of pride welling up inside of him, Levi shook his head and chuckled. "Okay, fine. Maybe I wanted to make sure my girl was okay while I wasn't around to do it myself. Can you blame me?"

The sound of the landing gear extending echoed loudly in the jet's cargo hold.

"I love you, Ahbah."

"I love you too, baby girl. I'll see all of you sometime later this week."

The line went dead and the jet jolted heavily as the first wheels touched down on the runway.

Levi sat in Brice's office, listening to the engineer read something off of a printout.

"Last year there was a fire at a chicken processing plant in Georgia, killing five workers and injuring dozens more. One month later, a fire at a meatpacking plant in Nebraska killed one and critically injured another. Soon after, there was a fire at a bacon processing plant in Iowa, killing two and injuring four more. Two months after that, a massive fire broke out at a food processing plant in Texas, destroying the entire facility and leaving over a thousand people without a job. That repeated itself again just weeks later in California. And it happened again in Ohio and Pennsylvania—"

Levi held up a hand. "Enough. I get the picture. Someone is not happy with our food supply. What's your point?"

"All of these incidents happened in 2021. And for each one of those incidents, I have an incoming email to Porchenko from an anonymous email address, talking about two things: a member of the House or Senate who needs 'convincing,' and a suggested target to 'send a message' in that congressman's state. Unfortunately, I don't have the more recent emails—nothing after late 2021. So I don't know what might have been happening since."

Levi leaned forward. "Wait. You're saying someone *else* made those suggestions to Porchenko? He's not the head of the snake?"

"Oh, he was the head all right. Or *a* head, at least. And this data puts us in position to create airtight convictions against many of the people he worked with. But we might be missing a lot of the guilty… and more importantly, this might be a multi-headed snake."

Levi motioned to the legal pad on Brice's desk. "Hand me that pad and a pencil."

Levi began writing a bunch of numbers on the pad. "When I was in Porchenko's office, I went through his phone. It had a list of the most recent two hundred calls made and received."

Brice's eyes widened. "Holy crap, Levi. You *memorized* them?"

"You know about that," Levi said, still scribbling.

"Sure, but it's still bizarre to watch it. Have you ever had your memory tested, by like, cognitive neurologists and such?"

Levi had. He'd had the results shredded and everyone involved sworn to secrecy. He certainly wasn't going to reveal all that to Brice.

"The docs say it's just something that sometimes

happens," he said casually. Changing the subject, he added, "When does Mason get back?"

"Two days. He got called to an emergency meeting of some kind over in Europe."

Levi finished writing down the numbers. Just as he was finishing up, he got a text from Dino.

We're ready. Things are on ice until you get here.

He pushed the pad over to Brice. "I've got to go. See if you can learn anything from these numbers—maybe there'll be someone here who isn't already on your radar."

Brice nodded. "I'll put this through the Utah Data Center. You never know."

Levi waved and headed out the door to meet up with Dino. He was going to owe the man a big favor, but it was definitely worth it.

As Levi walked into the soundproof room that the Marino family had arranged for him, the sole occupant of the room gasped. Tony Banks was strapped to a sturdy wooden chair bolted to the floor, and by the looks of him, he'd been there for most of the day.

Levi smiled. *Good.*

Dino was out in front of the building, eating dinner at a picnic table and joking around with his crew. This wasn't their problem.

Levi pulled on a pair of leather gloves. "Mr. Banks," he said. "It's interesting how the tides can turn, don't you think? You were playing games with me the first time we met, but now it's my turn. You really thought you had my number. And you know what? I'm not a petty man; back then, you weren't worth my time or energy. But things have changed."

"Listen," Banks protested, "I have access to a lot of cash. Almost eight hundred thousand dollars in unmarked bills. It's yours if you help me get out of this place. I won't say a word to anyone that this happened."

"Right. You won't say a word." Levi shook his head. "I'm not emotional about money. Unlike you, money doesn't rule my life. You know what I *am* emotional about? *My family.* I heard what you did, and I aim to know more about why you did it. Can you guess what I'm talking about?"

Banks shook his sweat-streaked head, his eyes practically popping out of their sockets.

Levi pulled out a gun and a knife he'd stowed under his fatigues, held them up for Banks to see, and then put them on the table. "You had a conversation with someone in Russia about my family. Do you remember that?"

Banks's jaw dropped.

Levi smiled. "You *do* remember! Excellent. You see, that does make me emotional. Angry, to be specific. For someone to even *think* about putting someone I love in danger—"

"But I didn't—"

The throwing knife whizzed through the air, flipping end over end, and slammed directly between Banks's legs. Banks cried out in fear, even though the blade didn't even touch him.

Levi walked over and yanked the knife free from the chair. Then he took a seat on a wooden table facing Banks.

"Where was I? Oh yes, putting someone I love in danger. And for that sin... you offered me *money*. There's no amount of money on God's green earth that can pay for that. I heard the conversation you had with your friend in Russia. You offered my daughter for the possibility of advancement in your friend's eyes."

Banks stammered, "H-he'd have had me killed if I didn't get him what he needed."

Levi nodded. "Interesting. Tell me, what was your friend's name?"

Banks froze.

Levi picked up the gun, racked the slide, and set it on his lap. "Go on, I'm waiting."

"Mr. P-Porchenko," Banks said. "I don't know his first name."

"How did Mr. Porchenko pay you?"

"One of his men would call me, and tell me to arrive somewhere. Like stand at the Washington Monument or something like that. And sometimes someone would bump into me and I'd find an envelope in my pocket. Or someone would break into my car and leave something under the seat. Cash. Always in hundreds."

Levi leaned back on his hands. "What do you know of his end goals?"

Banks cringed. "I know he was trying to get votes for his pipeline to be approved."

"But the US has nothing to do with that pipeline, right?"

"Well… not exactly." Banks's voice lost its tremor as he explained something that he clearly understood. "Congress votes in resolutions for supporting or not supporting such things. And through our State Department we use that to influence others in our voting bloc."

"And what did you do for Porchenko—other than offer up my daughter as bait?"

"I helped coordinate votes." Banks's chin quivered. "I was his eyes and ears inside Congress." Tears began to roll down his cheeks. "Please. Just let me go and I'll do whatever you want."

Levi stood. "Did you know I just came back from Russia?"

Banks shook his head.

Levi held up the knife and grinned. "You know, even though I cleaned this knife, it probably still has some detectable flakes of Porchenko's blood on it."

Banks's eyes widened.

Levi then smiled and held up the gun. "And this gun? It's

a SIG P365. The favored gun of Mr. Porchenko's bodyguard. You know how I know that?"

"B-because you killed him too." Banks was now sobbing. "Please… I'll do anything. Absolutely anything."

Levi sheathed his knife and walked closer to Banks. "All of what you've told me is information I already knew. I need you to tell me something I *don't* know about Porchenko."

Banks's eyes darted back and forth. "Um, I know he had others he talked with other than me. But I don't know who they are."

"How did he learn about you?"

Banks shifted in the leather straps holding him to the chair. "One day he just called me on my work cell phone. That was years ago. I was having money problems, and one of his people bumped into me, leaving me with an envelope that contained exactly how much I was in arrears to the bank on my mortgage."

Levi nodded. "What did he say about these other contacts?"

Banks shook his head. "Honestly he hardly ever mentioned them, and even then, it was always 'the others.'"

"Who do *you* think the others are?"

"I'm not sure. Probably other congressional staffers like me? Or even congressmen, though maybe he didn't really need to talk to them directly, if he had staffers. And I guess maybe lobbyists."

"Lobbyists?"

"You know, the folks on K Street. They're what special interest groups use to sort of do what I do. Talk to members of Congress about bills they favor or want to kill. It's all part of the swamp that is DC."

"What did you do that the folks on K Street wouldn't or couldn't?"

"Well, I have more access than they do. I'm allowed in some places where lobbyists aren't."

Levi felt a sudden loathing for the man in front of him. "Anything else?"

Banks pressed his lips together and was silent for a couple seconds. "Honestly, I think the more powerful ones can do just about anything. But I'm tenacious. Like those photos you gave me—they helped me sway the vote of a member of Congress."

"I saw you on the riverbank that day," Levi said. "You burned those photos. Obviously, you'd already used them. What brought you to the river that day?"

"You saw that." Banks said it as a statement, not a question, and shook his head. "I sometimes talk with people who —well, I think they're Russian intelligence, but they've never actually said that. I know they're associated with the embassy. The river is pretty easy. The way it was explained to me was that the lure on the fishing rod is an underwater transmitter. Someone in the vicinity, and it could be on the other side of the river, will have a receiver that records the signal I'm transmitting. But nothing above the water can even detect the transmission."

Levi nodded. It was a clever arrangement.

Banks licked his chapped lips. "Can I ask you one question?"

"Go ahead."

"Did you really kill Porchenko?"

Levi grinned. "The man's dead."

Banks frowned, and when he spoke, he sounded uncertain. "I don't know this for sure, but... I think he was getting his cues from someone who knows DC better than even I do."

Levi kept his voice steady, but for the first time he felt like the staffer might be picking at the scab of something new. "Why do you say that?"

"Well, there were a few times when he told me to talk to certain people. He knew they'd have the information I needed. And sometimes these were people, like, buried in some dungeon in the FBI labs who just happened to know something critical to what I was trying to help with. This happened at least half a dozen times over the last few years. Mr. Porchenko couldn't have known these people; he's in Russia. I don't think he's ever been in the US in his entire life. So I figure, someone in DC, someone who really knows DC, has to be feeding him things."

Levi's phone vibrated with a call. Before answering, he put the muzzle of his SIG nine-millimeter up against the staffer's right eye. "The moment you make a noise," he said, "I'll pull the trigger."

Levi then tapped his earbud. "Hey there. What's up."

"Dude, you won't believe what I just dug up."

Levi grinned as he looked up at the ceiling. "Let me guess: you think the other snake's head is a lobbyist."

"How the hell did you know that? Never mind, it doesn't matter. I correlated your phone numbers to the trace records the Utah Data Center keeps. Those NSA guys have a recording of just about any incoming call that originates outside the US. Most of the Porchenko calls were encrypted, but there was one phone number that didn't employ any of the end-to-end scrambling technology, and two calls were made involving that number. One was about three weeks ago. It was nothing but crap about Russian inside-baseball stuff. But the second one was from just before Porchenko bit it. Here, I'll play it for you."

A moment later, a new voice came over the line. Porchenko's.

"Alex, she's just like Anna. She's going to die, I can feel it. It's going to happen again. And then what will I do? I can't do this for much longer. She needs me."

Another voice answered, this one speaking English with an American accent.

"Stop it! Get control of yourself. This will be your undoing, and I need you to remain with the program."

"You're right. I know you're right. We're almost at the end, aren't we?"

"Yes. Things are lining up the way we need them to. I've sent you the contacts for what I believe will be five more influencers. The last set I sent you have been persuaded, and those votes are ours. We need five more in the House and two more in the Senate."

"I miss you. It's been forty years."

"Did you hear me? We're very close. Do what needs to be done."

There was a click, and Brice said, "And that's it. What do you think?"

"That was bizarre," Levi said. "What do you have on this Alex?"

"I traced the number to an address, which I just emailed to you. The home belongs to Alex Conway, the head of a lobbying firm on K Street. I pulled up his background, but I can tell it's been tampered with. It's too clean for someone working in his field."

"Forty years..." Levi said, thinking. "And an 'I miss you' tossed in there. It almost sounds like they were lovers. And if so, this K Street guy was clearly the top. What happens when he finds out about Porchenko?"

Brice's voice took on an ominous tone.

"That's what worries me. For the same reason we were worried about Porchenko going nutso if he felt the walls closing in on him, this guy probably has the same access to

senators, generals, and the like. Porchenko might have been doing a lot of the dirty work, but this Conway guy looks like the Svengali behind the operations: political unrest, leaking things that sow dissent within the public, pitting one side against the other… this is exactly the thing a lobbyist would be particularly skilled at—manipulating public opinion. With the right data leaked to the right places, one person can make the public lose confidence in their government. And if the public loses confidence, like if they begin to believe that their vote is meaningless…"

"You could get civil war."

"Exactly."

"So are you sending the storm troopers to his house?"

"I can't. We don't have a warrant, and this guy probably has every judge on his speed dial. It would take at least a few days even if it wasn't all classified data. But to get a classified hearing in front of the right judge… I need Mason to help."

"And all the while, this guy might be setting off virtual or literal bombs all over the place. If he thinks he's about to be a grease spot, he's going to pull all his pins."

"Right."

Levi smiled. "Hence why I have his address. Say no more. I'll be in touch."

He clicked off and returned his gun to its shoulder holster. The area around Banks's right eye was bruised from the pressure Levi had applied with the gun's muzzle.

"Okay, Banks, you said you have eight hundred thousand dollars."

The man nodded. "Yes. Well, about seven hundred and eighty."

"Where is it? This is your only chance. Tell me where it is, and how to verify that it's there, and you might see the dawn of another day."

"Thank you." Banks's breath came in ragged gasps. "It's in my attic. Under the insulation. I've hidden several brief-cases there."

Levi walked out of the room, slamming the door behind him, then went out front to where Marino's people were sitting.

Dino looked up. "Well?"

Levi grinned. "You picked him up from his house?"

Dino looked over at the other mobsters. "You momos pick up our stoolie from his place?"

The three mobsters nodded.

Levi crouched so that he was at eye level with Dino and spoke in a whisper. "Look up in the attic. Under the insula-tion he's got briefcases with almost eight hundred G's in them. It's yours. That's my payment to you and Don Marino."

Dino whistled appreciatively. "Nice." He tilted his head toward the building. "What about him?"

"You know." Levi spit into the grass. "He put my daughter in danger."

Dino held up a hand. "Say no more. It's done."

They shook hands.

"Always a pleasure doing business with you beach bums," Levi said.

Dino laughed. "I'll see you around."

Levi walked to his rental. He needed to get some supplies before driving across town.

Tomorrow was going to be an eventful day.

CHAPTER FIFTEEN

"Are you ready for this?" Brice asked.

Levi lowered the night-vision monocular over his left eye, and his surroundings turned varying shades of green. It was four a.m., and he was on the move near the home of the K Street lobbyist, Alex Conway.

He activated his throat mic and whispered, "You're entirely too smart to ask such a dumb question. I wouldn't be here otherwise. Has anything new happened since we talked a couple hours ago?"

"As a matter of fact, yes. The Russian media just announced Porchenko's death. I suspect our lobbyist doesn't know yet, seeing as it's the middle of the night here, but he'll surely hear about it later today."

"Great. What do you think his reaction's going to be?"

"It's hard to tell for certain, but we had one of our guys

who's a former FBI profiler go over what we have, and it's his opinion that Conway will either end up doing nothing... or he'll have a severe *reaction. There's no in-between."*

"Great. So a fifty-fifty shot that the lobbyist is going to be pissed his boyfriend got whacked and try to start a new civil war."

"It's not impossible. Anyway, Mason made a call from Europe. We need more data to secure the arrests of the major players complicit in this mess, and we need it quickly. I'll be interrupting internet access to this guy's office computers, and when the office gets in in the morning, I'll have a team on standby to go 'fix' things over there."

"Wait, you can do that? Then why the hell am I here again?"

"I thought I'd covered that. Crap, Mason's much better at this."

"You're not inspiring much confidence, Brice. Now tell me why I'm about to invade some guy's house when you seem to have a lock on his business already."

"Sorry. When Porchenko and this guy last talked, the cell phone records show that Conway was in the south wing of his house. And remember, he said that he'd just emailed something to Porchenko? So we believe there's key data there. We need those records—and anything else that's on his computer."

"If it's actionable, we act," Levi said, repeating the Outfit's motto. "Okay, let's do this."

"Good. I've borrowed time on a satellite hovering above our part of the world, and it's zeroed in on you. I've got a live image, and your GPS position shows you as a red dot. You're at a Y-junction near the end of the Potomac School Road, is that correct?"

"That's right. But why do I feel like I'm going to be an elephant lumbering through a china shop? I'm looking at a bank of mailboxes next to a narrow private road going into the woods. A sign says it's for private use and has no outlet. I don't get the impression there are mansions back there."

"Trust me, you're in the right spot. Don't waste the darkness. Go inside and burgle something, Mr. Yoder."

"Burgle, eh? Are you Thorin Oakenshield to my Bilbo?"

"You caught that reference, did you?"

Levi cut across the private road and entered the thick forest that bordered it. Keeping his trajectory parallel to the road, he found it slow going, as he had to weave through dense foliage.

"I did, and you do realize that Thorin never said that phrase. Maybe he said it in the movies, I wouldn't know, I didn't see them, but in the book, Tolkien made Thorin a lot more flowery with his language. Something like, 'Now is the time for our esteemed Mr. Baggins, who has proved himself a good companion...' and he went on and on, finally ending with, 'now is the time for him to earn his reward.'"

"I should have known that you've memorized the book.

I'm sure it's part of the Amish mafioso code to do that, right?"

Levi grinned. "You pick the weirdest times to develop a sense of humor."

"It's part of my charm. I get this way in stressful situations. And to be honest, my analogy is sort of backwards, because I'm the one trying to take Conway's secrets, you're just... just... "

"Helping?"

"Exactly. Okay, enough of the fun. What are you seeing?"

"Not much to see, to be honest. It's bizarre that I'm in McLean, Virginia, the epitome of suburbia, and I'm trudging through some seriously thick woods. Even with the night-vision stuff you lent me, I'm having trouble making out much. This place seems to have another tree trunk to skirt around every couple feet. I'm on the south turn of that private road and I just passed a home to my left. It's not a tiny one."

"None of those are. Our lobbyist is sitting pretty in an eight-bedroom, fifteen-thousand-square-foot mansion at the end of that road."

"I know, you sent me the floor plan images. What's the story with who's occupying those eight bedrooms?"

"Conway has four kids, but they're all grown and have moved away. They probably all have their own mansions to take care of. He's married, so I'm assuming there's a wife to

contend with, and with a house that size, maybe a live-in maid. But hopefully this will be just a couple minutes and you're in and out. I'll do the rest from over here."

"In and out," Levi said with a snort. "You make it sound like such a simple thing."

He glanced at his GPS tracker. His target was within two hundred feet. He slowed as he approached the edge of the woods. Sure enough, there was a mansion dead ahead.

"It looks like you're just west of the house."

Levi moved south and then swung east. "Roger that, I'm heading to the south side." He came around, then reported on what he saw.

"I see the window to the master bedroom. The lights are off. And the area beneath it has no windows at all."

This was expected. The floor plans had indicated that the office was a windowless room that could be accessed only by descending a set of private stairs from the bedroom directly above it. Probably a design that should never have passed muster with the housing inspectors; there had to be ordinances requiring rooms to have multiple exits or some such.

"As we thought. How are you at climbing?"

"I've seen it done before."

Levi removed his night-vision equipment—it wasn't doing him much good anyway—shrugged off his backpack, and retrieved his climbing rig and the connected rubber-coated grappling hook.

"Okay, Brice, I'm in position. Now we wait for our lobbyist to leave… and pray his wife doesn't like to hang out in the bedroom all day."

"It'll be fine. Sunrise is in fifty-five minutes, and after that I'll be able to give you a heads-up on anything I can see on satellite. In the meantime, I'm off to wreak havoc on K Street. If you need me, just squawk. I'll keep you on speaker."

"Roger that. Go do your nerd stuff."

───────────

It was just before seven a.m. when Levi, peering through binoculars, spotted a Rolls Royce sedan pulling out of the garage, driven by a woman with blonde hair, tied up in a ponytail.

"I'm thinking the mother hen just left the coop," he said.

"Well, that makes it easier, right? Bet she's off to her therapist appointment or something." Brice paused. *"I can't see her car on the satellite feed—the trees are too close to the road leading up to the house. But as long as she's gone, one less thing to worry about."*

"Her car was the only one in that garage bay." Levi swung his binoculars to the left to look at the other two-car garage. Just as he did, that garage door began rolling upward. "I've got motion in the second garage, and… well that's unexpected."

"What?"

"It's a Camry. If that's Conway, then I'm surprised he'd be driving that, especially with his wife driving a Rolls."

"Maybe it's the maid."

"I don't think so. There's no other cars in the garage."

Levi couldn't see the driver's face, but it was definitely a man's profile, and he had salt-and-pepper hair.

"Could be his car is in the shop and he's driving a loaner," Brice offered.

"Maybe. In any case, all the cars are gone, so that's my cue to move."

With the grappling hook in his hand, Levi moved across the yard and stopped just under the master bedroom's second-story window.

"Okay, here goes nothing on the grappling hook."

He lofted the three-pronged hook up toward the topmost part of the roof. It landed, hopped along the angled roof to the left, and fell off.

"Make sure you get a good solid connection, because you'll be messing around with those panes of glass, and they're heavy."

Levi made a second attempt, aiming slightly to the right of the topmost part of the roof. This time when he yanked sharply on the rope, he felt one of the hooks dig in. He pulled even harder to confirm the rope wasn't going anywhere, then looked down at the motor attached to his climbing rig. It seemed small.

"Are you sure this motor is good for my weight?"

"Unless you've gained a hundred pounds since last night, you're good. It's rated for three hundred pounds. Just press down on the lever and it'll winch you up. Flip the switch and it'll let out the line."

Levi squeezed the lever, and the quiet motor whirred and pulled the line taut. Then his feet slowly left the ground.

Two feet up.

Four feet.

At six feet, Levi could just reach the bottom of the second-story window sill.

At ten feet, he let go of the lever and hung with the window at chest height. He was looking directly into the bedroom.

From the side of his backpack he unhooked a device with a large suction cup on it. He placed it against the window and pulled back on a lever, applying a vacuum under the suction cup.

"Okay, I've got the suction-cup thing stuck to the window."

"Those windows are probably two or three panes thick. Let me know when you're done with the first pane."

Levi pulled the glass cutter from his belt, pressed the scoring wheel on the outer pane of glass, pulled it across the width of the window, and cringed when it made a high-pitched scraping noise. He continued until he'd scored a large enough square for him to enter through.

"Okay, done with the glass cutter. Moving on to the gas." Levi looked around, suddenly very conscious of how exposed he was, dangling from the roof. "I hope you're watching the front while I'm up here."

"Don't worry."

Levi took the can of compressed gas from his pack and sprayed it at the top right corner of the square he'd etched. Brice had said it would freeze the glass where he'd scored it, causing enough stress to make it break along the lines. Sure enough, the glass fogged up with frost, and there was a loud crack.

Levi, holding on to the suction-cup device with his other hand, grunted as its weight suddenly pulled on his arm.

"Okay, first pane is off."

He held the pane awkwardly to the side, twisted in the climbing rig, and flipped the suction cup's lever to the "release" position. The pane of glass dropped down below and landed on the dew-covered grass without cracking.

"Let me check on the alarm before you—oh, wow." Brice laughed.

"What?"

"We're in luck. Whoever left last didn't turn on the alarm. I mean, I guess it doesn't make a difference to you, it's just less hacking of the alarm system for me to silence it if you set it off and keep it from calling the sheriff's office."

"Well, I'm glad your job is easier."

Levi repeated the entire process with the second pane of

glass. When he applied the gas, the pane tilted into the house, trying to pull him in after it.

"I'm in," he said.

"Remember, in and out. Just get the virus installed."

Levi swung his left leg through the ruined window. The bed was directly underneath him, so he dropped the pane onto the mattress and released some of the cable that was holding him, lowering himself down onto the bed as well. After unbuckling himself from the harness, he stepped down onto the floor.

He saw the stairs going down and immediately went over to them. They were spiral stairs, leading into a darkened room below. He descended cautiously, and at the bottom the lights turned on automatically. A motion sensor.

Dark wooden bookshelves lined the room. It looked like a rich person's library, with a wheeled ladder attached to curved rails that ran along three of the four walls. A desk stood at the center of it all, holding a legal pad and a desktop computer.

Levi pulled out the USB dongle Brice had given him and plugged it into the back of the computer.

"I've plugged the device into the computer. I assume the computer needs to be on?"

"Yes. Turn it on and I'll start pulling as soon as it makes a connection."

Levi pressed the power button, and the desktop made a

single beep. As the Windows logo flashed on the screen, Levi kept his eye on the dongle. A red LED flashed once.

"Okay, it flashed red. Are we good?"

"One second... I'm checking."

Levi heard a double-beep sound from the room above. The same sound his alarm made when the front door was opened. Maybe a maid?

Precious seconds elapsed and he heard the creak of floorboards somewhere above him.

"I'm in! Pulling data now."

"Crap!" Levi grabbed the dongle, raced up the stairs to the bedroom—and skidded to a stop at what he saw.

This couldn't be.

"Levi, get out!" Brice's frantic voice barely registered in Levi's mind.

A man with a gun stood before him. A man who was supposed to be dead.

Porchenko.

"*You!*" Porchenko said, his face contorted with anger.

Levi held Brice's USB dongle in one hand, and his other was behind his back, reaching for his own gun.

He responded in Russian. "How are you not dead?"

"I was about to ask you the same question." Even though Levi had spoken in Russian, Porchenko replied in perfect American English. For a moment Levi was confused... and then suddenly everything fell into place as he remembered something Nadia had told him:

"There's talk on the street that he even killed his own twin brother over a girl they were both attracted to back when they were kids."

Total nonsense. He clearly had done no such thing.

Levi grinned. "Alexei Porchenko, I presume?"

A furrow formed between the man's brows. But he didn't answer Levi's question. "I'm sure there's an explanation," he said, "for why Ronald Warren, aka Lazarus Yoder, is in my bedroom."

Levi's hand wrapped around the grip of his Glock.

"Stop," Porchenko said. He held up a grenade. "I've already pulled the pin, Mr. Yoder. Or shall I call you Mr. Warren? It doesn't really matter which one you are. In fact, I'm thrilled to have you here. I owe you for my uncle, and just now I've learned about my brother, too. Your presence here tells me that was your doing as well. You are a plague on my family, and I curse you for ever having been born. Now here you are, I presume to finish the job.

"I have many questions, but none of them matter. We'll both get our wishes fulfilled today, don't you worry. Neither of us is getting out of this alive."

Levi had seen this type of grenade before—an old Soviet F-1. Porchenko was right about one thing: if he let that explode, it would kill them both. No question.

Porchenko's chin quivered, and for the first time he spoke in Russian. "I do want to know one thing before we're done."

Levi breathed in deeply, and just as he began to exhale, he whipped his gun from his waistband. Bullets flew in both directions, and as Levi felt something strike him in the shoulder like a sledge hammer, Porchenko screamed: "For Mother Russia!"

The spoon from the grenade fell to the carpet, and there was a loud popping sound.

Levi didn't hesitate. He jumped onto the bed, shattering the pane of glass that still lay there, then leaped through the window. A fiery explosion sounded behind him, peppering him with shards of pain, as he was launched into the open air.

The world turned black.

CHAPTER SIXTEEN

The spectacled, chubby face of Brice hovered over him as Levi lurched up from a hospital bed and gasped for breath.

"Whoa, Levi!" Brice put his hand on his shoulder. "It's okay. You're in one of our suites in Walter Reed."

His heart thudding loudly in his chest, Levi blinked and tried to make sense of his surroundings. His entire body felt bruised and battered, and his right shoulder was throbbing.

A physician walked in, holding a clipboard. "Yoder, we have got to stop meeting like this."

Levi looked up at the man. His senses were slowed, and it took him a moment to recognize the man. Then a smile bloomed on his face and he fist-bumped the doc with his uninjured arm. "Doc Spears, it's been a while."

Brice looked back and forth between the two. "You two know each other?"

Levi chuckled—then winced at the shooting pain coming from his shoulder. "I think the last time was a little operation in Argentina. Isn't that right, doc?"

The tall physician, who was not only a member of the Outfit but a former member of the Special Forces, nodded. "It's always good to bring home a victory for the home team." He patted Levi on his uninjured shoulder. "You're a tough nut to crack. I remember the first time you and I tangoed, you got hit not once but twice by a .338 Lapua, and all you had to show for it was a collapsed lung."

"You've got a good memory. But I think my condition back then read more on my body armor than anything about me." Levi lifted his right arm and felt tingles running from his shoulder to the tips of his fingers. "What's the damage this time?"

"We'll find out. Swing your legs off the gurney and face me. I need to do a few tests now that you're awake."

Levi did as he was told.

Doc Spears held up a pen. "Keep your eyes on the pen."

Levi allowed the doc to put him through a few basic motor skill and cognitive tests. When Spears was done, Levi turned to Brice.

"How long was I out?"

Brice looked at his watch. "It's not even lunchtime yet. I guess maybe a couple hours. I had a team extract you within ten minutes of the chaos you left behind."

"That wasn't my fault," Levi said. "You were supposed to be doing overwatch."

He rubbed at his arms. He'd been stitched up in at least a half dozen places. When he felt his face, he found some stitches along his jawline as well. "So, Doc, what's the verdict? Am I going to live? Do I look like Frankenstein's monster yet?"

Spears chuckled. "Considering you were too close to a freshly popped grenade and blown out of a second-story window, you're in remarkably good shape. Your CT scan came back normal. You've got plenty of stitches, but none of that's serious. And your shoulder will be fine, it's just badly bruised. I understand you were shot while wearing a bulletproof vest. I know that hurts, but no broken bones."

Levi moved his right arm. "What about this painful tingling? It's not a lot of fun."

"The bullet impact amounts to blunt force trauma, and it hit an area where a number of nerves are present. But while you were out we ran a nerve conductivity test, and you're within normal parameters. You're just feeling your body's reaction to the trauma. Consider it a reminder to take it easy for a while. If the tingling doesn't go away in a couple days, we can run some other tests, but I think you'll be fine once the swelling goes down."

"Does that mean he's okay to leave?" Brice asked.

"Most physicians would recommend he stay overnight for observation." Spears gave Levi a wink. "But I think our friend here is made of tougher stuff than that. I'll sign off on his release."

Before departing, Doc Spears left behind a bottle of Motrin. A yellow sticky note on it said, *If you're feeling a bit soft, take these for pain.*

Levi laughed, and winced, and laughed again. He liked that guy.

He turned to Brice. "Where are my clothes?"

"I'll go find a nurse and get them to you. And, hey, I'm surprised you didn't already ask, but… you did it. Thanks to you I was able to suck the home computer dry. The folks at the office are analyzing the data now. Mason's arriving later today. Let's get you out of here so we can brief him together."

Levi walked into the conference room wearing Russian-made street clothes. He had no other choice; his suit smelled like urine and his fatigues were shredded by shrapnel.

Brice and Mason were sitting at the conference room table talking about warrants, but when they saw Levi, Mason stood and walked over.

"Levi, are you okay?"

Levi smiled. "I'm fine."

"You sure about that? You look like a bunch of chewed-up bubble gum." The man looked genuinely concerned. "I'm really sorry the way things went down on this operation. This was a craptastic failure on many levels." He motioned toward the chairs. "Come on, take a load off."

Levi sat beside Brice, trying not to show his discomfort, even though his right arm still felt like a thousand ants were nibbling on it.

Mason sat opposite them. "I suppose the good news is that we might be at the end of this Porchenko nonsense. Brice, I need you to arrange for an AAR with the entire team, ASAP. The idea that we had someone get blown up isn't going to sit well with the folks I have to report to. But for now, give me the quick version."

Brice scribbled something on a pad, then angled his chair so he was looking at Levi and Mason. "Let's start with the lobbyist who DC knows as Alex Conway. We knew there was a relationship between him and Porchenko, and initially we even speculated they might have some romantic ties or something. That turned out not to be the case. Alex Conway was really Alexei Porchenko, Konstantin's twin brother, born in the Soviet Union and sent here almost forty years ago by the KGB as a long-term clandestine agent."

Mason frowned. "But the KGB fell apart with the fall of the Soviet Union in 1991. How did his cover not fall apart?"

Brice shrugged. "The Soviets had to have had someone on the inside. Conway had legit everything, even a birth certificate with a little footprint on it out of Bethesda." He hitched his thumb at Levi. "Levi put two and two together and guessed he was Porchenko's brother—"

"It wasn't a guess. I'd seen a picture of Konstantin Porchenko, and when I saw Conway, I literally thought I was seeing a ghost. Conway is the spitting image of Porchenko. And then I remembered our person in the Russian office mentioning a rumor that Konstantin killed his twin brother as a kid in a fight over some girl. I realized he really did have a twin, but he didn't get killed—and now we know what happened to him."

"Interesting," said Mason. "But again, how did the Soviets' fall not affect this KGB agent?"

Brice picked up one of his printouts. "The best I can tell is that he was embedded with the primary purpose of being a DC player. His earliest job record was as a clerk in one of the big K Street lobbying firms. My guess is that when the KGB was dissolved, he just continued his mission. He was earning a local paycheck and was self-sufficient by then."

"And obviously maintained contact with his brother," added Levi. "A pretty impressive feat to keep that secret over nearly four decades."

"Well, he was loyal to the cause," Brice said. "Just before the bedroom blew up, he shouted something in Russian. I'm sure Levi already knows what it meant, but I had to get the computers to translate it. It was 'For Mother Russia.' Literally his last words on this earth."

Mason shook his head. "And now I have to worry about

an army of ex-KGB officers possibly lurking in hidden nooks and crannies throughout the country. Sometimes I'd just rather not know these things. What's the status with the data analysis?"

"We're still working on it, and will be for a while," said Brice, "but the puzzle pieces are starting to come together. What's clear is that Alexei was the one to identify susceptible people in DC who might get influenced, and soft targets that could be used to influence the right people. He passed that info to Konstantin, who was the hammer, deploying the chaos."

"And even though the brothers are now dead, their contacts remain compromised," muttered Mason, drumming his fingers on the table. "We need to establish hard connections between the actors and get some arrests out of this."

Brice sighed. "I know. I pulled down nearly a hundred gigabytes of data off Alexei's home machine, and we're in the process of pulling literally terabytes of data from his offices on K Street. I just wish I had access to more of Konstantin's data. His contacts would be the ones we could most likely act on immediately. Or they would at least help us know what to look for."

Levi's eyes widened. "Hold up. I might have that contact list."

Both men turned to him in surprise.

Levi closed his eyes and recalled the few minutes he'd spent in Konstantin Porchenko's home office, flipping through the man's address book. The names, addresses, and phone numbers were global, but a good portion of them were in the US.

He opened his eyes and grinned at Brice. "I read Porchenko's address book. I just need a notepad and pencil."

"No effin' way." Brice stared at him. "You've memorized his entire address book?"

Mason laughed. "There you go, Marty. Levi's got your leads buried in his head. I think you know your next step. Get me names and addresses, and a list of the offenses for each. I'll start the paperwork rolling on the warrants. Sounds like we've got our plates full." He jabbed a finger at Levi. "But as soon as you write down what's in your head, you need to get some rest. If you like, you can have the use of our suite at the Waldorf Astoria that recently opened in DC."

Levi shook his head. "I'll just head back to New York City by way of Pennsylvania. I want to see my kids. Speaking of which, what's the story with the security on my mom's place?"

"Don't worry, we've got your family covered. You'll see what's in place when you get there." Mason stood, looking pleased. "Despite all the headaches and inefficiencies, it looks like we did manage to drain the DC swamp just a little bit."

Levi felt a wave of exhaustion wash over him as he thought about what had transpired over the last week. But despite all that had been achieved, he knew in the pit of his stomach that the job wasn't even close to done.

It would take a lot more than eliminating one corrupt ring of lobbyists and Russian assets to truly drain this swamp.

AUTHOR'S NOTE

Well, that's the end of *The Swamp*, and I sincerely hope you enjoyed it.

If this is the first book of mine you've read, I owe you a bit of an introduction. For the rest of you who have seen this before, skip to the new stuff.

I'm a lifelong science researcher who has been in the high-tech industry longer than I'd like to admit. There's nothing particularly unusual about my beginnings, but I suppose it should be noted I grew up with English as my third language, although nowadays, it is by far my strongest. As an Army brat, I traveled a lot and did what many people do: I went to school, got a job, got married, and had kids.

I grew up reading science magazines, which led me into reading science fiction, mostly the classics by Asimov,

Niven, Pournelle, etc. And then I found epic fantasy, which introduced me to a whole new world, in fact many new worlds, it was Eddings, Tolkien, and the like who set me on the path of appreciating that genre. As I grew older, and stuffier, I grew to appreciate thrillers from Cussler, Crichton, Grisham, and others.

When I had young kids, I began to make up stories for them, which kept them entertained. After all, who wouldn't be entertained when you're hearing about dwarves, elves, dragons, and whatnot? These were the bedtime stories of their youth. And to help me keep things straight, I ended up writing these stories down, so I wouldn't have it all jumbled in my head.

Well, the kids grew up, and after writing all that stuff down to keep them entertained, it turns out I caught the bug —the writing bug. I got an itch to start writing... but not the traditional things I'd written for the kids.

Over the years I'd made friends with some rather well-known authors, and when I talked to them about maybe getting more serious about this writing thing, several of them gave me the same advice: "Write what you know."

Write what I know? I began to think about Michael Crichton. He was a non-practicing MD, who started off with a medical thriller. John Grisham was an attorney for a decade before writing a series of legal thrillers. Maybe there was something to that advice.

I began to ponder, "What do I know?" And then it hit me.

I know science. It's what I do for a living and what I enjoy. In fact, one of my hobbies is reading formal papers spanning many scientific disciplines. My interests range from particle physics, computers, the military sciences (you know, the science behind what makes stuff go boom), and medicine. I'm admittedly a bit of a nerd in that way. I've also traveled extensively during my life, and am an informal student of foreign languages and cultures.

With the advice of some New York Times-bestselling authors, I started my foray into writing novels.

My first book, Primordial Threat, became a USA Today bestseller, and since then I've hit that list a handful of times. With 20-20 hindsight, I'm pleased that I took the plunge and started writing.

That's enough of an intro, and I'm not a fan of talking about myself, so let me get back to where I was before I rudely interrupted myself.

The idea of The Swamp came about from the uproar of many things happening across the globe at once. Whether it was Brexit, or the 2020 BLM riots, or the election of one president, or deposing of some other, the world saw what happens when politics are at play.

And a last-minute influence on some of this was

certainly the current (as of this writing) Ukraine/Russia conflict.

I by no means take sides on politics in my books, and it took a bit of creativity on my part to purposefully not give an indication of some political party being good or another side being not-so-good. But I did want to harp a bit on the undue influence that the media has on the public. Even from the opening scene where we had a crazy person influenced by the goings on from a New York Times article. Sadly, that scene is not so different than a real life scene that had played out in the recent past where a gunman fired on a bunch of congressman who'd been playing baseball.

Why did he do it? Because of the incessant messages received by the media the person in question watched.

I realize that our society has evolved in many ways, but in some ways not always for the good. I come from a time when the media, especially the news, they were charged with informing the public of current events. Giving you, the viewer, the news as it happened.

As Walter Cronkite used to say, "and that's the way it is."

I miss those days. It allowed the public to be informed, but not inflamed.

And today, too often we see the same thing playing out in America and abroad. Propaganda being broadcasted across airwaves. Depending on what channel, what country, what time of day, you may be getting very different messages, which causes polarization. It's not a healthy thing.

And from all this miasma of goo, came The Swamp.

I hope you enjoyed it.

As always, I'd love to hear comments and feedback.

Please share your thoughts/reviews about the story on Amazon and with your friends. It's only through reviews and word of mouth that this story will find other readers, and I do hope this book (and the rest of my books) find as wide an audience as possible.

Again, thank you for taking the chance on a relatively unknown author. After all, I'm no Stephen King.

It's my intent to release two to four books a year, and I'll be completely honest, I'm heavily influenced by my reader-ship on what gets attention next. An example of that being my first book, Primordial Threat, a book that was not going to have a follow-on title. But when I released it, it became a hit in the US and abroad, so due to demand, I released a second in what is now known as the Exodus Series.

I should note that if you're interested in getting updates about my latest work, join my mailing list at:

https://mailinglist.michaelarothman.com/new-reader

Mike Rothman
June 23, 2022

PREVIEW – NEW ARCADIA

The mist hung low in the forest, and the agent's footsteps squished through the damp ground, kicking up the aroma of peat moss—an earthy, dark, rich scent reminiscent of wet wool, with a hint of rot. In the distance, he caught sight of a barbed wire fence, the first sign of the high-security camp that wasn't supposed to be there.

Crouching low, the agent continued advancing toward the camp, but froze suddenly upon hearing a crunching and snapping sound underfoot. Dread consumed him when he recognized the sound of children's bones breaking.

The brittle remnants marked another shallow grave just outside the camp codenamed New Arcadia.

Despite the horror of the situation, the agent took another step forward.

He didn't hear the sniper round traveling at twice the speed of sound before it slammed into him.

The world turned black.

In a sound-isolated room fifty feet below Fort Meade, Doug Mason watched as two of his specialists worked on a patient lying on a hospital gurney.

One was a neuroscientist monitoring a flatscreen that had a bundle of wires attached to the patient's scalp. The other, a tiny bespectacled man who had been a practicing anesthesiologist before Mason recruited him into the Outfit.

A clandestine government agency that didn't officially exist, the Outfit and its members were an exclusive bunch, hand-picked for their special skills. These two both came from the private sector, and now served a higher calling… one that involved any number of unusual tasks, in all of which national security was at stake. Today was no exception.

Mason shifted his gaze to the head of the gurney. "Jerry, he'll be able to respond to questions, right?"

"Oh, most definitely." The neuroscientist pointed to the monitor, which displayed a variety of squiggly patterns. "We've got a classic EEG signature of unconsciousness at the moment. Mohan's going to chemically immobilize Agent

Xiang, and the sedative he's on should give up the ghost. Then he'll wake."

"It's got to be strange waking up and not even being able to blink," Mason said. He'd never witnessed a programming session before, mostly because it had only been done a handful of times, all when he wasn't on the premises.

"It's best that he can't move for a variety of reasons, but the most important have to do with the auditory and visual programming sequences." The neuroscientist adjusted a setting on what looked like a virtual reality headset the patient was wearing. "When we first began experimenting with neuro-programming, the subjects couldn't handle it. The results were miserable."

"What do you mean, couldn't handle it? Was it painful?"

The gray-haired man shrugged. "Hard to say. Before we started inducing paralysis in the subjects, they had an autonomic reaction to the process, flailed uncontrollably, and even when we strapped them to the hospital bed we couldn't get a complete lock on the programming. This is very fidgety, cutting-edge stuff. And the subjects usually don't even realize what's going on during the programming."

The anesthesiologist cut in, his Indian accent thick, yet intelligible. "Let's get things rolling." He cleaned the injection port on the IV with an alcohol swab, then injected a clear liquid into it. "This is Quelicin," he explained to Mason. "The good stuff. He'll be completely immobile. I'll attach an infusion pump to the IV so that he gets a constant four milligrams per minute throughout the procedure."

Mason watched the men work together smoothly as a team. Jerry Caldwell, was a neuroscientist, and Mohan Patel, an anesthesiologist. The two men already had a shorthand between them, and an easy, unspoken calm relationship. He didn't share their calm, feeling uneasy about this whole thing. He understood the necessity of the procedure—the news out of China looked grimmer by the day, and the Outfit needed Agent Xiang for a very special mission—but that did nothing to calm his nerves.

"I pushed a counter to the sedative," Caldwell said. "He should be awake now." He broke a capsule under the man's nose, and the smell of ammonia permeated the air. "Did he respond?"

"Yup. He's awake, Mohan," Caldwell said, eyes glued to the monitor.

Patel spoke, keeping his voice clear, and his speech measured. "Agent Xiang, this is Doctor Patel. Can you hear me?"

Mason couldn't make heads or tails of what was on the monitor, but it clearly meant something to the neuroscientist, who said: "He hears you."

"Agent Xiang, we're about to start the session. Just relax. You won't remember any of this when this is all over."

Caldwell pulled up a new screen on the monitor, this one flashing a series of patterns.

"Sending a baseline set of signals…"

A buzzing noise leaked from the agent's headset. A 3D representation of the brain appeared on screen, rotating, with portions of it highlighted.

"Do those highlights indicate where you're setting the memories?" Mason asked.

"Yes." Caldwell tapped on one of the highlighted areas of the screen. "This will be programming run one of three."

"Why do you have to do it three times?"

"We've found that repetition helps the memories stick. And it's not just pure repetition. On the third run we induce a slow-wave sleep to consolidate the memory—"

"I thought something like that required REM sleep," Mason interjected.

"No. The slow-wave sleep that comes right after you fall asleep is when memory consolidation occurs. So I induce that state with a slow-wave frequency generator and then trigger delta waves with about ten milliamps of current through the electrodes attached to the agent's forehead and the base of his skull.

"This isn't a great analogy," Caldwell continued, "but conceptually it's similar to when your computer gets an update and you have to reboot before it can process the changes. And sometimes you have to reboot it yet again once things have been configured. The brain has a similar process."

The scientist tapped some things on the screen, and text

scrolled rapidly past, along with images of places and people. All the things pertinent to an upcoming mission.

"Okay, Mohan, I've got the signals oriented. I'm about to hit go. Is he good?"

"Blood pressure is at a baseline of 115 over 78, oxygen is at 100%, and heart rate is 45. All good to go."

"Here goes."

A portion of the neuroscientist's screen blurred into streams of unrecognizable character patterns, not unlike the kind shown in the movie *The Matrix*. Mason looked over at the agent and saw Xiang's pale skin turning pink, almost as if he were having an allergic reaction or a hot flash.

The anesthesiologist adjusted the respirator, and its cyclic rate increased, giving the agent more breaths per minute. "BP is now 165 over 80, and heart rate has spiked to 115. We're still okay."

As the programming continued, the agent's skin went from pink to red, and dots of perspiration appeared everywhere his skin was exposed.

"How much longer?" Mohan said, adjusting the respirator once again, his expression tense. "BP is now 205 over 84, and heart rate is at 185."

Mason clenched his jaw as his gaze panned back and forth between the physicians and Agent Xiang.

"Almost done," Jerry said. "Five… four… three… two… one… done!"

The white noise permeating the room stopped, leaving

only the sound of the respirator trying to keep up with the demands of a patient they had put through the wringer.

Letting out a breath he hadn't realized he'd been holding, Mason felt a wave of guilt wash over him. No wonder the subject had to be immobilized for this. What kind of hell was he putting these people through? And was it worth it?

"Patient's stats are dropping back into normal range. BP is 135 over 78 and heart rate is 70. Both are drifting lower."

Mason turned to the neuroscientist. "Can he hear me?"

Jerry nodded.

"Chris? Agent Xiang, this is Director Mason. Are you okay to continue?"

The neuroscientist was watching his screen. "Can you ask your question again? I'm not sure the agent heard it. His brain is still processing the onslaught."

Mason leaned in closer. "Agent Xiang, are you okay to continue?"

The neuroscientist nodded. "EEG waves match the affirmative responses we recorded before the testing began. He's good to go."

Mason took a step back and motioned for the doctors to continue. There weren't any laws against what they were all doing, but he felt like there probably should be.

All in the name of national security.

The fires of hell didn't seem that bad compared to how Alicia's face felt as it burned from the chemicals she'd been sprayed with. She jogged in place and heard the other trainees coughing and struggling against the effects of the pepper spray. Blinking away the chemicals didn't even help; her eyelids felt like flaming hot sandpaper. She could only grit her teeth and try to ignore the pain as she bounced up and down on the balls of her feet.

"Move it, move it, move it!"

One of the instructors shoved her toward the track, and it took everything Alicia had to *not* send a back fist to the guy's temple.

She and a dozen other FBI Academy trainees were on a remote portion of Marine Base Quantico. She'd been integrated into this training class only three days ago. Yet despite the dusty surroundings, the chemicals in her face, and her complete physical agony, she knew there was one thing she *couldn't* do.

Let these bastards get the best of her.

"The more you sweat and suffer here, the less you'll bleed when on assignment. I want one and a half miles from all of you! That's six laps, for you people who aren't all that bright."

Blinking through the pain and tears, Alicia began running.

"Yoder, Sanchez, and Smith!"

Alicia and two other agents turned to the instructor.

He made a counterclockwise motion with his finger. "The other direction, numbskulls."

Alicia pressed a finger against the side of her nose, blew a seemingly impossible amount of snot in the instructor's general direction, and ran to catch up with the rest of the class.

Alicia felt much better after finishing the run—though she still felt a burning sensation in the back of her throat. She hadn't been the first to complete the six laps, but she had finished in the front third of the trainees, which would have to be good enough. Halfway through the run, she had developed a pain in her lower abdomen. It didn't feel like a normal period cramp, but what else could it be? She sure as hell wasn't going to mention it; as the only woman in this class, she wasn't about to allow that to be an excuse.

She had never run with anything more than two-pound ankle weights in college, and she'd never have imagined just how exhausting it was to run in full tactical gear. All the trainees had been completely kitted out, from military-issue combat boots to an advanced battle vest with ballistic inserts, load distribution system, and what the instructor called SAPIs and ESBIs—small-arms protective inserts and enhanced side ballistic inserts. The whole thing probably only weighed fifteen or twenty pounds, but

Alicia had felt every one of them over the course of the six laps.

The last two trainees came walking back from the track looking exhausted. Their eyes were bloodshot, and partially dried snot and Lord knows what else was streaked across their faces and into their hair. They looked like hell.

Alicia now knew the feeling—quite well.

When all of the would-be agents had completed the run and settled onto the benches, an instructor stepped in front of the group and spoke.

"Okay, trainees. We've got something special today."

He hitched his thumb toward the training site behind him —a dusty ghost town that had been constructed about a quarter mile away. It had been set up in a grid pattern, with a wide main street splitting it from north to south. Yesterday, when they'd used it to go through various close-quarters combat scenarios, corpses of burnt-out vehicles had lined the street. Today Alicia saw something else out there. Something metal. But she couldn't quite make it out from this distance.

The instructor smiled. "Some researchers out of DARPA have developed a new artificial intelligence unit, and we've plugged it into one of our EOD robots."

EOD was shorthand for explosive ordnance disposal— the bomb guys. And now Alicia realized what the metal object in the main street was. A couple weeks earlier she had worked with some folks from the Army's EOD group, and she'd gotten a chance to operate one of their remote bomb disposal units. It was kind of neat, reminding her of the robot from the cartoon *WALL-E*. It even had arms that she could manipulate through a remote control.

"With this new AI enhancement, the robot is supposed to detect and identify combatants in the field. It's been through quite a bit of testing already, but before it can be put out into the field, it's going to need a lot more work. Today is your turn to see if you can fool the robot. All you need to do is go up to it and touch the thing without it raising its red flag, meaning it saw you. Any questions?"

One of the trainees raised his hand. "Sir? How far can it see?"

"Good question. The robot will analyze anything coming within a thousand-foot radius."

A voice broadcast from what looked like a walkie-talkie on the instructor's utility belt. *"We're ready."*

The instructor spoke into a shoulder-attached mic. "Roger that." He then pointed at the man who'd asked the question. "Smith, since you're the curious type, you can go first."

The trainee launched himself from the bench and jogged north, skirting the edge of the makeshift town, then vanished between the buildings. After a moment the robot turned eastward, sensing him.

Suddenly the trainee raced into view, and the robot's arm shot upward, with something red hanging from it.

"Subject detected," the walkie-talkie squawked. *"Send the next agent."*

The instructor pointed at another trainee. "Darby, you're up next."

Scott Darby, a tall, blond, giant of a man, stood and tapped the shoulder of the guy who'd been sitting next to him. Carl something. "Hey, want to try and tag team Robo-Grunt?"

"Sure."

The two men spoke in hushed whispers, then took off at a sprint. They split up, approaching their target from opposite directions.

Was one of them going to sacrifice himself so the other could tag the thing?

As they converged onto the town, the robot seemed skittish, scanning back and forth, clearly sensing movement. But the men were ducking behind buildings before the robot could zero in on them.

Then Carl launched a rock past his target.

But instead of following the movement of the rock, the robot turned, raised its arm, then spun, kicking up a cloud of dust.

Alicia wasn't quite sure what had just happened, but the voice on the walkie-talkie said, *"Both agents identified. Send your next."*

"Cortez, you're up."

The man sitting next to Alicia jumped up and raced

forward. Like the others, he ducked behind the buildings and thus delayed his inevitable defeat. His tactic was to throw up a cloud of dirt to distract the robot. But the moment he leapt from cover, the robot flagged him.

Damn, that thing is fast.

"Yoder, you're up."

Alicia stood, then tilted her head to the supply shed. "Can I use the mosquito netting?" she asked.

The instructor shrugged. "Whatever's here, you can use."

Alicia unrolled nearly fifty feet of thick mosquito netting from the spool and wrapped herself with it. The instructor and trainees watched with confusion and interest as she created a puffy ghillie suit.

When she tied it off, she checked her shadow. She could barely see anything through the layers of mesh, but she'd created the desired effect: her shadow was round—not shaped like a human at all. Alicia hoped that the AI wouldn't know what to make of her.

Keeping her hands inside the suit, she pushed out the edges of the mesh, making herself look even rounder as she trudged northward.

She didn't bother skirting around buildings. She moved straight at the robot, her heart thudding in her ears as she wobbled forward.

It turned slightly as she got in range.

Alicia kept moving.

The robot shifted back and forth like it was suffering

from a nervous tic. It clearly sensed her approach. But would it identify her as a combatant?

Alicia heard the whoosh of the robot's hydraulics. She saw the red cloth clutched in its robotic grip.

It's about to raise its arm.

But it was too late. Alicia bumped directly into it and yelled, "I tagged it!" She felt a wave of triumph.

Two men stepped from the nearest building. They were dressed in street clothes and had picture badges clipped to their collars. One looked annoyed, but the other laughed.

"How did you know that your heat signature wouldn't be able to be detected through that mesh?"

Alicia shrugged. "I had no idea. I just figured if I didn't have a human outline, it might get fooled."

The other man grumbled, "Dumb luck."

"No, this was perfect," said the first man. He gave Alicia a thumbs-up. "I'd never have thought of this approach." He spoke into a handheld device. "It seems your trainee found a chink in our armor. We've got some work to do."

"Roger that. I'll dismiss the rest of the trainees for the day. Yoder, good job. We'll be back in the classroom at 0800."

As the scientists began unscrewing one of the panels on the robot, Alicia wriggled out of the layers of mosquito netting. Despite her little victory against WALL-E the Robo-Grunt, she couldn't help but feel anxiety over the training activities still to come. Unlike her classes in college, all of which provided a clear syllabus with what to expect, here she had been given absolutely no idea what the Outfit had in store for her.

She wasn't even completely sure what being an agent at the Outfit even entailed. The training seemed almost random. Last week it was working with some Marines on conditioning exercises. This week it was training at the FBI Academy. And next? Who knew?

She wished she at least had some grades to measure herself against, unsure if she was doing well or poorly. But that might change tomorrow. She had a mid-cycle evaluation with Mason at the Outfit's HQ, and she couldn't help but wonder what Mason would have to say about her performance.

It had been three months since Alicia had agreed to join the Outfit—a huge decision for her. It had not only meant moving to a new apartment in DC, it had meant leaving Princeton without having finished her master's degree in neuroscience. The unfinished degree didn't sit well with her, and now, as she drove past Lincoln Park, through the National Mall, past Foggy Bottom, and into old Georgetown, her mind was filled with doubt about her choices.

She placed a call on her phone and transferred it to the car's speakers.

"What's up, baby girl?"

The sound of her adoptive father's deep voice should have taken the edge off of her nerves, but it didn't.

"Dad, what the hell was I thinking? I feel like it was just yesterday that I was taking classes, an ordinary student, and now I'm training to be… hell, I don't even *know* what I'm training to be. Shooting drills, CQB training, and a few days ago they put me through an entire session on vehicle engagement tactics—learning how to drive and shoot at the same time, evasive maneuvers, anti-ambush drills… Dad, this is insane."

Her father chuckled. *"Alicia, take a deep breath. Where are you?"*

She took a deep breath and let it out. It did make her feel a little better. "I'm driving to HQ for my three-month review with Mason. My nerves have me all knotted up inside. Hell, I'm trying not to throw up right now."

"There's no reason for you to be nervous. You've got this. And besides, I've been keeping tabs, and everyone so far has had nothing but good things to say about your progress."

"If you say so. It's not like they would tell *you* if I'm doing poorly. You're Levi Yoder, Super Spy. I'm just… me." Alicia's throat tightened and her heart raced. "Dad, I… I can't remember what made me say yes to this. And I mean that literally—it's like total blanks in my head. I think I might be losing it."

"I assure you, you're not losing it. And those gaps... honey, let's just say that they're there for a reason."

"What do you mean?"

"It's hard to explain. Sometimes when people go through trauma, things get blocked from your consciousness. It's totally normal."

A chill raced through her, and she began feeling light-headed. "You don't have to explain to me how the brain works—I'm the neuroscientist, remember? Or I was *going* to be. But—what trauma, Dad? Was I"—she swallowed—"was I… raped or something? What am I blocking out?"

"No, no, it was nothing like that. You just... you managed to get mixed up in something that involved the Outfit. You kicked ass, Alicia. But it was hard on you. Mason and I thought you might lose some of those memories of the incident, and honestly, I'm glad you did. You're better off, trust me. And if you're nervous about it, talk to Mason. He'll totally understand."

"Maybe."

"It's your call. But listen—I'm in DC today for a quick meeting. Maybe you could meet me upstairs for a bite to eat? How's noon sound?"

"It sounds great, Dad." Alicia wiped tears of frustration from her cheeks. She took a deep breath in, then let it out slowly in an attempt calm the roiling fear, anxiety, and nerves. "I'm sorry. I'm acting like a baby. I'm just nervous and… freaking out a bit."

"Alicia, you have nothing to worry about." She could hear the smile in his voice.

They ended the call as she pulled into an open spot on the side of the road in old Georgetown. Traffic had been unexpectedly light, and she was an hour early for her meeting, so she tuned the radio to an oldies station and tried to calm her nerves.

Even the sounds of *Earth, Wind & Fire* couldn't banish the feelings pressing in on her. After thirty minutes, she gave up and got out of the car.

"Hey honey, you have any food I can have?"

She turned to see an old man in dirty threadbare clothing yelling at her from down the street. She grinned as she walked toward him. She recognized the "beggar" as a member of the Outfit, and the things he yelled were actually codes to notify anyone approaching headquarters if there was anything amiss. Asking for food was a sign that everything was clear. Had he asked for a drink… well, then Alicia was to leave the area immediately.

Ahead, Alicia saw a familiar sign. It featured a profile of a rooster on the left, and the head of a longhorn bull on the right. This area wasn't exactly upscale, but Alicia had gained some fondness for the dingy street front.

She walked into the Rooster and Bull, and the smells of stale beer and wood polish washed over her. The place was a dive bar… and also an entrance into one of the most secretive organizations in the world.

Dimly lit as always, the place's few tables and booths were all empty at this time of day. Behind the bar, a man toweled a glass dry. He nodded at her as she walked toward the back of the establishment.

Alicia entered the men's bathroom. A white-haired man sitting on a stool near the sink looked at her over his John Lennon-styled spectacles.

"Back again, little girl?"

She grinned. "Harold, how many pairs of tan slacks and plaid button-down shirts do you own? That's all I ever see you wear."

"Bah!" Harold held out a white towel. "My wife always harped about the same thing."

Alicia took the towel. It looked like an ordinary towel, but she knew it had a string of RFID tags sewn into it, and acted as a key of sorts.

"Sounds like your wife was a smart woman," she said, giving the old codger a wink.

For the blink of an eye, the old grump cracked a smile, then he muttered something unintelligible as he waved her away.

Alicia chuckled as she entered the third of the bathroom's three stalls—the one with an "Out of Order" sign taped to it. She shut the door behind her, then placed the special towel on the flushing lever and flushed the toilet.

Immediately the floor dropped—taking Alicia and the toilet with it. She put her hands on the tank to steady herself as she dropped with frightening speed down an incredibly deep shaft. She'd taken this route dozens of times, yet her stomach still lurched.

After a few very long seconds, the walls fell away and the toilet-elevator slowed nearly to a stop. Alicia focused on regaining her balance as she descended into a featureless room deep underneath old Georgetown. The platform settled softly into a recess in the floor, and Alicia stepped off.

Just as quickly as it had dropped, the toilet-elevator launched back up again, disappearing into the shaft in the ceiling.

Alicia tossed the hand towel in a nearby basket, then walked to the room's only exit: a steel door with a security panel mounted to one side. She placed her splayed hand on the panel, and a blue line passed back and forth. Then a green LED flashed, and a click echoed from inside the wall.

"Stand clear," warned a digitized voice.

Three massive locking bolts slid out of their retaining blocks on the right side of the door, and the door slowly opened outward.

Alicia remembered the first time she'd been brought here, by her father and Director Mason. The place had reminded her of a 1950s bomb shelter, except that no bomb shelters she knew of had a four-foot thick, tungsten-steel alloy door weighing eighteen tons at its entrance.

She walked through the opening, around a corner, and down a hall that ended at another door, this one with a retinal scanner. She put her eye up to the box on the wall, and with a flash of green light, the door clicked.

Alicia pushed it open and stepped into the inner sanctum of the Outfit's US headquarters.

She was in a room larger than most warehouses. Standing on a metal walkway about twenty feet above the floor, Alicia had a clear view of the cubicles arranged in a grid below her, stretching as far as she could see. No matter what time of the day or night she arrived, she always found men and women working like their lives depended on it. And very likely, somewhere out there in the world, someone's life *did* hinge on these people's work.

Four huge display screens, each fifty feet across, hung from the ceiling at the center of the space, displaying information, maps, photographs, satellite feeds, and more, and the walkway she was on continued around the edges of the giant room, leading to offices whose windows also looked down on the central work area.

She was reminded, not for the first time, of the headquarters in the movie *Men in Black*, except there were no aliens —at least, not that she knew of.

She walked down a flight of metal stairs, stepped into the cubicle bullpen, and started the long walk to the far side of the cavern-like complex. When she finally reached conference room C1, where she was scheduled to meet with Mason, the butterflies in her stomach were threatening to come flying out of her mouth.

Despite her early arrival, she found the director already waiting, studying a photograph. She looked up at the wall clock and saw to her astonishment that she wasn't fifteen minutes early, she was forty-five minutes *late*.

"Oh my God, I don't—"

"Daylight savings?" Mason said. "Did you forget the time changed early this morning?"

He stared at her with his pale, silver-hued eyes. He was in his fifties, with light brown hair and a receding hairline. Most men with his looks would have been dismissed by the general public as boring or average. Not Mason. Something in the way he held himself… his presence commanded attention. This man was the Outfit's most senior member in the US—at least, as far as she knew, and here she was showing up almost an hour late for her evaluation.

"I'm so sorry! Do we need to reschedule?"

Mason waved dismissively at her and slid the photo he'd been looking at across the conference room table. "Tell me what you see."

Alicia took a seat across from him and picked up the photo. It looked like some kind of business social. "Well, lots of Asian people, but I don't suppose you needed me to tell you that."

"Do you recognize anyone?"

She nearly shook her head when a woman caught her attention. She was only in profile, and she was a good distance from the camera, but…

"I'm not positive, but I think I do."

She felt a surge of apprehension. Her boss expected an answer—an *honest* answer—but Alicia didn't want to betray this woman's confidence. She was, after all, involved in the shady side of business.

"I… I think my father knows her."

"A very diplomatic way of putting it, young lady." Mason's stone-like expression softened, and he gave her a slight nod. "Very well, I'll talk to Levi in a bit."

He glanced at the wall clock and rose from his chair. "Unfortunately, I have another meeting at the top of the hour, so we'll have to postpone our review. I'll have my admin set something up." He walked to the door, put his hand on the knob, and looked back at Alicia. "And next time, don't be late."

She nodded.

As Mason opened the door, his phone rang, and he put it to his ear. "Hey, Levi. I'll be right up. My office." He looked back at Alicia once more. "This room is free for the next couple hours if you want to use it."

He closed the door silently behind him.

Alicia put her head in her hands. All her life she'd been an overachiever. She was always early for every engagement, meeting, class—everything. She couldn't believe she'd made such a dumb error. The training over the last weeks had been so intense, it had made her completely forget about the outside world… and ordinary things like *Daylight Saving Time*.

She'd been hoping that today's meeting would ease her anxiety. If she could just get some feedback on how she was doing—even if it was bad—she thought she'd feel more at ease. Instead, Alicia was almost an hour late to a meeting with one of the most important men in the entire Outfit. And had she not been wasting time sitting in the car, she'd likely have almost made it in time.

She remembered her father's advice, and took a deep breath.

It didn't help.

— end of preview —

If you're interested in ordering this novel, this link will take you to where you can order it: New Arcadia

ADDENDUM

If you've read my books in the past, you've come to expect this scientist to weave in some science regardless of what genre the book is. I don't like to be predictable, but here we are, once again, at the addendum, and as with most Levi Yoder novels, I've introduced some things that might warrant some explanations.

In *The Swamp* we see some new gadgets, and for anyone who has read the prior Levi books, I'd assert you're probably not surprised by that. I'll, of course, talk about the science behind those things. But strewn throughout the book I deal with current events which I would also like to talk about. And very much like in the novel, *Never Again*, I'll try to cover the fact vs fiction on what is portrayed in the media and at least try to put a spotlight on the issues, versus focus only on one flavor of the skewed viewpoints that most of the media feeds its audience.

The idea of *The Swamp* really came about from a series of events that showed how polarizing the media has become, and this seems to be a worldwide phenomenon.

Regardless of where you stood on any of these topics, some of the reporting was ludicrous: such as during the 2020 BLM riots across America where you literally had an MSNBC reporter, reporting on location from the Minneapolis protests where he characterized the demonstrations as "Not generally speaking, unruly." I'd note that as he said those words, a group of protestors had set a large building ablaze directly behind him.

I won't comment much on the strange media machinations outside the U.S. largely because I'm not close enough to the nuances to separate the wheat from the chaff. However, I can note the media's coverage of the Ukraine/Russia conflict—it's been nothing but hyper partisan, and varied greatly depending on what narrative was being supported.

There are some media outlets who are pro-Russia and would characterize the Ukrainians as Nazis and oppressors of the ethnic Russians who live within their borders. Naturally in this reporting, Russia is portrayed as the savior, coming across the border to save their people. I know people who are in Russia and this is exactly the narrative they've been told. Much of the foreign media influences have been blocked for citizens within the Russian borders, so they can't get other narratives.

Of course, there are many media outlets that show the Russians as aggressors who are using the so-called Nazis as a "manufactured" excuse to invade and attempt to annex a neighboring country.

This is just one example.

One that may be closer to home for many of us is the Covid coverage. During the earliest days of the Covid outbreak, a major political figure claimed that the virus's origin was from a lab leak in China. Wuhan, specifically.

At the time, it wasn't politically appropriate to say such things, and the politicians and media were heavily skewed against such statements. People were getting in trouble, being banned from social media, or even being accused of racism for even uttering such things. And this happened even on the main network news channels.

But today, much of the Western media has changed their minds about those "facts." Now such accusations of its origin seem to be common from all venues in the Western media. Where one year ago, saying something about the origin being in China would make you a pariah, now it's an accepted "fact" in much of the world.

Do we truly know what happened? Will we ever? What does China say?

Well, I happen to work with people in China, and I know what the people within China are told. They too have no access to Western media or other narratives.

Initially, the story within China was that the virus originated from infected meat that had been imported from Australia. Yes, many in the West don't know that, but for a long time, that was the belief of the citizenry in China, and what their media was telling them.

Later the Chinese news stated that the virus had been brought in by the US military during a training session.

Again, what's the truth? Who knows?

Either way, this just gives you some examples of how the media manipulates the public narrative to follow the story they want. People get upset, or have beliefs that may or may not be accurate. And unlike the days of Walter Cronkite where he would simply lay out the facts, the things that were known, and the public was allowed to build their own narrative, we are now being told what to believe.

And who are the puppet masters behind these narratives?

Often it is the politics of the moment. This doesn't just happen in America; it inevitably happens in all countries.

These so-called puppet masters are often part of the political infrastructure. Some are lobbyists, who are essentially paid by special interest groups to influence politicians. Others are the staffers and even the politicians themselves who are motivated to fulfill certain agendas. And to get public support, inevitably things are leaked to the media. Often the leaked items are juicy bits of gossip to support one side or another regarding a hot-button topic.

Unfortunately, such partisanship and the media's willing participation in being the political machine's megaphone can become deadly.

Some scenes in this book are based on real events. In fact, the first scene of this book is based on the 2017 Congressional baseball shooting, an incident where a ten-minute shootout occurred between a deranged individual who was motivated by hate induced by media reports, social media, and various newspaper articles. In the end, several people were shot, and at least one Congressman was critically injured.

That's enough of my mild-mannered rant about the often-harmful influence media can have on the public, let's get on to some of the specifics about a gadget or two:

Levi's Contact Lens:

The idea of a contact lens that can deliver real-time information to the human eye has been around in the movies for years, and a staple of many a thriller. But until recently, it's been a thing of science fiction, in that the technology hadn't been developed to properly merge the matrix of the contact lens itself with something that could deliver visual cues to its wearer.

But during CES 2022 (Consumer Electronics Show) just such a technology was presented by InWith Corporation. Its claim was to be the first company to develop the world's first soft electronic contact lens. The lenses work in conjunction with a smartphone or another device, presumably paired via BlueTooth, and it allows the lens to present real-time information.

The details are scant, but the real triumph in technology is the marrying of an smart-device with the contact lens, such that visual elements can be displayed onto what amounts to be the world's smallest TV screen—the contact lens itself.

And borrowing from concepts that already exist such as AR (Active Reality) – which is a form of Virtual Reality that takes your current sounding and overlays things that aren't really there.

An example of such a thing in today's world would be the game Pokémon Go. It's played by millions of people on their smartphones around the world and it allows users to look through their phones at their surroundings and the application overlays certain game elements to what the user sees. They might be looked at the beach in front of them, and a monster appears on the sand, as an example.

Well, with what has recently been developed, the contact lens that Levi is using can easily be envisioned to do something a bit more practical. In the software world, we have many algorithms to enable facial recognition and ultimately it works through a means of capturing an image of what someone is looking at (a person's face) digitizing it, and then using that algorithm to turn it into a stream of numbers.

These numbers would be communicated from the contact lens to the phone it's wirelessly connected to, and with an internet connection, the phone could use that hash of numbers, which represent the face, and search for a match.

Once a match is found, information about that person can be pulled from various online sources, and the information discovered can be broadcast back to the contact lens.

In other words, the contact lens acts both as a camera of sorts and as a miniaturized TV.

So, even though what I described in the book might have seemed fanciful, it is by no means science fiction. I'd even hazard to guess that in some classified sections of the Intelligence Community, we might have exactly this type of device deployed with our agents in the field.

Alicia's Flashlight:

Some of you might be wondering, "Hey! You had that scene where Esther, the ultimate Jewish grandma weapons dealer, devised a "weapon" that Alicia could have, despite the onerous limitations given her age and the location she would be going to school at. But she never got a chance to use it! Was that a mistake?"

This is where I as the author cackle maniacally and shake my head. It wasn't a mistake. I knew that I'd be using this device, but it's a device I'll be using in a book coming out soon after this book is released.

—Record scratch—wait, what?

The implications of what I just typed are many, but let's just say in the next book (which isn't a Levi Yoder book) called *Multiverse,* Alicia will appear in that novel playing a key role. And that flashlight of hers will come into play. And even though the book is very much a science-based thriller, we might see an appearance of Alicia's adoptive father.

I'll cover more about the technical details of the flashlight in that book's addendum, but I can say the device is very much inspired by a real object that is typically used in the medical field called a Bovie.

What is a Bovie?

Simply put, it's a device that is either powered through a large control unit, or in many cases, there are portable, battery-powered versions that are no bigger than a pen.

The business end of the device is handheld, and when activated, the tip glows red-hot.

It's used to cauterize wounds to stop the bleeding, typically during surgery.

The flashlight in its construction is very much styled as a tactical version of a Bovie, scaled up, and you can just imagine the kind of damage that could be done. It's a poor man's light saber, especially when it comes to contact with the skin.

I don't think anyone wants to meet the business end of Alicia's device.

And I promise, in that next book, you'll see it being deployed to great effect.

ABOUT THE AUTHOR

I am an Army brat, a polyglot, and the first person in my family born in the United States. This heavily influenced my youth by instilling in me a love of reading and a burning curiosity about the world and all of the things within it. As an adult, my love of travel and adventure has driven me to explore many unimaginable locations, and these places sometimes creep into the stories I write.

I hope you've found this story entertaining.

- Mike Rothman

You can find my blog at: www.michaelarothman.com

I am also on Facebook at:
www.facebook.com/MichaelARothman
And on Twitter: @MichaelARothman